"Only These Two Found."

The doctor of the military hospital at Valletta stooped and put his hand to her forehead. The fever had not abated. He doubted his ability to save her.

The other girl, who had been tied on top of the frail raft, had suffered less from the action of the waves. She might make it. Both sun-burned by the waves, their dresses battered to rags, they might have been sisters—the same long brown hair, matted with sea-water when they were brought in, now waved softly about the sleeping faces. And they were both tall, and well-built, with that delicate creamy Irish skin that suffered so cruelly from the sun and salt.

The doctor sighed and turned away. "Not a scrap on either one to tell us who they were, either. . . . Ah, well. The passenger lists will maybe help us."

Dear Reader,

We, the editors of Tapestry Romances, are committed to bringing you two outstanding original romantic historical novels each and every month.

From Kentucky in the 1850s to the court of Louis XIII, from the deck of a pirate ship within sight of Gibraltar to a mining camp high in the Sierra Nevadas, our heroines experience life and love, romance and adventure.

Our aim is to give you the kind of historical romances that you want to read. We would enjoy hearing your thoughts about this book and all future Tapestry Romances. Please write to us at the address below.

The Editors
Tapestry Romances
POCKET BOOKS
1230 Avenue of the Americas
Box TAP
New York, N.Y. 10020

Masquerade

Catherine Lyndell

A TAPESTRY BOOK
PUBLISHED BY POCKET BOOKS NEW YORK

An *Original* publication of TAPESTRY BOOKS

A Tapestry Book published by
POCKET BOOKS, a division of Simon & Schuster, Inc.
1230 Avenue of the Americas, New York, N.Y. 10020

ISBN: 0-671-50048-1

First Tapestry Books printing July, 1984

10 9 8 7 6 5 4 3 2 1

POCKET and colophon are registered trademarks of Simon & Schuster, Inc.

TAPESTRY is a trademark of Simon & Schuster, Inc.

Printed in the U.S.A.

Masquerade

Prologue

WAVES BATTERED AT THE PIECE OF WRECKAGE TO WHICH the two girls were clinging. Time and again the crests of water rose up above the frail planks and came crashing down, covering the girls with water while the boards spun crazily round as if determined to tip them off. Each time, Bridget ducked her head and held her breath until the renewed howling of the wind in her ears told her that it was safe to breathe again. She could hear Lady Charlotte on the other side of the improvised raft, choking and spitting out water after the waves passed.

Just "Charlotte" now, she told herself. Not so much of the "My Lady." Forget about the spoiled young lady who was going out to India to be married, taking along her Irish maidservant. Now they were just two girls trying to keep alive.

And if the storm would only blow itself out, if they could see land, they might have a chance.

The sun was coming up now. How long had it been since the storm blew the *Melbourne* off course on her journey from Gibraltar to Malta? The winds had begun just after sunset—she supposed that had made it worse. To her and Charlotte, locked in their cabin, there had been nothing but the ceaseless buffeting of the waves that threw them against the sides of their bunks, followed by the ominous silence that assaulted their ears as no additional noise could have done. The continual throbbing of the steam engine had been so much a part of their life in the last week that at first they could not comprehend what it meant when it stopped.

"It's the engines are dying." Strangely, it was Bridget Sullivan, ignorant little Biddy who'd never seen the sea before, who was the first to react. But then Bridget had faced death before. She hadn't survived the years of the famine only to die in this cramped room on the steamer that was supposed to be conveying her to India and safety.

And with that thought, clarity came. "I'll not be dying in this dark hole and never a sight of what's happening above. Come on, my lady. We're going on deck."

In all of Lady Charlotte Fitzgerald's pampered life, nothing had ever troubled her that could not be resolved by a command to one of the servants. The night-long pounding of the storm had made her first angry enough to strike Biddy for being slow in carrying out an order, then tearful and finally she had lapsed into this blankeyed incoherent stare that frightened Biddy worse than the anger. She'd been beaten by Lady Charlotte before and survived it. But this sleepwalker's stare was something new. Could a person really go mad from fear? If Lady Charlotte was incapable of going on to India, what would happen to them?

Back to Ballycrochan it would be, and John Kelly waiting for her there, twice as angry at the way she'd slipped free of him.

The thought had given Biddy the courage to urge her dazed and incoherent mistress out on deck. There the torrential rain and the milling, near-hysterical crowd of passengers had roused Lady Charlotte. "What are we doing here? Biddy, you know I cannot abide crowds! We will go below at once to wait out the storm in our cabin!" Her delicate ivory features were contorted with wrath, and she raised a hand to slap Bridget when she did not get instant obedience.

"There's no more waiting to be done," said a gentleman in a frock coat. He pointed into the murky blackness ahead of them. "We're driving down on those rocks. Get your mistress into a lifeboat. I'll help."

Bridget never knew his name, the man who'd helped her force Charlotte, hysterical with rage and fear, into one of the lifeboats. Before she could thank him, they were swaying down the side of the steamer in a dizzying journey that ended abruptly with the smack of a wave sending cold water into the lifeboat. She supposed he was dead now. Were they all dead—all but her and Charlotte? Mary Mother, no! There must be others like themselves, clinging to bits of wreckage in the water.

Charlotte had slapped Biddy for laying hands on her and forcing her into the lifeboat and, standing up in the crazily rocking boat, announced her intention of going right back into the ship where it was dry and warm. "She's not in her right mind," someone said. "We'll have to tie her down."

It was Bridget's task to tie Charlotte to the boat with strips of her own petticoats. Those bindings had saved Charlotte's life when the boat overturned and the rest

3

of the passengers were lost. And Biddy's too, for when she came to the surface, kicking against the folds of her wet skirt and choking on salt water, her hand still clutched the edge of Charlotte's billowing skirt, and that was what brought her back to the splintered planks which were all that were left of the lifeboat.

She'd had enough energy then to squeeze some of the water out of Charlotte's lungs and to tie them both more firmly to the remaining planks. Charlotte lay on her face on top of the boards, with strips of Biddy's apron and her own petticoat wrapped round her and the planks to make sure she did not slide off. Biddy herself lay half in the water, only her head and shoulders supported on the improvised raft. But one oarlock remained on the piece of the boat that they lay on, and she had taken the precaution of passing a strip of linen under her arms and around the oarlock several times, so that she could not be shaken off by one of the waves that inundated their little raft.

At the time it had been only a precaution. All Biddy's fierce energy and desire for life had gone into the grip of her strong young arms round the planks, and she would have sworn that nothing could make her let go to slide into the water! But the ceaseless battering of the waves had worn her down to the point where she hung limply supported by the bindings, just conscious enough to control her breathing when the water broke over her head.

As the sun rose and the winds died down from their twenty-four-hour frenzy, Bridget Sullivan was too tired even to notice their going. She lapsed into unconsciousness, her head lolling on the splintered planking, and let the night winds carry them where they would. Before the sun had burned off the morning mist she was burning with fever.

Four hours later they were picked up by a fishing boat that had set out from Malta to search, without much hope, for survivors of the wreck.

"Only these two found," said the doctor of the military hospital at Valletta, with a kind of gloomy relish. "All the passengers and crew of this mighty ship gone to the bottom, and two girls saved. And this one'll likely no' live." He stooped and put his hand to her forehead. The fever had not abated. He doubted his ability to save her.

The other girl, who had been tied on top of the frail raft, had suffered less from the action of the waves. She might make it.

Both sunburned, their dresses battered to rags, they might have been sisters—the same long brown hair, matted with seawater when they were brought in, now waved softly about the sleeping faces. And they were both tall, and well built, with that delicate creamy Irish skin that suffered so cruelly from the sun and salt.

The doctor sighed and turned away. "Not a scrap on either one to tell us who they were, either. . . . Ah, well. The passenger lists will maybe help us."

Chapter One

Calcutta, 1850

"Look, Charlotte, you can see the shore now!" Agatha Lanyer clutched her new friend's arm and pointed. "Do you recognize your Keith yet?"

Charlotte straightened the seams of her borrowed dress one more time and leaned over the railing of the steamer again, anxiously seeking a red uniform in the crowd that awaited the docking. Her palms were moist and she was having trouble breathing, though that might be because Agatha Lanyer, whose dress she was wearing, was smaller and thinner than she was, and they'd had a mighty tussle with the laces to get her into the dress at all. But Aggie had been adamant.

"It's a romantic story," she said. "Shipwrecked on the way to meet your fiancé! It's only fair you should be properly dressed for your first meeting. That rag they gave you in the hospital is not the thing at all."

So she'd been laced into the pink tarlatan, with its full bell-like skirt and layers of starched petticoats fluffing it out. She was almost afraid to move for fear she would be tipped over entirely.

"You don't want your Keith to see you looking like a dowd, do you?" Agatha reached up to straighten one of the pink silk roses that bordered Charlotte's bonnet. "There! What are you looking so worried for? You're perfectly beautiful. Keith will love you."

"If he recognizes me."

"Bound to." Aggie was all brisk practicality now. "Didn't you write that you'd be traveling with me? And you can't have changed all that much since you were sixteen. It's only been five years. Of course he'll know you."

The statement was not as reassuring as Aggie had doubtless meant it to be. She strained her eyes until it was time to transfer from the steamer into the flat-bottomed wherry that would take them closer to shore. The complications of getting over the ship's side in a crinoline were a welcome distraction. But as the boat pulled closer to the docks—no, not docks; Aggie called it the Chandpal Ghat—she began searching the crowd again. There! Among the shouting, white-clad bearers and the other dark-faced people in their strange colorful costumes were two young men in uniform. One was short and fair, with sunburned skin and a snub nose. The other was half a head taller, tanned almost as dark as a native, with black hair combed close to his head. One of them must be Keith.

Agatha clutched her arm. "That's James M'Laughlin." She pointed to the fair-haired man. "I met him at home. How nice of him to meet the boat!" She raised herself on her knees and waved and yoo-hooed vigorously.

Both men glanced toward the boat. The one called

James M'Laughlin said something to his companion, and then Keith leaned forward and surveyed the passengers with new interest. His gray eyes, curiously light in the tanned face, seemed to fasten on her as a hawk seizes his prey. She felt a strange weakness overcome her as she gazed back into the tanned, aquiline face. Unsmiling now, totally serious, he held her gaze for twenty seconds across the distance of splashing muddy water.

Then the palanquin bearers were running out into the knee-high water, all shouting and wrangling at once for the patronage offered by the new arrivals, and she could not see him anymore. Aggie hired two sets of bearers to take them on shore, using the scraps of broken Hindustani she remembered from her childhood, and within minutes they were swaying toward the shore in curtained palanquins borne on the shoulders of half-naked men.

Keith Powell had not been overly anxious for his reunion with Lady Charlotte. He felt he had done his duty in coming down to the docks to meet the girl and in arranging a place for her to stay. Now his resentment at the way he was being pushed into this marriage surfaced and he lounged on the docks, refusing even to look for the steamer as it drew up the muddy Hooghly River, while his friend James M'Laughlin cracked jokes and tried to win him out of his depression.

"I don't even like the girl," Keith said for the third time. "Never did. But her aunt and my mother were always talking about a match. Well, talk—that means little enough. Especially when I'm in India and don't have to listen to it!" A flashing grin lit up his tanned face and showed momentarily why the ladies of up-country stations were so friendly to a mere lieutenant. Then he frowned again and drove his fist down on his other hand.

"But I never bargained for having my hand forced like this. 'Dear Keith,'" he quoted in savage falsetto mimicry, "'your Charlotte is old enough now to carry out the marriage we refused when you left for India.' Refused, hell! I never asked her to marry me. They were all taking it as a settled thing. I thought my going to India would let them understand how I felt about it. Now they're shipping the damned girl halfway around the world to me. Making sure I don't get the letter until it's too late to write back and stop her. And then she gets herself shipwrecked off Malta, loses her aunt and uncle, and does she have the sense to go home then? No, the good English colony on Malta has to take up a collection to send her on to me. What am I going to do now? Send her back on the next packet?" His face fell into its previous lines of brooding discontent.

"Well, you wanted leave anyway," James offered.

"Yes. To apply for a political appointment. Not to squire some pallid damsel round Calcutta. Balls! Masques! Garden parties!"

James had to laugh at his friend's evident discontent. "Some of us wouldn't take it as a prison sentence, laddie. Try to smile now. You're not likely to be stuck with the girl if you don't want her, you know. A season in Calcutta and she'll have other suitors, even if she's fish-faced and flat on top."

Keith brightened. "She's not plain—at least not when I last saw her. You think she might marry someone else?"

"Bound to," James said. "Just explain to her the difference in income between a poor dog of a soldier and a gentleman on the Civil List; settle her in at the

10

Lanyers', introduce her around, don't say anything about this talk of an engagement and go back to your station. She'll have snapped up a three-hundred-a-year dead-or-alive man before the cold season is over.''

Keith was forced to laugh at his friend's description of the Civil Service men, considered matrimonial prizes because of the pension of three hundred pounds a year which was guaranteed to their widows. "I hope you may be right . . . James! What's the matter?"

His friend was showing all the signs of an incipient apoplexy: bulging eyes, stuttering speech and a rich roseate hue suffusing his face. Keith sprang toward him with some vague idea of loosening his collar, but James waved him away. "I'm all right," he said. "Is that her?"

Keith spared a glance over his shoulder at the wherries approaching from the steamer. In the nearest one he saw two ladies at the rail: a pretty girl in pink and a thin, sandy-haired female. The sandy-haired one was waving and calling to James. "Must be the one in pink," he said. "Charlotte's a brunette, I think. Besides, she would never lower herself to wave and shout in a public place."

"Has to be," said James. "T'other one's Aggie Lanyer. Met her two seasons ago, just before I left England. Didn't you say your Charlotte was traveling with the Lanyer chit?"

Keith nodded and looked up again. The boat was much closer now. "Yes, but don't call her . . ."

For a moment he stopped, unable to go on. Charlotte had been a pretty girl when he left Ireland, but who'd have thought she would develop into such a beauty as this? The two girls in the wherry were quite clearly visible now, and it was also quite clear that from the shining coils of her brown hair to the tips of her aristocratic fingers, Lady Charlotte Fitzgerald was a

11

beauty who would take Calcutta by storm. Her skin was
a clear ivory just touched with gold from the sun of the
voyage; her eyes were wide-set, dark and promising;
her mouth might be a trifle too wide for classical beauty
and her chin too firm; but together with those clear eyes
they gave an impression of strength and sweetness that
might have bowled over a lesser man than Keith Powell
had he not known that impression to be utterly false.

". . . my Charlotte," he finished, feeling somehow as
breathless as though he had just sprinted onto the
docks.

The palanquin bearers were mobbing the boat now;
he lost sight of Charlotte in the crowd and felt his
strength of mind returning. "Because she's not. Call
her your Charlotte, his Charlotte, any man's but mine,
and I'll agree."

"You're a fool," said James equably, "but we'll not
quarrel over it. There are not so many English girls in
Calcutta that I'll object to any man who passes up his
chance at one."

"You're the fool," Keith retorted, "if you take those
pretty looks at face value. She's poison, James. A
pretty, beguiling, nicely wrapped bundle of poison, I'll
grant you, but let her beguile someone who doesn't
know her already!"

And then the girls were beside them, and Keith
swung round wondering if Charlotte had heard anything of what he had said. If so, she was too well-bred
to show it. There was a faint tinge of pink in her cheeks,
and she was breathing shallowly, but that might have
been due to the commotion on the docks. Still, Keith
felt guilty for his rudeness. He put out both hands to
greet her.

"Lady Charlotte. I hope you are not too much
fatigued from your journey?"

12

That was enough. Then a slight bow, and he could excuse himself on the score of dealing with the luggage while James entertained the girls.

That had been his plan. The moment his palms touched Charlotte's cool fingers, an electric shock ran through him that quite put out of his head any plans for cool greetings and quick excuses. Instead he lingered, staring at her like some country booby while her dark eyes widened and the tinge of pink flowered on her cheeks. She was looking at him with her lips slightly parted, as if she wanted to speak but could not. But those wonderful eyes spoke for her. There was mystery in those eyes, and the promise of adventure, and laughter and all the gifts with which he endowed his dream woman in the lonely nights up-country. Keith felt an intoxication like wine running through his body from the tips of his fingers where he touched her.

Then she inclined her head slightly and withdrew her hands. "I am glad to see you in good health, Mr. Powell."

Yes—that was Charlotte. She might have come half-way across the world to marry him, but she would not waste her gracious airs on him till she saw how the land lay. That self-centered possession had been one of the traits he'd most disliked about her when they were children.

The spell was broken, and Keith was glad enough to busy himself with arranging for bearers to take up the trunks as they were delivered from the ship. There were more than he'd expected for Miss Lanyer and none at all for Charlotte.

"The shipwreck," she explained. "There's nothing I have but the clothes on my back—less than that, even. Agatha was after lending me this dress to . . ."

To make a good impression on him, Keith finished.

13

Of course! Far be it from Charlotte to arrive looking like the bedraggled victim of shipwreck. He wondered just how she had bullied it out of sandy-haired little Miss Lanyer. He gave Agatha a speculative glance and she grinned at him. "The color is far more becoming to Charlotte than to me. And Mama was so generous in sending me money for this trip, I have far more dresses than I need. There is a green watered-silk ball dress in one of those trunks. I hope it may not have been too sadly crushed in the journey! I brought it hoping for a ball at Government House before the hot weather."

She continued to chatter about anything that came into her head, covering up Charlotte's reserved silence. Keith found it difficult to get a word in edgewise. By the time they had got the trunks loaded into a wagon to follow the Lanyers' barouche, he was happy enough to let James sit beside Miss Lanyer and listen to her stream of inconsequential chatter. He found himself thinking that there was something to be said for Charlotte's cool reticence after all. Still, you'd think the girl would notice something about her surroundings! Here she was getting her first sight of the mysterious East and not a word to say about it. Well, that was Charlotte. Nothing impressed her so much as her own consequence.

Just then she leaned eagerly out of the carriage as they passed a group of natives decorating one of their statues with wreaths of marigolds and turned back to him with delight in her eyes. But before she could speak, Aggie leaned over the back of the seat and directed her stream of talk at them. "Oh, they must be preparing for a festival! Which one is it, Mr. M'Laughlin, do you know? I have been away so long that I cannot remember. It would be famous if we could show Charlotte the Diwali celebrations. Would you not like to see all the little lights floating down the river, Charlotte? Oh, there is the Burra-bazaar. My *ayah* used to take me there for sweetmeats when I was very little. Do you ever go into the native town, Lieutenant Powell? I wonder if they still have those beautiful Kashmiri shawls . . ."

She went on in this vein, never giving anyone a chance to answer her numerous questions, and Charlotte's dark eyes danced at Keith as if inviting him to share the joke. He ran a finger round the inside of his stiff uniform stock. It might be the cool season, but he was finding the day uncommonly warm all of a sudden.

When Aggie settled down in the front seat again, it was as if a water tap had been turned off in full spate. The silence that fell was too much for Keith.

"Do . . . do you find the climate very fatiguing, Charlotte?" he asked.

"No, Mr. . . . Lieutenant Powell," she replied. She seemed to be thinking about each word before she brought it out. Was it so much effort to converse with him? "Like Agatha, I find it delightful, but I am informed that will change soon."

"Yes, the hot season begins in March or April," Keith agreed. He frowned. Better not to pursue the subject. Charlotte would likely throw a fit when she found he was planning to leave her at the Lanyers' and go about his business; it would only be a worse fit if she knew how hot and miserable it would be in Calcutta by next month. Well, best to get it over with.

"There are very few accommodations fit for a lady in the city," he said. "I have arranged for you to stay with Mr. and Mrs. Lanyer, Agatha's parents. They have a very pleasant house in Chowringhee, where most of the English families in Calcutta reside. I think you will be quite comfortable there." There, it was done, and she was only smiling at him as if she were quite happy to be left at some strangers' house like a piece of unwanted luggage. Oh, but he had not done. "I will do myself the honor of calling in a few days to see how you get on. Unfortunately, my duties do not permit me the leisure of visiting daily. In fact, I may be called up-country again very soon."

Was that a flash of relief he saw in her eyes? Keith had no time to consider the matter, for James had turned round in the front seat of the barouche and was about to speak. Doubtless he wanted to ask what these "duties" were, since he knew very well that Keith was on leave and had nothing to do but kick his heels while waiting for a political appointment. Keith scowled horribly at his friend and made several grotesque faces intended to convey the message, "Shut up, I'll explain later."

Finally James turned back to Miss Lanyer and Keith relaxed. He stole a glance at Charlotte to see if she was preparing to throw a fit. He'd seen her go into a rage over fancied slights to her dignity when she was only a child. He shrank from imagining how she would respond to this quite real slight. But, incredibly, she seemed to be laughing. As he looked at her she hastily smoothed her countenance to express nothing but well-bred vacuity. But the laugh had been there. Keith yanked at his suddenly too-tight uniform collar again and wondered if she'd seen him making faces.

Fortunately, it was not far to the Lanyers' residence in Chowringhee. At least, Keith thought, Charlotte could not complain of the style of her accommodations. This district of beautiful detached houses surrounded by gardens was one of the most pleasant parts of Calcutta. The Lanyers' house and garden, like most others, was surrounded by a high wall to keep out thieves. Within, the beauty of the meticulously tended garden with its flowering shrubs and carefully raked sand paths and the gracious charm of the house with its deep verandah on three sides were bound to appeal to Charlotte.

Keith was pleased to note that she drew a deep breath as the barouche rolled in through the gate. "Sure, and it's lovely!" she cried with spontaneous pleasure. "Never did I think to be seeing something so beautiful as the flowers and birds along the river, but this has them all beat!"

Agatha giggled. "Really, Charlotte, your accent is quite *Irish* sometimes."

Charlotte blushed and sat back, gripping her hands together so tightly that the knuckles turned white. Keith was moved to speak in her defense. He might not care for Charlotte personally, but he was Irish too, he reminded Agatha, and not ashamed of it.

But it was strange. She had sounded for all the world like one of the servant girls on the estate.

Keith mulled it over for a few minutes, wondering if Charlotte had developed low tastes on her return from school to the Fitzgeralds' country place. It did not seem like her. Charlotte had always felt herself above the rest of the country gentry, let alone the villagers.

But it was a trivial matter after all, and he forgot all about it in the strain of the next few minutes. All his social ingenuity was required to greet the Lanyers, make just the minimum amount of conversation required for politeness and extricate himself without either giving active offense to Charlotte or acting like a man who considered himself engaged to be married. It was his devout hope that if this "engagement" were to go unmentioned for a while, Charlotte would find herself another suitor in his absence. And so whenever

Mrs. Lanyer inquired about his immediate plans or directed a beaming glance of approval on the recently reunited young couple, Keith changed the subject.

It should have been a source of satisfaction to him that Charlotte seemed no more eager to discuss their engagement than he was. She was positively helpful in avoiding the subject. When Mrs. Lanyer asked Keith how long he would stay in Calcutta, it was Charlotte who said that a soldier was hardly master of his own time. And when she suggested that the two of them take a turn in the gardens, Keith excused himself on the grounds that Charlotte was greatly interested in nature and would doubtless prefer to walk with someone like Colonel Lanyer who could tell her the names of the flowers. Charlotte took her cue and immediately looked up at Colonel Lanyer with such a pretty, beseeching expression that he laughed and twirled his mustache and called her a naughty puss.

Oh, they made a great team, working together to avoid being thrown together. Keith knew it was illogical, but he could not repress some feeling of pique.

"Tell me, have I broken out in a disfiguring attack of prickly heat?" he asked James M'Laughlin when, their farewells made, they were returning to their lodgings in Calcutta. "Is my uniform spotted and grease-stained? My person unpleasing, my manners unacceptable?"

"You don't want her either," James pointed out. "What's your complaint?"

Keith gave an uneasy laugh. "I don't know. Nothing. Help me dig up some Civil Service gents for her to meet."

James's steps slowed and he threw a quick glance at his friend. "I hope you didn't mean that literally."

"What d'you mean?"

"Johnson died last night."

Keith slowed his steps to match James's pace. "Damn! That's two this week. Cholera?"

James shrugged. "I don't know. There's sickness in the native quarters. But when isn't there?"

Keith frowned and broke a twig from a flowered bush, absently twirling it in his hand. "It's too early for cholera. The worst outbreaks are in the hot season."

"I know."

Neither of them was completely reassured by this agreement.

The Lanyers' elegant house in Chowringhee was deserted—if one did not count the two or three dozen native servants who dozed, squatted in corners or lackadaisically pounded rice for the evening meal. Agatha Lanyer and her parents had gone out to take a turn in the garden. Agatha had invited Lady Charlotte to go with them, but she pleaded the fatigue of the journey and said she might take a short nap.

Now she wandered through the house, tired and restless, relieved and excited, unable to sleep and curious about the household arrangements. She had expected something like the Fitzgeralds' gracious Regency house in Ireland with its lower floors full of elegant antique furniture and its upper story of cramped little rooms for the servants. This was entirely different.

She wandered through spacious, high-ceilinged rooms opening one into the other by means of ceiling-high folding doors and windows. The walls were covered with white plaster and the floors with some sort of coarse brown matting. On the lower floors, green-painted blinds of bamboo slips hung over the doorways

19

that opened onto the verandah. Upstairs, the room she had been given was screened by silk hangings with curious painted figures on them.

Beyond the verandah there was the glare of the sun, the ceaseless hum of countless insects, the subdued murmur of two or three servants who squatted on the verandah to gossip. The air in the house smelled of spices and sweet flowers, dust and sun. Nothing more different from damp, green Ireland could have been imagined.

She took a deep breath of satisfaction and gave an impudent grin to her reflection in the wide, slightly wavy mirror on her dressing table. She watched her own gestures in the mirror as she unpinned the flowered silk and straw bonnet whose unaccustomed weight made her head ache. Once it was loose, she flung it up across the bed where it caught and dangled on a trailing curtain of mosquito gauze. She picked up the full, hampering skirts and essayed a brief jigstep, heels clicking against each other and sinking into the soft matting again without a sound. "You've done it!" she whispered exultantly to herself. "Bridget Sullivan of Ballycrochan, it's yourself that's the fine lady now and no danger at all of being sent back, the way you've fooled them all so rarely!"

Suddenly demure again, she let her skirts fall, crossed the matting with little, precise steps, and called for an ayah to get her bonnet down and unhook her dress. It was complicated, this lady business, but she'd manage. God wouldn't let her get this far and then let her down.

Chapter Two

THE LIQUID BROWN EYE SEEMED TO BE STARING STRAIGHT at her with a disdainful expression, as though it saw through her pitiful pretense to being a lady. Bridget clenched her hands around her riding crop and stared back, giving as good as she got. After a moment, her adversary turned away with a snort.

So far, so good. But now, Mary Mother, she was expected to climb on this crazy contraption called a sidesaddle, instead of riding with her two legs clamped around the sides of the horse the way the Lord meant a sane person to ride. Bridget shut her eyes and uttered a silent prayer. Sure, it was broken in pieces she would be! But it was that or confess her deception to the Lanyers and suffer humiliating exposure.

She had already tried every excuse she could think of to avoid joining Agatha on her early-morning rides.

"I detest early rising."

Agatha had briskly disposed of that one. "Nonsense. By next month the hot weather will begin and the only times one can get out at all then are before dawn and after sunset. You may as well get used to it now."

"I have no horse," Bridget had tried next. This time it had been Colonel Lanyer who foiled her.

"Plenty of hacks in the stables, getting fat for lack of exercise! What do I pay all those grooms and grass-cutters for, if they can't saddle up an extra horse for Aggie's little friend, eh?" He'd pinched her cheek. "Have to keep the roses in those cheeks!"

Then she'd pleaded her lack of suitable clothes. All she had were the two dresses donated her in Valletta by the Hospital Society and Aggie's pink tarlatan.

"The *durzee* can alter my old riding habit," Mrs. Lanyer had said, measuring Bridget with her eyes. "A little taken in at the waist and the bodice let out a little, should do it. And while he is working, I have a length of Berhampore silk in my dressing room that should be just the color for you. We will have it made up into a day dress. And there is that white muslin I bought at the Burra-bazaar, Lord knows why, I'm long past the age for white . . ." She'd drifted off to find the durzee who spent his days sewing for the household, and Bridget had succumbed to the cumulative effect of the Lanyers' generosity. Perhaps, she thought optimistically, it wouldn't be so bad. She had seen Lady Charlotte riding sidesaddle many a time at home, and she looking as comfortable as if she were sitting in an armchair.

But that was before this cool dawn when she stood face to face with a great stupid beast twice the height of her father's little donkey, and Agatha and James M'Laughlin and Keith Powell waited for her to leap onto its back the way Lady Charlotte would be doing.

Worst of all, Mrs. Lanyer had dragooned Keith into

joining them when he came yesterday to pay a brief duty call. Bridget thought that she would rather die than confess her masquerade before Keith and watch the boredom in his eyes turn to open contempt.

She looked up nervously at the horse. Up close, it seemed very big.

Bridget set her teeth and accepted Keith's help in mounting. Fortunately she had had time to watch the other ladies doing it. He leaned forward with his hands interlaced and she put her left foot on them, her hand on his shoulder, then straightened her leg while he lifted her to the saddle.

Only it didn't quite work. She scrambled for the saddle, felt herself falling, then his hands were about her waist and he lifted her into the saddle like a child.

She hooked her knee about the crutch of the saddle and smoothed her skirts down. Keith placed her left foot in the stirrup. His hand rested on her ankle. She felt the warmth of his touch all through her body. Why didn't he leave off fussing with the stirrup and let her go! He didn't even like her. All right, so it was Lady Charlotte he didn't like. Came to the same thing, didn't it? Humiliating, to feel this way from the touch of a man who avoided you whenever he could. She wanted to lean over and smooth his dark hair back from his temple. No, she didn't. She didn't care a rap for him.

He stepped back at last, and Bridget got her first good look at the ground. It seemed so far away, and she felt so insecure perched up here! Not much like riding the little donkey out in the soft green fields, with no saddle to get in your way and a good soft turf to fall on. Her leg was about to go numb, the way she was bending it about the crutch of the sidesaddle, not to fall off.

The *sais* who held her horse's head passed the reins up to her. She held them tightly, one in each clenched fist. A titter from Agatha warned her. That wasn't the way. She slid a sidewise glance at Aggie and tried to copy her way of holding the reins, casually, passed loosely through the fingers.

The damned horse snorted again and shuffled sideways. Bridget slipped to one side and had to grab the saddle to pull herself upright again. While she was studying the reins, Keith had mounted and come up beside her. She eyed his great chestnut horse uneasily. It seemed to have a wild look in its eye. So did hers, if it came to that. Merciful saints, what if the creature ran away with her? She'd just have to forget propriety, throw her right leg over its back and clutch the mane. It would take Calcutta a long time to get over laughing at that, the Irish servant girl galloping flat-out through town in her borrowed riding habit. Bridget clenched her teeth and gave Keith a determined smile.

"Ready, Lady Charlotte?"

Bridget inclined her head. She was afraid to speak lest her trembling voice give her away.

It wasn't so bad as she had feared, once they were moving. The animal seemed to respond to the touch of her reins, and that great horn sticking out of the saddle, that they called the crutch, did give her some sense of security. After a few moments, she was even able to make light conversation with Keith. What would Lady Charlotte have said?

"Is this not delightful beyond anything, Keith? I cannot tell you how I missed my morning ride while we were on the steamer!"

Keith inclined his head slightly. Bridget felt a shiver of unease at the smile in his eyes. But his words were unexceptional. "I am glad to hear it, Charlotte. You looked so pale, I feared you were not enjoying yourself."

Bridget seized on and embroidered the excuse his words gave her. "To tell the truth, I am not feeling perfectly well. Perhaps it is the change of climate. I was determined not to miss a chance to ride, but now I fear I may have made a mistake in coming out at all."

She wished that Keith would quit looking at her in that puzzled, calculating way. Was she making some mistake in her imitation of Lady Charlotte? Her mimicking of the folk at the Great House used to send the other servants into peals of laughter, and they vowed she could "take off" Lady Charlotte to perfection. But perhaps that wasn't very good training for this masquerade, any more than a few years spent learning gentle ways as Lady Charlotte's maidservant were adequate training for pretending to be a lady herself.

Fortunately, Aggie provided a diversion. She had ridden some distance ahead with James M'Laughlin. Now she wheeled her horse and raced back to where Keith and Bridget were talking, making a showy stop inches from them that raised the white dust on the Esplanade.

"Is this not famous?" she cried. "Only think, Charlotte, here we can gallop as far and fast as we like, and no one to lift her eyebrows and call us hoydens! Oh, how I missed this during those dreary years at school! Will you race me to Government House, Char?"

She was off again as soon as she had spoken, with James in attendance on her mad gallop. Bridget's horse threw up its head and pawed the ground as though it wanted to dash after them. She felt the reins slipping through her hands, made a desperate snatch to retrieve them and inadvertently yanked the horse's head back again. It reared up and she tumbled to the ground with an ignominious thump that knocked the breath out of her.

Blackness, stars, light, somebody lifting her up. "Charlotte! Are you all right?"

Unable to speak for lack of breath, she grinned at Keith to reassure him. "Okay . . . just . . . winded," she managed jerkily. The constricting stays kept her from getting a good breath. Hard work, being a lady. Bridget was exhausted already, and it not yet seven in the morning!

She gave in to the enervated feeling and let her head fall back against Keith's shoulder. He was supporting her. That should help. But everywhere that he touched her just increased the delicious, dangerous lassitude that ran through her entire body. Her lips were very near his tanned cheek. She felt a sudden mad impulse to press them to his face. What would it be like if he turned his head and kissed her? Not like that time John Kelly cornered her behind the stables, that was for sure.

He was looking at her in that way that made her forget everything. A puzzled, questioning look was in his gray eyes—almost wounded, as if he wanted her so much that it hurt him. And then, without warning, his arms relaxed around her and he left her to support herself.

"Charlotte! Are you all right?" This time it was Aggie, back from her brief gallop and bending over her anxiously. And behind her, James. Bridget stood up and shook her skirts free of the clinging white dust. "Sure, and I'm not so fragile as to break from a bit of a toss," she assured them with a broad grin to cover up how shaky she felt inside. "Haven't I had worse at home, many a time? Why, once when—"

She bit off the sentence. It would never do to be telling these fine folk of the time she tried to ride standing barefoot on the back of her father's donkey.

What was Lady Charlotte doing on an Irish peasant's donkey, they would ask. And then the fat would be in the fire for certain!

"It does not signify in the slightest," she said, this time remembering to hold her mouth tight as if speaking pained her, the way Lady Charlotte would be doing. "Agatha, I am afraid the sun is too much for me." What a stupid excuse. The sun was barely up. But nobody contradicted her. "Perhaps I had better return to the house and lie down."

The Lanyers' house was barely half a mile away. She'd thought to lead her horse back there—no persuasion was going to get her up on it again!—and leave the rest of them to enjoy their riding, if enjoy it they truly did. But it seemed this was impossible. Charlotte could not go back to the house unescorted; Keith would have to go with her. Charlotte and Keith might walk without a chaperone, since—Agatha giggled, earning black looks from both parties—everybody knew they had an Understanding. But it would not be *comme il faut* for Agatha to ride alone with James.

"And what mischief would they be getting up to, and them on horseback?" thought Bridget scornfully. "Sure, and it's all they could do to keep their limbs whole, without getting to entangling them round each other!" But she kept this thought to herself. Something told her Agatha would think she was being coarse, though what could be coarser than the way fine folk were forever thinking of the ways people could get into bed, and the ways to keep them out of it, was beyond her entirely.

Complicated, this lady business.

At least she didn't have to ride again. Evidently it was also unthinkable for a lady to walk a few hundred yards, but Agatha suggested that since poor dear

Charlotte was feeling dizzy, Keith should take her up before him on his horse.

That was almost worse than riding. She sat primly stiff and gazed out over the Maidan, trying to pretend she didn't notice his arms on either side of her, his breath against her neck. She forgot her fear of the horse in an older, more potent fear. The warm touch of his body, his arms brushing against hers, tempted her down unknown ways. She could turn her head and kiss him. He would be shocked. She could confess that she wasn't Lady Charlotte, and then maybe he wouldn't dislike her anymore, but he would laugh at her, and that would be worse. She could throw herself off the horse to escape being so close to him and feeling so strange.

She could sit perfectly still and stare in front of her and not speak a word that might give her away.

"They are called adjutant-birds," Keith said.

"What?"

He raised his right hand and pointed at the large, ungainly birds stalking about the green ditches alongside the Maidan.

"Oh!"

"I thought we might as well pretend to talk about something," Keith explained. "You would scarcely want to be recollecting stories of our childhood?"

The cold dislike in his voice chilled Bridget to the bone. It was no worse than she'd heard before, but in this inescapably intimate contact it hurt her more.

"No," she said. God knew, the last thing she needed was Keith Powell in a reminiscent mood! But she couldn't think of anything suitably Lady Charlotte-like to add to the bald monosyllable, and so it hung there.

Keith reached around her and transferred both reins into his left hand. Then his right hand passed slowly, caressingly up the curves of her tight-fitting basque. Bridget felt her breast tingling beneath his touch, and her breath came shorter for some reason. She glanced to her left. Agatha and James were riding a few paces behind, leading her horse. Keith's movements were lost on them.

Lady Charlotte would say "How dare you!" and slap him. Bridget knew that without a doubt. But she wasn't Lady Charlotte. She was Bridget Sullivan, and she'd never felt anything like this before, or known a man like this, whipcord-tough and lean and confident. She let her head fall back against Keith's shoulder. The rhythmic pounding of his heart was loud in her ears. She sighed with the pleasure of his caress as he daringly sought out the sensitive areas under her cloth basque.

A low chuckle from Keith brought her back to her senses. His hand dropped away. "Since you don't talk, I had to take other means of seeing if you were alive," he explained. "The experiment seems successful. Imagine Lady Charlotte purring under a furtive caress, just like the servant girl on the back stairs!"

"How dare you!" said Lady Charlotte, and slapped him.

They reached the Lanyers' compound without another word spoken on either side. Keith handed Bridget down before him to a waiting sais.

"The *memsahib* is unwell," he said. "Call her ayah." He bowed to Bridget. "I shall do myself the honor of calling this evening to assure myself that you have suffered no ill effects from our excursion."

James and Agatha were just riding up. Bridget went into the house without a backward look. Let Keith be insulted by her rudeness if he would! They had nothing to say to one another. He was a detestable man and even if he weren't dangerous to her, she would be glad to see the back of him.

In the semi-privacy of her bedroom, with its open doors on all sides screened by silk curtains, she wearily faced the truth. Detestable he might be, but she could not learn to detest him. Their few brief meetings had left her with an image against which she compared every other man who came to the Lanyers' house and found them all wanting.

But she would have to learn better. The attraction she felt for this man was dangerous. It could destroy her whole plan.

Bridget stared into the mirror while the ayah unpinned her masses of brown hair. They tumbled down around her face, framing her flushed cheeks and starry eyes, and turned her from the dignified Lady Charlotte back into Biddy the maidservant. She closed her eyes against the sight. How had she gotten herself into this? It had seemed so easy at first!

She'd never meant to spend weeks masquerading as a lady in Calcutta. When the doctor in Valletta checked the passenger lists, greeted her as Lady Charlotte and gave her the sad news that her uncle and aunt had died, as well as her maid, she had been too tired and weak to explain to him. Only later, as she lay in the sickbed, did it occur to her that while Bridget Sullivan might be put on the next packet back to Ballycrochan, Lady Charlotte Fitzgerald could quite reasonably travel on to India to meet her fiancé as planned. And so the daring impersonation had begun. But it was only intended to last as long as the voyage. Once in Calcutta, given a few days to look about her, she would slip away and take service with some English family. She wasn't afraid of hard work, just so it was honest work.

But there were a few things she hadn't reckoned on in that plan. One was the friendship of Agatha Lanyer, thin, plain little Agatha who was going back to India to visit her parents and who invited "Lady Charlotte" to travel with her. Talkative, generous, tactless and loving, Agatha would be sorely hurt if her new friend disappeared without a word as soon as they reached Calcutta.

Bridget sighed. She still hadn't figured out how to break the news to Agatha. But that would have to wait until she solved the second problem. There were so few white women in Calcutta that she would find it almost impossible to vanish. And none of them kept white servants. Every family had its thirty to fifty Indian servants—what did they need with one Irish maid? The Indians had their own homes to go to, got their own food and were content to squat for countless hours in some out-of-the-way corner waiting for the moment when they might be called upon. She couldn't compete with that.

The only Englishwomen in Calcutta were the wives of officers and civil servants and a few girls like Aggie, come out to marry. So that was what she would have to do. Find a nice, not too observant young man, preferably one serving in a back-country station where her social deficiencies wouldn't be too noticeable, and marry him. Quickly. Before one of her many lies caught up with her.

And that brought her back to why she mustn't give in to the strange new feelings that Keith Powell stirred in her. He was the one man in India who had known the real Lady Charlotte, the one most dangerous to her. She would simply have to stop thinking of the way his eyes crinkled round the corners when he laughed, the deep tones of his voice, the lean, brown hands that had held the reins before her with such control. She would have to avoid him at all costs.

Fortunately, Bridget thought, he seemed equally determined to avoid her. Even if he'd promised to call again, he'd made it perfectly clear that he regarded it as a distasteful duty.

That should make her feel better. For some reason it didn't help. In fact, she felt like crying. She screwed her eyelids together to stop the tears and squinted into the mirror, willing her face back to the icy composure suitable for "Lady Charlotte."

She wondered what time Keith would be calling that evening.

Chapter Three

THE WIDE STREET CALLED THE BURRA-BAZAAR WAS crowded with traffic of every description, from bullock carts prodded along by half-naked coolies to palanquins shrouded in red silk from which a brown hand and arm, covered wrist to elbow with clashing bangles, reached out to finger some merchant's wares. Keith thanked his good fortune that he had had the sense to stop the Lanyers' barouche at the end of the street, and cursed his ill luck that his dutiful evening call on Charlotte had somehow been transmuted into an excursion to show the young ladies around the bazaar.

It was Aggie Lanyer's fault, he decided—her indefatigable enthusiasm, and her interest in James M'Laughlin, and his unlucky habit of taking James with him whenever he called on the Lanyers, as a shield against being left alone with Charlotte to make his formal proposal. Somehow Aggie had seized upon a chance remark of his about the native town and embroidered it and decorated it and pulled it this way and that until she made out that he had invited her and Charlotte to come for a ride down to the native bazaar. And as soon as they left the carriage, there went Aggie on James M'Laughlin's arm, leaving him to entertain Charlotte.

Keith glanced at the girl on his arm with a sigh of regret. Her profile, framed in the pink bonnet and brown ringlets, was enough to lead any man on. And if she'd been any girl but Charlotte Fitzgerald, he would have been exercising all his charm to make her turn her head and bestow a full-face smile on him, maybe even to say something. But Charlotte—no! Only vinegar came from those sweet lips. He was perfectly happy to stroll on with her in silence.

Perfectly happy.

Really.

If only she didn't look so damned enchanting! Keith groaned. The girl was a lovely, temptingly baited trap, waiting to lure him into one careless word that she could embroider into a marriage proposal. And then what? Could a pretty face compensate for a lifetime of the acidulous, desiccated marriage that the older Fitzgeralds had enjoyed, and that Charlotte bid fair to reproduce with the man luckless enough to take her? No, he would have to control his desires. Rise above lusts of the flesh, and remember how much he would dislike being stuck with her for life.

Just then Charlotte glanced up at him and smiled, and Keith groaned again. The flesh was hard to control. Cold showers, that was the thing. Cold showers and exercise and maybe a discreet visit to the native quarter. . . .

"Mr. Powell?" That was Charlotte's voice, icy-sweet, controlled, and yet with something of the unfamiliar

timbre in it that had got him off-balance once or twice.
"Are you unwell?"

"I?" Keith met her inquiry with a look of bland
unconcern. "Why should you ask?"

"I thought you groaned."

"I . . . ah . . . you must have heard a conch shell."
He pointed at a stall full of shells and other merchan-
dise of the sea. "The natives blow them for, ah,
religious reasons. Temple ceremonies. That sort of
thing."

Charlotte looked up and down the crowded street. "I
see no temple here."

"The stallkeeper was just demonstrating one to a
customer." Keith improvised wildly. He stepped over
to the stall and snatched up the largest shell he could
find. He set his lips to the small end and blew,
producing a sound like a lovesick cow with the glan-
ders.

Charlotte laughed until she had to clutch at his arm
for support. "Oh, Keith, that was wonderful! Do it
again!"

He obliged with another mighty honk, and then
another, until he was red-faced and gasping for breath.
Then he gave in to an irrational impulse and tossed the
stallkeeper a few *pice*.

"Here." He handed the conch shell to Charlotte. "A
souvenir of your first visit to the bazaar."

She laughed again and tucked the large pink shell
under her arm.

They wandered on, stopping wherever Charlotte or
Agatha saw something to catch the eye. There was
entertainment in plenty at the Burra-bazaar, from the
intinerant sweetseller with his brass tray of confections
to the Kashmiri shawl merchant seated amidst a rain-

bow of fine yarns. Agatha stopped to turn over a pile of the rich warm shawls. "Oh, look, Charlotte! Does not this deep gold color suit you to perfection?" She held the glowing cloth up to Charlotte's cheek, where it echoed the gleam of the setting sun in her warm brown hair and the gold flecks in her eyes.

"Indeed it does," laughed Charlotte, "but I prefer the color of these spices!" She moved on to the *bania*'s shop next door. Stooping over an array of brown sacks, open at the necks to display their wealth of sweet and pungent spices, she pointed to one sack full of a deep gold powder.

"That is turmeric," Keith told her. "It is used to flavor the native curries. If you want a paint, you should buy some of this." He lifted a small bag full of brownish-black grit. "This is henna. The native women stain their palms with it." He lifted her hand and traced out a design with his forefinger to illustrate what he meant. The small, squarish hand trembled in his own, and he laid his palm flat against hers for a moment. The unplanned contact was a point of sweetness that spread through his whole body.

Charlotte dropped her eyes. Her voice was low and troubled. "And . . . should I . . . emulate their example?"

"No," Keith said. He dropped her hand before he could give in to the insane urge to press kisses on the white palm. "No, you are . . . quite all right . . . as you are."

He turned away and pushed through the crowd, leaving Charlotte to make her own way behind him. What had come over him? Next thing, he'd be fancying himself in love with the girl! That just showed what too long on an up-country station, seeing no new faces, could do to you. It was long past time for him to come on leave. As soon as he got these girls back to the Lanyers' house, he and James would go out and have some real fun, cut a swathe through the native town and find some dark-skinned girls with henna-dyed hands and bells on their ankles to keep them company.

The thought didn't appeal to him as much as it should have.

By the time they had passed a few more stalls, Keith had noticed a pattern. Agatha looked, and bought, and pointed things out to Charlotte. Charlotte admired everything and bought nothing. James was loaded down with the pretty shawls and silks and glass bangles and brass trays that Agatha had picked up, not to mention the basket she had bought for him to carry things in and the quilted silk *rezai* that Keith had to carry because James's arms were full. Charlotte had nothing but the conch shell.

"Look, Charlotte!" This time it was a stall full of silver bracelets.

"No, but look, Agatha!" Charlotte turned away from the tempting display of jewelry and pointed to a marriage procession wending its way down the street, the bride in a curtained palanquin and the groom decked with flower wreaths from head to heels.

An uncomfortable thought struck Keith. When they were collecting the luggage the other day, Charlotte had said she had nothing but what she wore. How literally did she mean that? He knew that on the Fitzgeralds' death, the estate passed to a distant cousin. If Charlotte had had nothing but the money and baggage she brought with her on the trip, and all that went to the bottom of the Mediterranean, she must have been counting on Keith to take care of her once she reached India. Instead of which, he had left her to depend on the charity of strangers.

Keith flushed a dull red under his tan. It was one thing to say he didn't want to marry the girl. It was another to be her only acquaintance in the whole of India and to leave her in a strange house with an empty purse.

"These bracelets are really beautiful, Charlotte," he pressed her when Agatha turned back to the stall. "Why don't you buy one? They're only a few rupees."

When she looked away and made an evasive answer, Keith had all the confirmation he needed. On the spur of the moment, he improvised a plan and set out to execute it.

"Look, Charlotte," he said the next time Aggie, darting away like a little fish in the stream of humanity, drew James after her to examine some new gaudy trinkets.

Then he stopped and tugged at his uniform stock. This was harder than he thought it would be.

"Look," he began again. "I fear I have been remiss in a matter of business that lies between us." All this beating about the bush was getting him exactly nowhere. He took a deep breath and plunged right in. "When Lord and Lady Fitzgerald wrote to me that they were escorting you to India, they asked me to make some arrangements for your stay here."

"Yes, I know," Charlotte said absently. "The Lanyers have been very kind. Oh, look, Keith, what are they doing over there?" She pointed at a narrow alleyway leading to an open court where a circle of half-naked women were dancing, emitting shrill cries in time with the drum and slapping themselves as they pranced up and down.

Keith took her shoulder and turned her away from the sight. "Never mind," he said. Thank goodness she hadn't been in India long enough to recognize what she saw! He had seen hundreds of women in that frenzied dance last hot weather, dancing to placate the goddess who sent the cholera. There were only a few dancing now, but it was impossible to tell how quickly the disease—and the panic that accompanied it—might spread through the city. They should never have come down to the bazaar. He would have to find James and get the girls out of here. But first he wanted to finish his explanation to Charlotte.

"The Lanyers are good sorts," he agreed. "But your aunt and uncle expected to be here with you. They wanted me to procure a house and servants for you all. Lord Fitzgerald sent me a bank draft for the money and I deposited it and then forgot all about it when we heard the sad news of the shipwreck. It comes to . . ." he hesitated, trying to weigh a reasonable figure against what remained of his sadly depleted quarterly allowance, "two thousand rupees that I owe you." That was enough to hire a small house and pay for a modest establishment of servants—say, twenty or thirty—for a year. More would hardly have been credible.

Two thousand rupees! Bridget sucked in her breath as she contemplated the sum. With that much money, she might be able to fulfill her original plan of disappearing. She could afford to go to some other city and rent lodgings while she tried to find work. She need never see Keith Powell again, never risk his exposing her imposture.

The thought didn't appeal to her as much as it should have. It was almost with relief that she discovered the loophole. The money was in some bank. To get it, she would have to go to the bank and sign some papers in Lady Charlotte's name. That was fraud or something.

You could go to jail for that in Ireland. She didn't know what they did in India, but it was probably something gruesome like cutting off your hand.

"Oh, but I couldn't be taking it," she blurted out in her relief, "and it not really my money at all." Then she stopped with one hand half-raised to clap over her mouth. Bridget Sullivan, when will you learn to keep your big mouth shut? And talking Irish, to boot!

"That is," she amended, "I . . . I don't feel as if it is right. Being from the estate, you know."

Keith eyed her suspiciously. Her first speech had been unforced; the second sounded lame. Had she seen through his stratagem so easily as that? Impossible! He was going to be a master diplomat some day. Everybody said so. Why else was he kicking his heels in Calcutta, waiting for the governor-general to grant him a staff appointment? He bent his energies to persuading Charlotte to accept the mythical bank draft.

Bridget could have kicked herself for her unwary words. She thought she had covered up well enough, but why was Keith looking so suspicious? Afraid of saying something else that would give her away, she nodded her head and meekly agreed to his plans to transfer the bank draft into her name. She was somewhat relieved when he offered to take care of the business aspects himself. Because there were no bank notes in India, he explained, it would be inconvenient for her to carry the entire sum in rupees. It would be better if he cashed a part of the draft so that she could have some money while she was in Calcutta and left the rest as notes of credit on the bank.

Fine. She would deal with the problem of the notes of credit later. For now, there was no denying that a little money in her purse would be welcome, enough to save her from depending on the Lanyers' charity for every stitch she wore. There wouldn't be enough to finance her disappearance; that would have to wait. Bridget gave a sigh of relief and turned back to the crowded bazaar with real pleasure.

But now Keith seemed to be in a hurry to get back to the barouche. So, Bridget thought. He had only brought her out here to go through his little speech about the money. As soon as that was done, he was eager to be rid of her. Well, she would show him she wasn't easily pushed around. She deliberately dawdled from one stall to the next while Keith conferred with James M'Laughlin in the background.

"Cholera here?" James gave a low whistle.

"I don't know. The native women think so. They were doing that dance, you know the one. We saw it often enough two years ago." The shadows in the bazaar seemed to be deepening ominously. Keith did not like to remember that season of death. "I saw them down a side street. And there was Johnson . . ."

James nodded. "It's early yet for the cholera epidemics, but we'd best take no chances with the ladies. Let's get them back to Chowringhee."

He took Agatha's arm and escorted her back down the busy street to where their barouche had been left in the charge of a groom, while Keith scanned the crowd for a sight of Charlotte. Damn the girl, where had she got to? Turn his back for a minute, and . . . ah!

He could just see her pink-trimmed bonnet in the dark arcade where the goldsmiths squatted over their charcoal fires. The displays of gaudy bracelets and filigree earrings must have drawn her across the street.

Before Keith could cross to get her, two dark-skinned bearers carrying silver maces dashed down the street, clearing the way for their master's entourage. After them came two coaches, the second draped with red cloth to conceal the women within from men's eyes. Keith tried to shove his way between the slow-moving vehicles and was pushed back by a bearer trotting beside the women's coach. His anxiety was increased by hearing shouts and cries of alarm from the other side of the street.

When the coaches passed, he could see that the crowd had backed away to stand in a rough semicircle around the goldsmiths' arcade. He pushed his way through and saw a red-coated figure staggering to and fro in the semicircular space, waving his arms and shouting incoherently. Wherever he moved, the crowd surged back.

"Cholera." The whisper passed from man to man in the crowd, and they shrank back even farther.

Keith could just see Charlotte, standing at the entrance to the arcade. "Let me through!" he shouted, pushing blindly at the men nearest him. He was hemmed in by greasy, sweating, frightened humanity and the warmth of their bodies oppressed him. The odor of rancid oil, sour butter and human sweat filled his nostrils and his fear for Charlotte filled his mind. The fear of cholera could turn this tense, uneasy crowd into a blindly shoving beast with a thousand heads, trampling people and smashing property in their panic. And if they decided to blame the Europeans for the sickness brought into the bazaar by the red-coated soldier, he and Charlotte might be their first targets.

By the time he broke through the crowd, Charlotte was kneeling in the dust beside the soldier, loosening his coat with expert fingers.

"Charlotte!" he called. He seized her shoulder with

some thought of dragging her away by main force. "Come away. You don't know the danger. He may be sick." He dared not repeat the dreaded word *cholera* lest it be picked up by the crowd.

Instead of obeying him, Charlotte bent to sniff at the soldier's face. She turned a smiling countenance up to him. "Sure, and it's only blind drunk the poor fellow is," she cried. "I've loosened the collar on him, and he'll be all right when he's slept it off."

An elderly, white-bearded native with a pair of scratched spectacles perched on his nose nodded and translated Charlotte's words to the hushed crowd. "The *Angrezi* soldier has drunk himself into a stupor, as is the habit of the Europeans. Because the fools make their men wear heavy clothes that pinch them in the neck, he has fainted."

A hefty bearer in the front of the crowd grumbled his disbelief, and the goldsmith raised his voice again. "If he were sick with the cholera, would the white woman be tending him? There is nothing to fear! I, Gul Ram, tell you there is no sickness here!"

There was a vast sigh from the crowd of onlookers, a collective release of tension, and even as Keith watched they melted away to resume their occupations. He, Charlotte and the goldsmith were left standing around the soldier's body.

Gul Ram started when he saw the young officer who was rumored to speak fluent Hindustani and began apologizing for his impolite references to the *Angrezi* sahibs, whom all the world knew were the most generous, the most understanding and—he peered up through his scratched spectacles—the most forgiving of all sahibs?

"No need for forgiveness, my friend," Keith said. "It

43

is we who should thank you for ending what could have been an ugly situation."

Gul Ram bowed. "The thanks are due to your *memsahib* here. She understood the situation and acted while I was still staring stupidly. If my small understanding of the Angrezi tongue has enabled me to help by translating her words, I am already rewarded. Now . . ."

He whistled to the boy who drove the bellows for his charcoal fire and motioned to him to drag the English soldier into the arcade. "He can be taken from there to the hospital in an hour, when it is dark."

"To the hospital? But if he is only drunk . . ."

Gul Ram interrupted him. "He is not drunk, my friend. It is the cholera. I have seen many die." He sighed. "And now we will see more. But thanks to your memsahib, there will be no riot today. At least we have been spared that much."

"The cholera," Keith repeated. Reflexively, he stepped back from the soldier's body as the boy dragged it past into the shadowed arcade. "Then . . . you were mistaken, Charlotte." He took her arm and drew her away from the arcade. Her head was bent so that he could not see her face, only the straw bonnet with its border of silk roses next to the curve of her cheek. He felt an irrational desire to put his arms about her, as if that could protect her from the infection. His fear transmuted into anger. "What a rash thing to do! Didn't you think?"

"Oh, yes," Gul Ram said softly. "She knew the danger. When the soldier began to stagger around, I told her, 'He is sick. You must go back to your friends. When the people see that he has the cholera, they will be very much afraid and bad things will happen.'"

Gul Ram put one hand on his breast and nodded emphatically. "She knew!"

Keith's mind was a jumble of chaotic emotions on the short drive back to Chowringhee. He felt embarrassed to speak to Charlotte again after scolding her for what had turned out to be a courageous action. Fortunately, he was not required to say anything. Agatha and James had observed the scene from the barouche. They spent the entire drive exclaiming over Charlotte's courage.

It was very strange. The Charlotte he had known in Ireland would not have stepped out of her way to help a dying laborer, still less have risked herself to stop a mob. Keith stole a glance at Charlotte's face, still averted under the rose-trimmed bonnet. Perhaps his memory was failing him. The firm line of the jaw, the generous curve of her wide mouth, formed no part of his memory of Lady Charlotte Fitzgerald. Perhaps, in maturing, she had changed.

Keith had no chance to mull over the matter any further. They were met at the gate of the Lanyers' compound by Mrs. Lanyer herself. Without waiting to hear the tale of their adventures in the bazaar, she called to Agatha and Charlotte to come inside and change their dresses.

"Such exciting news, my dear!"

It was to Charlotte that she addressed herself.

"You remember Bishop Gairdner, your uncle's good friend? He is making a tour of our Indian missions, and he will be in Calcutta in a few days' time. I was visiting Lady Dalhousie this afternoon when the runner came with his letter. He happened to mention how much he enjoyed visiting all of you in Ireland last summer and that he was looking forward to seeing you again when he arrived in Calcutta. Naturally I sent a message back inviting him to stay with us."

Mrs. Lanyer bustled off, fairly clucking with joy at the social *coup* of achieving not only a titled Irish lady, but now a bishop, in the very same week.

A faint sigh alerted Keith a split second before he turned to hand Charlotte down from the barouche. She had slid down against the seat, looking white as the outer rim of that silly conch shell he had purchased for her in the bazaar.

Chapter Four

BRIDGET STARED UNSEEING ACROSS THE EXPANSE OF THE Lanyers' garden. Butterflies darted over the white sandy paths in the shade of the giant *peepul* tree, and a daring leaf-grasshopper decorated her skirt with its gauzy wings, but she might have been sitting in a cold Irish drawing room for all the attention she spared for the wealth of nature around her. Her hands were tightly clasped round a small leatherbound book from which she had been attempting to teach herself enough Hindustani to communicate with the servants. That book and the rupees Keith had promised her were the two feeble crutches on which her hopes for independence rested—an independence she was going to need very soon.

Bishop Gairdner had been a guest at the Fitzgeralds' country house only the previous summer. Bridget had only seen him from a distance, but she well remembered Lady Charlotte's complaints about the hours she had to spend entertaining the dull old man with his never-ending talk of ignorant heathens and native missions.

She could not possibly get away with meeting someone who had seen Charlotte so recently. This Bishop Gairdner would take one look at her and denounce her for an impostor. The only solution was to be out of the Lanyers' house before the Bishop arrived. And before she betrayed herself any more to Keith. Well, that was safe enough. She wasn't likely to have another chance to see Keith at all before she had to slip away and, even if she did, she could hardly tell him good-bye.

Bridget opened the Hindustani book at random and forced herself to concentrate once more on the crabbed print, partially obliterated in many places by spots of mildew. The words seemed to dance before her eyes until the tiny specks of print had no more meaning than the flyspecks that liberally decorated the page.

"The aorist tense is generally preceded by an adverb or conjunction."

Now what did that mean? Bridget flipped through the pages of the book, lost patience and flung it down again. There were a number of sample sentences in the back. Perhaps she could just use those.

She might not need to know that much Hindustani anyway if her plan worked. She had recently heard of a woman living up-river, a Mrs. Trenton, who was worried about the way her children were growing up speaking more Hindustani than English. Bridget's half-formed plan was to use the rupees Keith had promised her to pay her passage up the river and present herself to Mrs. Trenton as an English-speaking governess. What she would do if Mrs. Trenton had already found someone or wanted references, she refused to think. It was better than waiting here to be exposed and laughed at as the Irish servant girl who tried to play the lady.

A shadow fell across the immaculately swept garden path.

"May I sit down?"

Without waiting for an answer, Keith Powell picked up the discarded Hindustani grammar and ensconced himself on the bench beside her. He had plucked a sprig of *kamalata* creeper on his way through the garden, and now he twirled the long stem with its red starlike flowers between two fingers before dropping it, like an offering, on the white skirts of Bridget's simple muslin dress.

"I hope I do not intrude," he said. "The *khansamah* told me that Mrs. Lanyer and Agatha had gone for a drive, but that you were walking in the garden." With some embarrassment, he drew a small leather bag from his pocket. "This is a small part of the money your uncle sent to me. I can withdraw more from the bank whenever you need it."

Bridget's fingertips brushed his hand as she accepted the bag. His skin was firm and warm, as if he had incorporated some part of the Indian sun into his very being. "I . . . thank you," she replied at last, stammering slightly. Why must her wits flee her whenever she spoke with Keith? Well, that was not a problem that would trouble her much longer. "I do not think I shall be requiring more."

Keith laughed. "Not immediately, perhaps. But you are sure to see some trinkets you would like in the bazaar."

A neat, plain dress suitable for a governess, Bridget thought bleakly. Passage on a boat going up-river.

She forced herself to return his smile. If she never saw Keith again, at least she would have the memory of this last, unhoped-for meeting. She would not spoil it by fretting about the future.

"You are right," she exclaimed with forced animation. "For instance, I have been longing for one of those Kashmiri shawls such as we saw the other day."

Keith's eyes lit up. "No. I don't think you should buy yourself one of those." He took a flat parcel from under his coat and unwrapped it with a flourish.

The deep, rich colors of the shawl, all gold and brown, glowed with the warmth of the setting sun against the blue tints of evening. Bridget put out a finger and stroked the soft fabric wonderingly. "For me?" she whispered.

Keith looked embarrassed. "Well . . . I went back to the bazaar to see how Gul Ram was getting on and to find out if there had been any more outbreaks of the cholera. There have been one or two more cases, but nothing severe. He promised to send me word if there was any trouble. But I spent quite a long time talking with some of the shopkeepers, and it seemed only fair to buy something to recompense them for their time."

"Oh . . . of course. How thoughtful." Bridget felt unaccountably dashed by his explanation. For a moment she'd had the foolish notion that he'd gone to the bazaar especially to get her the shawl. But her spirits revived as she stroked the rich fabric with its glowing, jewel-like colors. A cooling breeze swept through the garden, fanning her bare shoulders in the low-cut gown, and she shivered. Calcutta in February might be as warm as Ireland in August, but the evenings were still chilly!

"May I?"

Without waiting for permission, Keith arranged the shawl around her shoulders. His hands lingered over her, adjusting the folds with unnecessary precision.

Bridget shut her eyes and pretended that what she felt was a lover's caress, his hands resting gently on her shoulders before he turned her head for a kiss.

When she felt Keith's breath on her cheek, the fantasy was so real to her that she turned and pressed her lips to his without thinking.

The touch of his lips sent her swaying into a dark and perilous world from which there was no escape. She strained upward, seeking the sweetness she had found, while his hand on her back pressed her close to him. His darting tongue invaded her mouth and sent ripples of pleasure through her body. With her free hand she caressed his cheek, wondering at the masculine feel of his close-shaven skin and the warmth which emanated from him.

He let her go and she dropped back onto the marble bench, clutching the shawl about her. The air was sweet with the scents of night-blooming flowers that only now opened their waxy petals to the evening. Only when the time came. Bridget looked up at Keith, and there was singing inside her. How had she ever thought she could go away from him? There would be some other way to handle things. There had to be.

"I'm . . . sorry . . ." Keith said. His voice was rough and wondering. He brushed her cheek with one finger. "I did not intend—"

Bridget interrupted him before he could say anything to spoil the moment they had shared. "I was only wanting to thank you for the shawl." She hugged it closer to her and caressed the soft folds again with delight. "Nobody ever gave me anything before."

"What?"

Keith's shocked tone recalled Bridget to her masquerade. Biddy Sullivan might have come of a family too poor to waste their coppers on gifts, but how could she have forgotten Lady Charlotte's never-ending stream of birthday gifts and name-day trinkets and Christmas presents, gold lockets and ivory combs and silver-backed mirrors?

". . . that I liked half as much," she went on as if she were just finishing the sentence.

Keith stroked his mustache and regarded her with a half-smile that made her distinctly nervous. She reached for her Hindustani grammar to change the subject.

"I have been trying to learn the language," she told him, holding up the book as proof of her efforts. "It seems very difficult, though."

"Really? That's wonderful! Very few of the women who come out here ever bother to learn more than a few phrases for speaking to the servants. How far have you got?"

Bridget looked down at her hands. The small hands with their blunt-tipped fingers, so capable with a paring knife or a sewing needle, looked incongruous folded round this leatherbound book from a gentleman's library. "Not . . . too far," she confessed. "I'm not . . . I find it hard to learn things out of books."

Keith took the book from her. "Oh, it's not so hard once you get into it. And I admire you for making the effort, Charlotte. I really mean that." His gray eyes looked into hers with a peculiar intensity that made her feel at once helpless and very powerful. As though what she did mattered to him.

Bridget laughed to dispel her uneasiness. "You'll be thinking I'm stupid, though. You speaking it so well and all."

"Oh, that's different," Keith said quickly. "It's part of my work. Everybody who applies for a staff appointment has to pass examinations in Hindustani and

Persian." He took her hand and stroked the backs of her fingers lightly, absently, while he talked. His touch sent little quivering shocks of pleasure running through her. She felt weak and helpless and utterly unable to pull away.

"I'm better at languages than most, but that's not the only thing when you're going for a staff appointment." He grimaced. "Pull counts, too. But my colonel thought it was worth the try. All of us clever chaps go into the staff, you know, it's the only way to get ahead. If I'm lucky, I might be assigned to some remote spot where I can take on a lot of responsibility and make my mark in the service."

Some remote spot. She remembered now that when they'd met, he had been talking about going away. It was hard to accept, with his hands warm on hers.

"Your friends in Calcutta will miss you."

Keith's hand pressed hers very lightly. "When I became ambitious . . . I did not know what it might cost me."

He cleared his throat with unnecessary vigor and flipped the Hindustani grammar book open. "Well! Shall I help you to get started?"

He put one arm around her to hold the book open before them. Bridget shivered involuntarily at the touch of his arm on her shoulders. A little turn, and he could be kissing her again, instead of reading that stupid book. The pages of close-set print blurred before her eyes.

"The pronunciation is often the hardest thing for a beginner," Keith announced. His breathing was uneven, as though he had been running. He cleared his throat and ran a finger down the page. "Why don't you try repeating the words after me? *Chiragh*, lamp. *Bachcha*, child. *Khush*, happy."

"Chiragh," Bridget repeated obediently. What were the other things he had said? She bent her head over the book to read the list of words and her cheek brushed against Keith's. *"Bachcha."*

His hands were tanned almost as dark as a native's, with long, sensitive fingers. She remembered the feel of those fingers spread out on her back, pressing her to him. "And . . . ah . . . *kush.*"

"Khush," Keith corrected her. He put one hand over hers, covering the pages of the book. "You should . . . learn the difference between the different *k* sounds. There is the soft *Kh* as in *khush,* the hard *k* as in *dak,* which means a journey, and then there is the *q* sound." His arm tightened round her shoulders and he lifted her hand, playing with the fingers, tracing lines on its back that sent shivering pleasure through her. "As in *ishq.*" He turned her hand over and pressed a kiss on the palm. "Love."

Bridget raised her face to his, but he loosened his hold on her shoulders and moved slightly away from her. "Charlotte, I owe you an apology. Several apologies. I must confess that when I heard you were coming out here, I resented your presence. I have to be honest. When I knew you at home, I thought you were a spoiled brat and not likely to improve with age. I was going to leave you on your own at the Lanyers' and hope you found a civilian to marry."

"Yes," Bridget said. She had been unhappy to find how much Keith disliked her, even though that dislike was really directed at his memories of Lady Charlotte. But now it was all right. Wasn't it? A bird called in the garden, and the harsh grating sound seemed a precursor of loss. "You made that perfectly clear." Her own voice sounded far away in her ears.

Keith had the grace to look down. "Yes. Well

. . . what I wanted to tell you was that I admire the way you've changed. The way you handled that situation in the bazaar, for instance. The Lady Charlotte I knew would have screamed and run away from anybody who might give her the cholera. She would probably have been angry with the poor soldier for exposing her to infection. But you . . . you were magnificent!" He raised his eyes to her face. "Charlotte, I was proud of you. I want to apologize for the things I thought when you first came out. From a spoiled little girl, you've become a woman. A woman who is capable of handling the best and the worst that India has to offer. A woman that any man in India would be proud to have as his wife."

He took her hand and lifted it to his lips. "A beautiful woman," he whispered. His mustache just grazed the back of her hand. "Charlotte, my darling."

Bridget closed her eyes in anticipation of his kiss. But instead he began talking again. "I can't believe how much you've changed. You are almost a different person from the one I remember."

Here was dangerous ground. Bridget stared at the garden path, afraid to let Keith see her face. "Do . . . do you mind if we don't talk about the past very much, Keith? I have tried to change. I don't want to remember what a horrid, spoiled little girl I used to be."

Keith squeezed her hand. "Of course, my darling. I understand perfectly." He settled himself more comfortably and began toying with her fingers once more. He looked up at the deepening sky and sighed. "Just look at that perfect, clear, deep blue! And any minute it will be night. A far cry from our lingering Irish twilights, all mist and rain. You're right, Charlotte. Everything is different now. I shouldn't expect you to be the same girl I remember from that day beside the Liffey."

He looked at her as if expecting some intelligent response. When she said nothing, he went on.

"Charlotte, darling, I know you don't want to talk about the past. But we have to talk about that. Even if it's painful, I have to know how you feel about it now."

Dublin. The Liffey river. Bridget's mind went blank. Charlotte had visited Dublin from time to time, but she had never been invited on those excursions. She couldn't begin to imagine what could have passed between Charlotte and Keith to make him so angry at the mere recollection.

"As a matter of fact, I don't remember anything particular about that day," she said with as cool a countenance as she could muster. "How would I be recalling every little thing, and it all those years ago?"

Keith's face changed. All in a moment it seemed to have become as hard as the stone wall around the compound. He dropped her hand and turned away from her as though he couldn't bear even to look at her. Rising from the bench, he paced back and forth on the sandy path.

"She doesn't remember," he said, addressing the shrubbery. He gave a low, bitter laugh. "I can't believe it, Charlotte. I can't believe that even you could put something like that out of your mind."

He wheeled and stooped over her again. "In fact, I don't believe it now. I'll tell you this, Charlotte. You have just saved me from the biggest mistake of my life. I was ready to forget and forgive; I thought you might really have changed since you came out to India. God help me, I was beginning to fancy myself in love with you! But if you don't even have the common honesty to admit your wrongdoing, if you can pretend the whole affair was of so little moment to you as that, well, I am just disgusted. Thank God I saw my error in time!"

Bridget felt as if she would crumple under the force of his accusations. Only the sound of his booted feet, crunching on the sand of the garden path as he marched away, roused her from her disbelieving stupor. She jumped up from the bench and ran after him, the shawl trailing from her bare arms. She caught at his sleeve and forced him to stop.

"Keith, wait!" she begged breathlessly. The tears were making damp tracks down her cheeks, but she didn't care. All that mattered was removing the hard light in his eyes. "Please believe me, Keith. It's the God's own truth I'm telling you, Keith, whatever it was happened that day, it's gone clean out of my mind. Can you not believe that much? Please, Keith, I cannot bear for you to be going away and your face set against me!"

Keith stared at her as if at a total stranger. "Do you really not remember? Very well. I shall tell you." His voice was low and hurried, and he looked out into the darkness of the tropic night like a man reliving scenes against his will.

"You were at school in Dublin, and I was about to leave for India. Your aunt and my mother had settled it between them that I should take you out for an afternoon before I left, and I was too weak-willed to go against them. We drove around in a hired carriage for the afternoon and had tea. It was when I was taking you back to the school that it happened.

"A ragged little urchin was running across the street, trying to dodge between the horses. He tripped and fell right under the wheels of our carriage.

"I shouted at the coachman to stop and jumped out to see if I could help the child. The wheel had gone right over his leg and the bones were crushed. All I could think of was getting him to a doctor as quickly as possible. I picked him up to put him into the carriage, and you screamed at me to get the filthy urchin out of your sight, that you wouldn't have him near you, getting blood and dirt on your dress and probably crawling with bugs!

"When I told you that I would not consider leaving the child, you ordered the coachman to drive on. You reminded him that he was your uncle's servant and threatened to have him discharged if he didn't obey your orders.

"You drove off and left me standing in the street with the boy in my arms. I walked from there to the nearest hospital. They were able to save his life, but the leg had to be amputated. The surgeon told me that if he had received immediate treatment, they might have been able to save the leg."

Keith fell silent. Bridget stood frozen with one hand still on his sleeve. No wonder he despised her so! If only, if only she could explain!

"I . . . did not know," she murmured. "Perhaps someday you'll understand . . . it was not like . . . it is not what you think."

His face unmoving, Keith heard her out to the end. Then he reached over and removed her fingers from his arm, one by one, like somebody plucking a loathsome insect off his sleeve. "No more, Charlotte. You had me almost believing in you for a moment. I don't mean to make that mistake again."

And then he was at the compound gate, shouting to the sais to bring his horse round, and Bridget lacked the heart to follow him farther. She stood alone on the path, the silly tears streaming down her face until the quick tropic night had fallen and the twinkling lights of the fireflies came out in the trees.

The worst mistake of his life. Yes, marrying her would have been that, but not for the reasons he was thinking.

It wasn't her he hated, not really. It was Lady Charlotte, who had died of the fever in Malta. It had nothing to do with her, Bridget Sullivan.

She wandered back down the white garden path that led toward the house. A dark line across the path caught her eye, and she stooped to pick it up. It was the sprig of kalamata creeper that he had brought her, its delicate red flowers now crushed beyond repair.

Chapter Five

By night the Burra-bazaar was a different place. The flickering of hundreds of little earthenware lamps illuminated the shops, while here and there half-naked porters gathered over a small open fire to cook their evening meal. Crouching over the fires, their bodies cast monstrously elongated shadows across the hard-packed earth of the street and the walls of the shops.

Wherever Bridget passed the whispers began. She caught the words "memsahib" and "Angrezi," buried in sentences whose import she could only guess at. A skinny dog with the ribs starting through its sunken sides followed her for several paces, whining and sniffing at her skirt. A *fakir* with one withered arm held high above his head lurched out of an alleyway, spinning crazily, and blocked her way for a full minute while he stared into her face with glittering dark eyes. Then he was gone, but the crowd of street urchins and loafers at her heels had grown.

Bridget held her head high and marched down the street with a firm, determined stride. She hoped that she presented a bold appearance. Truth be told, she was afraid to stop, even to inquire the way to Gul Ram's shop. She only prayed that she would recognize the arcade by night. Things looked so different in the deep shadows and glares of light produced by the open fires.

Her bundle was slipping; she hitched it up without pausing and prayed the things would not spill out before she reached the goldsmith's shop. It was an awkward load to carry, all wrapped up in the gold and brown Kashmiri shawl.

She breathed a sigh of relief when she saw that Gul Ram was still working. By night the goldsmith's shop took on an unearthly appearance, lit from within by the forge fire against which the old jeweler and his helper stood forth like black shadows in a demon play. But to Bridget it was her only refuge.

At first Gul Ram refused absolutely to aid her.

"It is not right for an English *mem* to travel by herself," he said. "Wait for your friends! Where is Powell sahib? Why does he not do this for you?"

But Bridget was as adamant in her way as Gul Ram was in his. "You must help me," she insisted. "Please, Gul Ram, it's yourself is the only one can help me, and a small favor indeed I'm asking of you, only to come with me and help me to hire a pinnace. I want to be going up the river as soon as can be."

"You cannot leave at night," Gul Ram tried next. "The river is full of sand bars and very difficult to navigate. Sail in the day, tie up at night. If the matter is so urgent, Powell Sahib should rent you a palanquin to travel *dak*."

"Powell Sahib has nothing to do with this!" Bridget

61

snapped. "And I . . . I prefer to travel by water." The truth was that her slender purse would not stand the charges of a palanquin journey to Berhampore, with the necessity to pay a new set of bearers at every stage. She could not even afford the steamer fare; all she could manage was the hire of a country boat.

Bridget moved closer and placed her hand on the old jeweler's sleeve. "Please, Gul Ram! If yourself will not be helping me, then I'll go down there by myself and see will the boatmen take me up-river now or will I sleep on the boat tonight."

And with a sinking heart she turned and made as if to march off into the darkness. The thought of going down to the docks by herself, armed with nothing but Hunter's *Hindustani Grammar*, terrified her. But not as much as the thought of facing Keith again.

No wonder he disliked her so much, thinking she was the Lady Charlotte he remembered from Ireland! The wonder was that he had brought himself to be civil to her at all. True, in a day or two he would know better. Bishop Gairdner would expose her imposture, and then he would know he had been making love to Biddy Sullivan, the upstairs maid at Ballycrochan. Then he wouldn't hate her anymore. She would merely be beneath his notice. That would almost be worse. No, she had to get away, whatever the cost!

"Wait a moment." Gul Ram studied his visitor's flushed face and unnaturally bright eyes. She was shabbily dressed today, in a plain old cotton gown that had seen many washings. And that ridiculous bundle! White mems did not travel like this, on foot and with a bundle wrapped up in an old shawl. They went in carriages or palanquins with many, many servants to carry their many trunks.

The answer came to him. This memsahib had quarreled with her lover—well, nothing new in that. But new to India as she was, the strain had doubtless brought on an attack of brain fever. This was the first stage, this ridiculous fancy about traveling up-river by herself in the middle of the night. Soon, no doubt, she would be raving and calling on her God, like the soldiers who were struck down from standing too long in the sun.

Gul Ram sighed and turned up his palms to signify acquiescence.

"Wait," he said again. "I will come with you. Only let me shut up my shop. I have many valuable things here. I must be careful."

Bridget's sigh of relief never reached her lips, but it was as heartfelt as any prayer she had ever made. "Only let me get safe away, and I'll burn a candle every day to the Blessed Virgin," she vowed and stifled in her heart the contradictory prayer that some magic would happen to stop her before she left Calcutta—and Keith Powell—behind forever.

Gul Ram fidgeted around the shop for some time, packing away his tools and jewelery. Bridget thought she would die of impatience by the time he had finished putting everything away, giving some incomprehensible Hindustani commands to the bellows-boy, and checking over his accounts for the day's work. Finally they were ready to go.

He led her through the winding, narrow streets of the native town. A white mem hurrying through the native quarter attracted some attention, but no one actually followed them. Bridget was glad of Gul Ram's company.

It seemed a long way that they had to go to get to the river. After a few turns in the dark alleys she had lost all sense of direction. It was so confusing that she actually felt as if Gul Ram was leading her around in circles.

He paused before a shadowed doorway set into a brick wall partially covered with flaking plaster. "We go through here. It is a shorter way." He unlocked the door and waited politely for Bridget to pass before him.

There was a small courtyard, then another door leading into what appeared to be a private residence. Bridget paused, uncertain. "Go on, go on," Gul Ram encouraged her. "We must hurry to catch the boatmen before they go to sleep for the night."

She stepped inside and looked about in perplexity. A single earthenware lamp burned in a corner, emitting a flickering light from its wick of twisted rag dipped in *ghee*. In the dim light she could see only four mud walls and a roof of close-set poles. There seemed to be no door other than the one she had just entered by.

She turned to ask Gul Ram for guidance and saw only the door softly closing behind her. There was a metallic clang from outside and a soft rustling in the straw at her feet.

She felt a creeping fear that attacked at the back of her neck, like something quivering all down her spine. A clammy draft of damp air brushed her neck. She whirled to face this new danger and saw nothing, heard nothing but the rustling at her feet.

"Gul Ram!" She raised her voice and called again. "Gul Ram, where are you!"

The door moved as much as half an inch outward when she pushed at it; then it came to rest against some obstacle that she could not push aside. Another draft whispered through the room, bending the tiny lamp-flame onto its side and making it quiver until Bridget's shadow danced crazily up and down on the mud walls.

"No, no!" A wild unreasoning panic came over her.

She dropped her bundle and attacked the door with her fists, shouting for help. All the whispered stories retailed over dinner or tiffin at the Lanyers' came back to haunt her—tales of strange sacrifices and heathen rites, stories of travelers who disappeared and were never heard from again. "His bearers said he died of a fever, but we never found the body." And the palms turned upward, a slight shrug of ignorance.

What did she know of this mysterious continent, that she had thought she could make off alone in it? There were men who worshipped a black goddess called *Kali*, who was made happy for tens of thousands of years by the sacrifice of a man. There were women burned alive on the deaths of their husbands, and fakirs like the one she'd seen in the street who held one of their arms above their heads until it withered in that position and the fingernails curved round and grew through the paralysed hand.

There were her hands beating on the door until the knuckles were raw and bruised. But no one came, and the door only sagged half an inch outward again, then rested solid and immovable.

Slowly Bridget's hands ceased their frantic pounding, and she backed away from the door a step at a time. She stood very still in the center of the room and clasped her hands together. At least the rustling had stopped. Think—she had to think. There must be some other way out of here.

The little lamp still flickered brightly, a reassuring point of light in the shadows that surrounded her. She wrapped her hands in a fold of the cotton skirt and picked up the lamp to explore the room. The hot earthenware saucer transmitted its warmth through the folds of cotton. She could only hold it a few minutes before it scorched her fingers. But those few minutes were enough to show her that there was no other way out, no window, no door but the one she had entered by, now unaccountably blocked.

She stooped to set down the lamp. As she freed her hands from the skirt, the rustling noise in the straw startled her again. She jumped back and the sound seemed to follow her, together with the little wisps of straw that had caught on her skirt hem.

Bridget looked down and laughed. Of course! These long skirts that real ladies wore almost brushed the floor. Hadn't she been forever afraid she would trip over them when they first gave her this dress in Malta? The full petticoats held the skirt out somewhat, raising it an inch from the floor. But she had discarded most of her bulky petticoats for this journey, and the cotton skirt hung limply down to the ground, where it caught on the straw and dragged one wisp against another to produce the furtive rustling noises that had worried her.

Discovering the false alarm gave her renewed confidence. Gul Ram's little trap might have done very well for a lady, but she, Bridget Sullivan, had more courage and ingenuity than to be defeated by four walls and a roof. She would simply have to explore more.

There was a native bed, a *charpoy,* in one corner, the only furnishing the room boasted. Bridget sat down on the bamboo frame with its "mattress" of tightly interlaced cotton strips and opened her bundle to see what tools she might have.

There wasn't much. She had not wanted to bring any of the things "Lady Charlotte" had been given by the Lanyers. That seemed like cheating. Besides, what would a governess be doing with a pink silk tarlatan dress and bonnet trimmed to match? But now Bridget sighed for the sewing scissors she had left behind with her workbasket. She would have felt better for a weapon of some sort.

All she had was the other cotton dress from Malta, Hunter's *Hindustani Grammar* and the big, spiky conch shell Keith had given her as a jest. She had used the Kashmiri shawl to wrap up the things.

"If it came to that, I suppose I could always hit someone with the conch shell," she mused. But it didn't seem an effective weapon. She would do better to read Hunter's *Grammar* to any assailants. That would put them to sleep!

Bridget grinned and rose to her feet again. Whatever foulness Gul Ram planned for her, she'd no mind to sit patiently and wait for it. She gave the wall a thump with her fist. Solid. If she had the tools she could maybe be breaking it down.

No tools. She took inventory of her possessions again, and stopped when she came to the earthenware lamp. Fire was a tool. And the door was wooden. . . .

The door was also, examination disclosed, constructed of at least three layers of some extremely hard wood that barely charred in the lamp flame. And there wasn't very much ghee left in the lamp, either. It would be out long before she'd made an impression on the door. But the roof was also wood.

Bridget looked up again at the long but spindly poles, laid side by side, that constituted a roof. Even when she climbed on the charpoy, she could barely reach them with the tips of her fingers, and could not exert enough force to give them a good push. But if they were weakened by fire, she might be able to break one or two, then she could turn the charpoy on end, climb up and wriggle out through the space she had made.

She had already scorched her fingers by trying to hold the lamp in a fold of her dress. The only thing she had that was thick enough to serve as a lampholder was the heavy Kashmiri shawl.

Very illogically, Bridget smoothed out the folds of the shawl and laid her lips against the soft fabric before she wrapped it around the base of the lamp. Then she climbed on top of the charpoy and reached upward, straining into the darkness so that the wisp of flame could attack the roof poles.

After dinner Keith rejected an invitation to go riding with James M'Laughlin in favor of staying in his lodgings and brooding. James's cheery conversation, his invariable ability to find a bright side to the darkest situation, got on his nerves at times. James was sure that if Keith had not yet received the staff appointment for which he had been recommended, it was only because the governor-general was waiting for something worthy of his friend's linguistic and political talents. And if Keith told him about his encounter with Charlotte, James would either make excuses for her behavior or tell him that he was well out of it.

At the moment he was not sure which response would be more irritating.

So he stretched out alone on his charpoy, threw a boot at the *khitmutgar* when he came in to trim the lamp and swore in three different native dialects at the omnipresent mosquitoes. None of this was particularly relieving to his feelings. He stared at the unpainted beams of the ceiling and went over, one more time, the train of events that had fooled him into believing that Lady Charlotte Fitzgerald could ever be anything but a spoiled, heartless brat.

Even now he could not reconcile the two images of her that he carried in his heart. One was the selfish girl he had known in Ireland, concerned with little but her own consequence. The other was the woman who had come to Calcutta, the one who had risked the anger of the mob to tend a dying soldier.

The two images blurred into one when he remembered her casual dismissal of the affair in Dublin. "You cannot expect me to remember every little thing that happened all those years ago." Charlotte! Keith groaned and flung an arm over his eyes, as though the light of the single lamp was too much for him to bear. That day was etched on his mind as though by acid. And she could still call it a "little thing," that her selfishness had caused a boy to lose his leg.

He tried now to find excuses for her, as James would have done if he were there. It hurt so much to lose the Charlotte he had come to know and love in India. Warm, delightful, enticing Charlotte. No, cold Charlotte, who brushed a boy's ruined life out of her memory as easily as she would brush a grasshopper off her skirt.

But she had looked genuinely stricken when he retold the story. Was it possible that she truly had forgotten? Or was that just a clever piece of acting? Keith pressed his arm down over his eyes. No, she couldn't have forgotten. The tragedy that ended that day had left every detail etched on his mind. He could even remember the earlier part of the afternoon, when he sat in agonizing boredom, his hat balanced on his knees, in the parlor of the ladies' seminary while Charlotte played the piano pieces she had learned in the last year. He could remember the watery sunlight filtering through the lace curtains, the buzzing of a fly in insolent counterpoint to the piano and Charlotte's long, white, delicate fingers reaching over the keys with such precision.

Keith sat up so quickly that he seriously frightened

his bearer squatting in the corner and two mosquitoes who had been planning to dine on his outflung arm. Now two images were blurring together again in his mind, but this time there was no way he could make them fit. How could he have been so blind? That very afternoon he had been kissing her hand. Her small, square hand with the blunt fingertips.

"By God! She really didn't remember." He laughed. "That part was absolutely true. How could she remember? Why didn't she tell me?" He stood up and began buttoning his uniform jacket. Halfway through he paused, doubting his own deductions. If only there were some way to be sure!

He could hardly charge into the Lanyers' house and charge her with it. It was a delicate matter to bring up. And she might possibly be angry with him after the way he had left that afternoon.

Keith was still standing in the middle of the room, his jacket half-buttoned, frowning as he tried to work out the best way to approach Charlotte, when a messenger arrived who temporarily drove all other thoughts out of his mind.

"It is a boy from the bazaar, sahib," the khitmutgar announced reluctantly. He kept most of his body on the other side of the door in case the sahib should be inclined to throw his other boot. But the boy had been most insistent that he should speak with Powell sahib at once. "It is to do with the white mem who was with him at Gul Ram's shop," the boy had said.

Chapter Six

THE RATTLE AT THE DOOR CAME TOO SOON.

One of the roof poles was half charred through and ready to break, but the second one was only blackened around the edges. Bridget pushed frantically upward, but the pole held firm.

The door was slowly being pushed open. The flickering lamp in her hand gave just enough light to make out the dim outlines of a human form.

Bridget raised the lamp over her head and threw it at the widening opening.

The throw went wide. Burning oil spattered the room in a wide arc, landing harmlessly on the earthen floor, while the earthenware lamp shattered on the far wall and left the room in darkness.

"Charlotte!"

It was Keith's voice. Bridget gave a long shuddering sigh and collapsed against the wall. She could feel her heart pounding with the fear that had overtaken her when the door began to open.

"Are you all right?"

He was feeling his way forward in the darkness. Bridget forgot the humiliation of their last meeting, her vow never to see him again, in her relief. She jumped down from the charpoy and fell into his arms.

Kisses on her tangled hair, hard arms around her holding her tight and safe, a man's rough cheek grazing hers. Haven.

She drew away. "Keith? We'll have to be running for it. Are they outside? Can we get away?"

His voice was deep, amused. "What are you talking about, darling?" He drew her toward the charpoy in the corner, felt ahead of him in the darkness until he found it. "Here, sit down. We don't have to run anywhere, darling. There's no one outside but Gul Ram. This is his house, you know."

"Gul Ram!" Her voice rose to a near shriek. Was he waiting for them? The fear returned, palpable as the blackness that pressed down around them. "He's the one who locked me in here. Please, Keith, don't let him . . ."

Keith stroked the tumbled hair away from her face and pressed her head down against his shoulder. "There, there, darling. It's all right now. You're perfectly safe. Didn't Gul Ram tell you he had sent his boy to fetch me?"

"N-no." Bridget felt herself shamefully near to tears. She drew a deep breath and sat upright in the protecting circle of Keith's arms. "No, he told me this was a short way to Prinsep Ghat. Then he locked me in here and just left me. I thought . . . I don't know what I thought." Her earlier imaginings seemed too foolish to admit.

"The ghat!" Now it was Keith's turn to sound surprised. "What did you want to go down there for? At this hour, too." Gul Ram's boy had only said that the memsahib wanted him and that she was waiting at Gul Ram's house. Now it seemed there was more to the story.

"Oh, it doesn't matter," she said wearily. "Gul Ram didn't think I should be going down there either. Promised to guide me, he did, but I suppose he meant all along to send for you. I wish I'd known what it was in his mind. I was trying to get out when you came."

Keith thumped the mud wall behind them with his fist. "Never make it. Unless you happened to have a pickax in your reticule, by any chance? These walls are solid as rock in the dry season. Only way to get out is to excavate . . . or wait till the rainy season. In June when the rains begin, half a dozen houses dissolve in the water every year."

Bridget gave a watery giggle. "I don't think I could have waited that long. I'm too impatient. I was trying to burn through the roof poles with that . . . that oil lamp thing he left here."

"A *chiragh,*" Keith said absently.

"Yes." Now she remembered the word. He'd taught her how to say it only that afternoon, sitting in the Lanyers' garden. Bridget felt a lump in her throat. She couldn't bear to remember that. "It took a long time, though, because the lamp was so small and hard to hold, and oh, Keith, I scorched a hole in your beautiful Kashmir shawl!" Suddenly that trivial misadventure seemed the worst of all. She had meant to keep the shawl forever, in memory of those brief moments in the garden. Now that, too, was ruined. Everything was ruined.

To her shame, she burst into noisy, hiccuping, unrefined sobs. Keith held her and rocked her back and forth like a child until the shuddering sobs calmed down.

"There, there, it doesn't matter," he soothed. "We'll buy another one. Dammit, I'll buy a cartload of them!" He put one hand down on the charpoy for support and yelped as something spiky bit his finger. "What the hell . . ." He trapped the unknown object. It was cold and hard, vaguely conical, with a ring of flaring spikes at the broad end. By God, it was the conch shell he'd bought her in the bazaar!

Keith put both arms round Charlotte and held her while he stared over her head into the darkness. Now why would she be going down to Prinsep Ghat with a conch shell tucked under one arm? The absurdity of it touched him. Did she treasure his foolish gifts so much?

She must have been running away. His inner conviction hardened. There was no reason for Charlotte to run away. But was this girl in his arms Charlotte?

"Feeling better?" he asked when her shoulders stopped shaking.

She sat up and scrubbed the sleeve of her dress across her damp face. "Yes. Sorry I am, that I should be making all this trouble for you."

"Oh, I'm used to it," Keith said. He paused and weighed his words carefully before he went on. "Actually, this reminds me of the time your governess whipped you for insolence, and you ran away across country with your pony and came to me to hide you."

"I did?" Bridget was startled. She had never credited Charlotte with so much independence. "I mean . . . yes, I remember." She couldn't very well claim to have forgotten every incident Keith brought up. Look how much trouble it had gotten her in last time!

"Speaking of your governess," Keith went on, "how is dear old Miss Cherry these days? Is she still very badly troubled with the rheumatism, poor old dear?"

Bridget frowned in the darkness, searching her memory. What a mercy Keith couldn't see her puzzled face! She had never been up at the Great House in the days before Charlotte went to finishing school in Dublin. It was while Charlotte was away that her parents had died, her brother emigrated to the Americas and the Fitzgeralds had taken her into service at the Great House.

She could just vaguely remember a governess who used to take Charlotte out walking through the village, but she had been a young woman. This Miss Cherry must have been some old retainer, pensioned off when the new governess came.

"I do hope Miss Cherry is all right?"

No more time to think. "Oh, the rheumatism is much better since she retired," she hazarded.

"Really? I'm surprised to hear that. That cold, damp country where her sister lives can't have done it any good."

Bridget closed her eyes and prayed for guidance. She would have to make up something else now. "Oh, but they did not stay there. It was too cold for Miss Cherry. The last I heard, they had gone abroad. To . . . to the south of France. No one has heard anything from them since."

"How strange. I wouldn't have thought two old ladies like that could have afforded to travel."

"I believe she received a legacy," Bridget improvised, wishing she had killed Miss Cherry off at the beginning of this conversation instead of being drawn into more and more absurd fantasies.

Thank God, Keith didn't seem to question that. "Oh, of course. From her brother in India, I suppose."

"Yes." Bridget thought that if she heard one more word about Miss Cherry, she just might revert to screaming and pounding on the walls. "Keith, can we not go now?"

"Of course." He seemed to be laughing very quietly, but in the dark it was hard to tell. He stood up, took her hand and pulled her to her feet. "I'll take you back to the Lanyers' at once."

"No!" Bridget scrambled around the charpoy in the darkness, feeling for her possessions. She tied her bundle up again with shaking hands. "No, if you can just take me to Prinsep Ghat. . . ."

Keith took the bundle from her and set it down in a corner. He put his hands on her shoulders and turned her to face him. "Charlotte, you cannot go down to the ghat this late. You're not still angry at me, are you? Darling, I know I was hasty this afternoon."

"No," Bridget said. "You were right." Tears prickled behind her eyelashes and she blinked them back. "I don't see how you can ever respect me after the way I behaved in Ireland. Besides, I . . . I . . . Oh, never mind. I just have to get away. I cannot stay with the Lanyers any longer."

"Just for tonight," Keith said. "Charlotte, we have to talk. Please, let me take you home for the night. Tomorrow we can talk, and if you still really want to leave the Lanyers', I promise I will help you."

"You will?"

"On my honor as an officer," Keith replied. That was safe enough. Tomorrow he could explain everything to her, tell her that he knew she could not be Charlotte because there had never been an old governess called

76

Miss Cherry. No, she wasn't Charlotte Fitzgerald, and thank God for that! And whoever she was, whatever she'd done to force her into this impersonation, didn't matter to him. He loved her and he intended to marry her no matter what she called herself.

Only a man could hardly go on his knees in this muddy hovel. It was neither the time nor the place for such explanations. He didn't want to risk frightening and humiliating her so that she ran away into the darkness of the native town. He had already hurt her enough that afternoon, with his careless anger. He would have to go very slowly and very gently from now on.

And he couldn't repress the wild, irrational wish that she would tell him herself who she was, choose of her own free will to give up this playacting.

"I promise," he repeated as she stood, irresolute, under his hands. "If you still want to go away after we have talked, I will help you."

Her shoulders rose in a deep breath of relief. But he could feel the tension transmitting itself through her body to the palms of his hands. What madness was she planning now?

"But you," he added, "must promise not to do anything foolish until you see me tomorrow?"

"I . . . can't promise that," Bridget said in a low voice. The most foolish thing she could possibly do would be to go back to the Lanyers' now, gamble one more day of the masquerade for one more day with Keith. "But I promise not to run away tonight."

Keith could feel her relaxing under his hands, like an unstrung bow. All the soft tenderness of her that had so recently been in his arms . . . Keith yielded to temptation.

"It is customary," he said, "to seal a promise." His voice sounded hoarse in his own ears. His hands slipped down from her shoulders, along her back, drawing her against him. He lowered his head and tasted the sweetness of her mouth.

She put her arms round his neck and pressed closer to him. Her body molded against his so perfectly. He could feel all the softness of her through the thin cotton dress. Lord, it must be all she was wearing! Instead of the customary barriers of stays and crinolines, he could feel all the generous curves of her, pressed against him and driving him wild with the imagined thought of the lush beauty under her dress. And her mouth was open to his invasion, sweet, demanding, consuming.

There was a roaring like the sea in his ears. Somehow, he never knew how, they stumbled back in the darkness and fell upon the charpoy. Then he was pulling at her bodice, and her trembling fingers helped him to loosen the maddening row of tiny buttons. He buried his face in the sweet warmth of her breasts. She smelled of woman-scent and jasmine, India and home mixed together, a seductive brew that was too much for his will.

The desire he had been holding in check since his first sight of her now possessed him. He gave way to it with a savage exultation, parting her willing thighs and pressing his manhood, aching with desire, into the warm and welcoming center of her. She cried out beneath him and wrapped her arms and legs around his plunging body.

The intimate contact excited him unbearably but he forced himself to slow down until he could feel that his rhythmic movements had brought her to the edge of the same ecstasy that he was feeling. Then he plunged over the edge, carrying her with him, spiraling down and down into a flaming space where the only sounds were her half-smothered cries of pleasure. Then there was silence, darkness and the breathing of two bodies momentarily sated.

"My darling, my love," Keith whispered when he could speak again. He laid his head on her breast, where he could hear the pounding of her heart. "You must never go away from me. I love you. I'm going to marry you." The pounding was louder. Was he frightening her? "It doesn't matter . . ."

"Gul Ram!"

She started up, pushing him away and fumbling at her bodice with fingers made clumsy by haste.

"What?"

It took Keith a moment to adjust to the fact that even now, sitting up, he could hear the regular knocking that he had taken for Charlotte's heartbeat. But now he realized that sibilant whispers were coming through the darkness.

"Powell sahib? Sahib? Your *ekka* is here."

"Oh, Lord," Keith moaned, and he made a dive for his trousers. "No, don't bring us a lamp, Gul Ram! Hold on, I'll be out to talk with you in a minute."

Charlotte was sitting all huddled up on the charpoy, as quiet and still as a frightened animal. Keith realized that since he had spoken in Hindustani, naturally she did not understand what was going on. He struggled into his clothes and said over his shoulder, "It's all right. I told Gul Ram to find me a carriage to take you home in. All he could get in this quarter was an ekka. I hope you don't mind?" He straightened his coat and marched toward the door, once more the masterful white officer in thorough command of himself.

He wondered if she had heard and understood his confession of love.

Bridget used the moment of Keith's absence to comb through her hair with her fingers and push it back into a big knot. She was under no illusions as to what she must look like—tear-stained, with rumpled clothing, and now with other stains on the clothing as well—but she might as well try for a semblance of decency.

Gul Ram's interruption had rudely shocked her back into the real world. For a few moments, while Keith lay on her breast, she loved and was loved. She could even pretend that somehow everything would be all right, that he would never find out about her deception or would love her anyway.

Now that he was outside, she could no longer hold on to her dream. This was reality: a hard-packed mud floor, straw sticking to the hem of your dress and a harassed young officer who was in a hurry to get dressed before a native caught him in an embarrassing situation.

She could not blame him for what had occurred between them. She knew what went on between a man and a woman; growing up in a one-room Irish peasant's hut where man and wife shared sleeping space with seven children of all ages left little room for the illusions that a well-brought-up young lady like Lady Charlotte was supposed to cherish. And she'd known well enough what sort of response she was inviting when she pressed herself into his arms under the excuse of the token kiss. She had brought it on herself, deliberately, thinking to have at least this much to remember. And now she had only herself to blame if she had been overtaken by a passion too powerful for her to fight, older than time itself.

Dry-eyed, Bridget bit her lower lip and stared into the darkness, as if seeking some comfort there. "I didn't know, Mary Mother, I could not guess 'twould be like this!" she thought.

Keith's love had blazed into her heart with a fury that would leave only ashes behind.

How could she leave him now?

No, how could she marry him, when she loved him so, and knew how he would despise her when he found out the truth? It would be a thousand times worse than anything he thought of Lady Charlotte, when he found out how she had lied to him and tricked him. He would think she had deliberately set out to trick him into marriage to advance herself in the world.

It turned out that an ekka was a tiny little two-wheeled carriage, hardly more than a rickety cart. The driver gave her a curious glance as she emerged from the walled courtyard, but it was mercifully too dark for the extent of her disarray to be clear.

They spoke but little on the way back to Chowringhee. Keith held her hand and dropped kisses on the top of her head from time to time, and Bridget could not bring herself to speak and break the spell of love that was around them. Tomorrow would be time enough to explain. Tomorrow she would tell Keith who she really was. Perhaps he would be disgusted; but perhaps he would listen long enough to understand the fear that had driven her to it. If he understood, it would not be quite so bad.

But she would have tonight to remember. And these last precious minutes of the ride home were part of it. She bargained with God in her mind. If she told Keith tomorrow, wasn't she entitled to tonight?

That rationalization lasted until the gatekeeper let them into the Lanyers' compound.

The sound of the ekka's arrival was all but drowned out by the buzz of conversation in the Lanyers' brightly lit drawing room. Mrs. Lanyer, moving among her guests in her new silk gown, was too occupied with making all the presentations to Bishop Gairdner in the proper order to pay any attention to the muffled noises outside.

"Yes," she said for the fourth or fifth time, "it was so kind of Lady Dalhousie to bring the dear bishop over right after dinner!"

So inconsiderate, too. She had barely had time to scrawl chits to a few dozen of her friends in Calcutta, turning what Lady Dalhousie had intended as an informal visit into a crowded soirée where every one of Mrs. Lanyer's acquaintance could thank her for this chance to meet the bishop.

"Such a pity that dear Lady Charlotte is unwell," she said for the fourteenth or fifteenth time. "I know she is eager to see Bishop Gairdner again. But you know how the climate here affects these young girls straight from England. I have left her in her room with strict instructions that she is not to come downstairs until she is feeling quite recovered."

The guests smiled and agreed and discreetly over-looked the fact that the hot season had not begun yet; this evening was positively chilly! Doubtless Lady Charlotte was really troubled by some feminine complaint which it would not be proper to mention in mixed company.

Mrs. Lanyer knew what construction they would place on her vague words. The lie was paid for in little pinpricks of pain that radiated from her right eye down her cheekbone. Mrs. Lanyer sipped a glass of wine discreetly laced with laudanum and prayed that her headache would go away. Where *was* Charlotte? How could she be so careless as to go out alone at this time of night? Her reputation might never recover. And tonight of all nights, when Bishop Gairdner had come expressly to see her again!

The bishop sat in state in the midst of all this gaiety, a shriveled figure almost buried in the opulently padded wingchair in which Mrs. Lanyer had installed him. He peered at the assembled company through thick spectacles with heavy lenses and said polite things in a voice hardly stronger than a thread.

Mrs. Lanyer was presenting her third cousin once removed, a Mrs. Jameson from up-country who was hardly worthy of the honor, when she noticed a stir by the door. Good manners required her to remain by the Bishop's side until the introduction was completed. Then she swept toward the door to see what new problem had arisen.

But by then it was too late.

Charlotte's bedraggled form, the disarray of her hair and the buttons missing from her dress were taken in with open enjoyment by the assembled guests. The girl looked as if she wanted to run upstairs, but Lieutenant Powell was gripping her arm in a way that made that impossible.

The sibilant whispers were heard throughout the room, as of course they were meant to be.

"My dear, only *look* at her dress!"

"Out alone, at this hour of the night; well, one knows what to think."

"These Irish girls are so dreadfully *fast*."

"I thought she was supposed to be upstairs?"

Keith bowed to the ladies. "What a fortunate coincidence that so many of the shining lights of Calcutta society are here to welcome us," he said. "I hope you will all wish us happy. Lady Charlotte has just agreed to become my wife."

The murmurs of pleasurable shock gave way to somewhat disappointed congratulations. One granted some license to young people once they were actually engaged to be married.

Mrs. Lanyer pushed her way through the crowd and took Charlotte's hand. "My dear, I am so happy for you. Now you must come in and meet the dear bishop."

She noticed with some annoyance that Charlotte was perfectly white. Was she going to faint now and round off the debacle of the evening? And that impossible dress! ". . . as soon as you change your dress," she tacked on to the end of the sentence.

The girl nodded, whispered something unintelligible and almost ran up the stairs.

Bridget had been seeking the safety of her room in hope of a chance to think. But there was no privacy there. Agatha Lanyer followed her and laid out a suitable dress while the ayah combed out her hair and unhooked the stained cotton dress.

"I told Mama that I had known where you were all along," Aggie announced. Her pale cheeks were flushed and for once, in the vicarious excitement of the moment, she looked almost pretty. "All the old cats were gossiping downstairs. You never heard such a fuss! That Mrs. Jameson would have it that you were eloping with Keith but he changed his mind and brought you back. I don't know where she gets these ideas. Just because Mama didn't know where you were! So I told her I had known all about it, that you wanted some time alone with Keith to decide whether you really wanted to marry him and you asked me not to tell anyone."

"Oh, Aggie," Bridget said while the ayah combed her hair. "You didn't have to do that. Now your mother will be angry with both of us." She would be even angrier in a few minutes, unless Bridget could think of some way to put off going downstairs to meet this bishop. She put her hand to her head. "I feel faint. Perhaps I should not go down."

Aggie shook her head. "No, Mama's already used that. She had to come up with some story for the bishop for why you weren't here. Even if you're really about to faint, you'd better pull yourself together for a few minutes. Cheer up. It won't be so bad. Those gossiping old tabbies are just mad because you've got the handsomest man in Calcutta. I'd be jealous myself if . . ." She stopped and fussed with the frills of lace covering her bosom. "Well, never mind. You are looking pale, now I see you." She pinched Bridget's cheeks to bring out the color.

"If what?" Bridget asked. She stepped into the yellow silk skirt and held her breath while the ayah pulled on her corset strings.

Aggie's averted face and unbecoming, freckly blush gave her the answer. "Is it James?"

"Don't tell anyone," Aggie whispered. "Mama will never agree. . . . She wanted me to marry a Collector or a Resident. Someone with a good salary and a pension. James is only an ensign, and he's not brainy like your Keith. He'll never get a staff appointment. He'll always be just a soldier. But I don't care. We love each other and I'm going to marry him!" She burst into tears.

"Of course you are," Bridget soothed, patting Aggie on the head and mopping her face with a linen handkerchief. "It will work out . . . you'll see." She felt guilty for wishing that Aggie would go away and leave her a few moments of peace before she had to go downstairs. If only she could get a minute to think! There must be some way out of this tangle.

Keith had said they were to be married. In front of all those people. And now the same people were waiting for her to come downstairs and meet her old friend, Bishop Gairdner.

Bridget cast a wild look at the doors opening onto the verandah. Fantasies of kicking aside her crinoline and skirts, running onto the verandah and climbing down the outside of the house flashed through her mind. Anything was preferable to going downstairs and drawing Keith into the net of ridicule that was waiting for her.

She edged closer to the open door. A shadowy figure in white uncurled from a sleeping mat and made a *salaam.*

"Missy Sahib want to send message?"

It was a *chuprassi,* one of the letter carriers who ran all over Calcutta with Mrs. Lanyer's notes to her friends. Beyond him were other servants, waiting for orders.

At this hour of the night she could hardly pretend to be going out for a stroll in the compound, as she'd done that afternoon. There was no way she could escape unobserved, even if she got rid of Aggie.

Bridget turned back into the room and let Aggie clasp a string of pearls round her neck and thrust a pearl-bedecked comb into her hair. The stiff yellow silk of her skirts rustled whenever she moved.

At least, she thought, she was going down to her defeat in style.

Chapter Seven

DOWNSTAIRS, KEITH HAD ACCEPTED A WHISKEY AND SODA with gratitude. He accepted congratulations on his engagement with somewhat less comfort. He hadn't meant to rush Charlotte that way, but what else could he do under the circumstances?

Not Charlotte. That was a relief—but confusing. His head was whirling. Dammit, he didn't know anything else to call her! They would have to have a long talk. Tonight. No, tomorrow. For tonight, there was this Bishop Gairdner to take care of.

Keith felt the sweat springing out on his brow. There was too much to deal with all of a sudden. No wonder the girl had gone white. This Gairdner fellow had stayed with the Fitzgeralds in Ireland. He'd know she wasn't Charlotte.

Keith was tempted to let the farce play on. This Gairdner fellow might know who his "Charlotte" really was. But even so—no, he didn't want it to happen this way, to have the truth forced out of her before this staring crowd. Tomorrow they would discuss things calmly, reasonably. He still cherished a hope that she would tell him herself.

But first he'd have to stop this Bishop Gairdner from spilling the news in front of everybody, and as yet he had no idea how he was going to do that. Some quiet time for reflection might help, but he wasn't going to get that. A good stiff drink might help even more.

He swallowed the rest of his whiskey and soda at a gulp and half-turned, glass in hand. "Bring me another drink!"

Instead of the answering murmur of the white-robed steward who had been at his elbow a moment earlier, Keith heard a good-humored chuckle.

"Delighted to, m'boy, but the damned khitmutgar's disappeared again."

Keith found himself next to the portly figure of Major Bouverie, the military secretary to the governor-general. He started so violently that if his glass had not been empty, he would have sprayed them both with its contents.

"B-beg pardon, sir," he got out at last, in a strangled croak. "Didn't see you."

Major Bouverie chuckled again and took the glass from Keith's shaking hand. "Obviously not. Nerves, eh? To be expected. Newly engaged, and all that. Cupid's snare, eh, young Powell?"

"Ah—quite so, sir." Keith straightened his collar and groped frantically for something to say that would impress the major. He knew that all requests for staff appointments, although nominally in the hands of the governor-general, went through the military secretary's hands. Only yesterday he had been cursing his luck that he knew no one in Calcutta who could recommend him to Major Bouverie's attention. Now here he was standing next to him and all he could do was stammer and spill things!

"Remember when I got engaged myself," the major rumbled on. "She was a dainty little thing in those days . . . wouldn't think it to look at her now, would you?" His eyes followed the massive, corseted figure of Mrs. Bouverie.

"Ah . . . no, sir. I mean, yes, sir." Keith's first lesson in the army had been that one of those two answers would apply to every occasion. Now he reflected that he could have done with a little more training in when to apply which answer.

The khitmutgar glided up with a tray of filled glasses. Keith took one and emptied it at a gulp. His throat seemed to have gone dry suddenly. He tried to peer unobtrusively around the major's considerable bulk. Any minute now Charlotte might be coming down those stairs, and he still hadn't figured out how to save her from meeting the bishop.

"She'll be down in a minute," the major said. "You'll survive. After you've been married forty years, you won't be so eager to see her." He exhaled a wheeze of gusty laughter and cleared his throat several times before going on. "Quick thinking you showed there. All those old cats ready to start a scandal 'bout you being out alone with the girl. You really plan to marry her?"

"Yes, sir." At least that was one question he could answer unequivocally.

"Good, good. Like a young man that knows his own mind. Some of my colleagues don't hold with a political officer being married, but I say it's a good thing. Steadies 'em. Not so likely to go native. Some of these fellows, you send 'em off to a damned rajah's hill court for a few years, they start thinking like the natives. Taking their side! Pretty thing. What's a political good for if he doesn't protect British interests?"

Keith hardly took in what the major was rumbling on about. All his faculties were concentrated on the agonizing effort to peer around the major at the stairs Charlotte would be coming down and to think of some way he could get away and stop her without offending Major Bouverie permanently. But the cessation in the rumbling warned him that some sort of reply was expected.

"Er . . . quite so, sir." Was that a woman's dress rustling in the upper hall? Keith cast an agonized glance behind him at the wingchair where Bishop Gairdner had been settled. The old man was laboriously working his way to his feet.

The major laughed and clapped him on the shoulder. "Good man. Come by my office tomorrow morning. Might have something for you. Know anything about Guahipore? Well, find out. Tomorrow morning. Ten."

Keith's throat seemed suddenly to have gone dry. "Yes, sir. A small native state bordering on Kashmir, isn't it? Mohammedan. Thank you, sir. Language a variant of Urdu with some Tibetan words. Ten o'clock. Thank you, sir. Excuse me, sir."

Charlotte was standing in the doorway, newly arrayed in a gown of yellow silk that spread around her like the petals of a flower. And the knot of people between her and the Bishop was slowly parting to let her through.

Bishop Gairdner had completed the painful ascent from his chair and was polishing his glasses with a thick white handkerchief while he gazed around the room with the amiable, unfocused smile of the very nearsighted. Keith turned to put his glass down, seemed to stumble, and cannoned into the khitmutgar who in turn bumped into the bishop's stick and knocked it out from under him. Keith barely caught the old man before he went down on the floor; the glasses skittered away from them both.

"Terribly sorry, sir." Keith put the bishop's cane back in his hand and backed away from him. "Do let me find your glasses—went somewhere over here, I believe—"

A crunching of glass announced that Keith had indeed found the spectacles. He put one hand to his bootheel and regarded the large piece of glass embedded therein with obvious dismay. *"Terribly* sorry," he repeated. "Dreadfully clumsy—excitement of the moment—overjoyed by my engagement. . . ."

He went on backing up and babbling apologies, while behind him he heard Mrs. Bouverie's penetrating whisper. "Positively inebriated. And on the very night of his engagement! I pity Lady Charlotte."

Keith turned to Charlotte with a lopsided grin, holding out the twisted and mangled ruin of the bishop's spectacles. She looked past him to Bishop Gairdner, now sketching a bow in the general direction of Mrs. Bouverie.

"Charlotte, m'dear," he mumbled. "Terrible tragedy —y'r poor uncle. Aunt, too. Very sorry to hear."

Mrs. Lanyer redirected the bishop's attention with a gentle push on his elbow. "That's Mrs. Bouverie, the military secretary's wife, Bishop. Lady Charlotte is over here."

Bishop Gairdner gave his head a quarter-turn and nodded amiably at a spot equidistant between Charlotte and the door. "Pleased to see you again, m'dear. Terrible tragedy, y'r poor uncle. I've said that already, haven't I? Never mind, then. Tell you about my native missions." He half closed his eyes and appeared to reflect. "Didn't tell you all about my missions already, did I? You were quite interested last year, as I recall. Might get bored with hearing it all again."

"It will seem like the first time," said Bridget with perfect truth. She was feeling a little dizzy and there was a sort of singing noise in her ears as it dawned on her that she was not, after all, to expect immediate exposure. She placed her fingertips on Keith's arm as she had seen other ladies doing and gave him a brilliant smile. "Keith, dear, would you be so kind as to procure me something to drink?"

Keith exhaled and placed the ruined glasses in his coatpocket. "With pleasure, my love. Bishop Gairdner, I cannot sufficiently express my regret for this unfortunate accident. I trust you have a second pair of spectacles in your luggage? No?" He gave an unobtrusive sigh of relief. "You must let me see to the replacement of these. No, no, I insist. I will see to it myself." If necessary, Keith thought, he would see to it that the replacement did not come through until Bishop Gairdner was safely on his way home.

He procured a glass of wine for Charlotte and a third whiskey and soda for himself, oblivious of the whispers and disapproving stares of Mrs. Bouverie and her friends. He had earned it.

There was no chance to talk alone with Charlotte again that evening, although often he felt her eyes on him, waiting, questioning. Once he squeezed her hand while Bishop Gairdner was explaining how his spare spectacles had been swallowed by a crocodile one day when his bearer borrowed them without permission. The bearer had also been swallowed, but he was somewhat easier to replace.

"Tomorrow," he whispered to her.

Tomorrow, after his appointment with Major Bouverie, he would see her and tell her his news. Keith's blood was singing in his veins. He had made love to a beautiful girl, and he was about to get his coveted staff appointment. What more could life offer? When it became clear that there would be no more chance to get Charlotte alone that night, he excused himself so that he could walk home. The nights were still cool, the stifling heat of spring had yet to close down on the city, and there was too much in his heart for him to go to sleep yet. He walked for hours through the sleeping city, watching the moon on the rooftops and spinning dream palaces for himself and Charlotte to occupy after he had made his mark on the Indian civil administration.

Bridget watched him go with only a trace of regret. The evening was dull without Keith; but seeing him only reminded her of the reckoning due the next day.

She wished that she could withdraw herself. All she wanted to do was to lock herself away in her room and remember the little mud-walled hut in Gul Ram's compound where Keith had become her lover. But Bishop Gairdner had an inexhaustible fund of mission stories to tell her, and all of Mrs. Lanyer's friends wanted to talk about her engagement to Keith. Bridget smiled and nodded and said the right things while her heart was miles away, dreaming of the mud hut that had become a palace.

She did not even flinch—or not very much—when Mrs. Bouverie turned her congratulations on the engagement into a ten-minute monologue on the importance to young men of marrying the right sort of wife and how much difference it could make to their careers.

"A true lady, Lady Charlotte, one such as you or I, can be of inestimable service to her husband by her attention to those little social details which make or break him in the eyes of his superiors. I think I may venture to say that even Lord Dalhousie would not occupy the exalted position of governor-general were it not for the discreet influence of Lady Dalhousie. The intimate little dinner party, a word dropped in the right ear—these things can make a man's career, Lady Charlotte, just as an alliance with a coarse or vulgar female can ruin it."

"Yes," said Bridget. "I am well aware of that."

Mrs. Bouverie did not take offense at the stiff way in which Lady Charlotte uttered these few little words. Was that not just the manner of the true aristocracy?

Her speech had only underlined what Bridget had known in her heart all along. Keith could never marry such a one as her. To have courted her would make him a laughingstock if the truth came out; but marriage—that would ruin his life.

Oh, if only she had not loved him! If only he could have been someone else who did not know the real Lady Charlotte! But here she was, engaged to the one man in India who was bound to find her out in time. And more fool she, she loved him. Too well to marry him. That was what she would have to explain, and perhaps he would not think too badly of her.

"Tomorrow," thought Bridget.

Chapter Eight

THE HOURS OF THE NEXT MORNING PASSED WITH AGONIZ-
ing slowness for Bridget. Mrs. Lanyer had proposed
taking her into the town to shop for stuffs for her
trousseau, but Colonel Lanyer vetoed the proposed
expedition.

"Three more cholera cases in the hospital," he said
over his newspaper. "Thinking of sending you and
Aggie to the hills. Don't want you traipsing around the
bazaars."

So instead of a fascinating foray through the shops of
the Calcutta merchants, Mrs. Lanyer had to send for
bolts of cloth to be sewn up by the durzee who sat
cross-legged on the verandah. Bridget supposed this
was a good thing. If they went shopping, she might be
out when Keith called for their promised talk. It was
better to tell him at once and get it over with. She knew
that.

She had lain awake for most of the night, dry-eyed, evolving her plans for dealing with this latest emergency. Bishop Gairdner had accepted her as Charlotte, but it could be only a matter of days until he got his new spectacles. And at any moment some reminiscence of his might trip her up.

She must not still be engaged to Keith when the truth came out. When he came to see her today, she would confess everything, throw herself on his mercy. They could put it about that she had jilted him, and perhaps he would help her to get up-country to take that position as Mrs. Trenton's governess.

Unless he despised her too much to have anything to do with her, once he found out. No—Keith wasn't that sort. He was a decent man; he wouldn't abandon her here. He might even feel himself bound to hold by his offer of marriage.

Would that be so bad? She loved him, truly she did, and she could make him happier than ever Charlotte could have.

No. It was bound to come out sometime. And what would the scandal do to his career? Bridget remembered the way Mrs. Bouverie had gone on and on about the importance of the right connections to a young officer's career. No—even if Keith were willing to stand by her, she couldn't let him sacrifice himself that way.

Then, having reasoned her way to an irrefutable conclusion, she had finally cried. Very quietly, so that the servants who were everywhere should not hear, she had lain staring open-eyed at the punkah above her bed while the tears filled her eyes and overflowed.

Now she was tired and heavy-eyed from lack of sleep. A glance in the mirror showed a pale girl with dark eyes too large for her face, whose wide, generous mouth drooped a little at the corners.

Not a face for a newly engaged girl to show the world. Bridget thought with grim humor of all the amusing memories that she could call to mind. Let's see, there was the time Paddy Reilly's pig got drunk on the sour potato mash, and the ridiculous stalking dignity of the adjutant-birds on the Maidan; and . . . and . . .

It was Keith who had pointed out the adjutant-birds to her.

She burst into tears again.

"Nerves," Mrs. Lanyer decreed. "Laudanum," she prescribed and poured Bridget a glass of sticky-sweet wine heavily laced with the drug. "Go and lie down, my dear. You must be in good spirits when your Keith comes to see you."

Bridget carried the wineglass up to her room with her. Once there, she realized that she was thirsty and that she had forgotten to ask for any soda water. Of course she could call for it from her room, but the thought of hearing the chain of commands relayed from one end of the house to the other and back made her head ache worse than before.

She sipped the wine cautiously. It was too sweet, but not so bad when you got used to it. The sweet taste must be that loda . . . laude . . . whatever Mrs. Lanyer had said. It did make her feel better, but her head was still aching. Well, if a little was good, a lot must be better. Bridget drank down the full glass and lay down fully clothed on her bed.

The quantity of laudanum poured out by Mrs. Lanyer was what she used for her own headaches. But then, Mrs. Lanyer had been having headaches since the day she arrived in India, twenty-five years earlier. There was enough laudanum in the wine to put Bridget out for hours.

At first the influence of the drug only sent her off into a half-waking state in which nothing seemed to matter very much anymore. The portion of her mind that was still operating noticed that the day was growing hot, cooperated with the ayah who loosened her dress, approved when the punkah began its lazy scooping motion across the room. Then the hot room with its accompaniment of buzzing insects, the swish of the punkah and the chatter of Agatha and Mrs. Lanyer in the next room all faded away.

She dreamed through the next few hours, oblivious to the scurrying feet of the chuprassi, Mrs. Lanyer's exclamations as she broke open and read the chits from her husband and from Keith Powell, the bustle of the household as clothes were lifted from tin boxes and aired in preparation for packing.

The cholera cases in the native town had reached epidemic numbers. Colonel Lanyer, afraid for his family, had directed them to leave at once for Simla, where they normally lodged during the hot weather. Lady Charlotte could go up with them; young Powell could follow when he'd finished his business in Calcutta.

Keith Powell, closeted with the military secretary, was also unaware of the hasty preparations being made in the city as dozens of English families decided to follow Colonel Lanyer's lead and remove to the hills. And even if he had been aware of them, the rumors of yet another outbreak of cholera would have seemed unimportant to him next to the destiny that Major Bouverie unfolded before him.

He too had been up half the night, searching his books and buttonholing fellow officers for information about Guahipore, with the result that this morning he was able to follow the major's somewhat disconnected briefing with a semblance of intelligent attention.

"Won't be an easy post," the major warned him. "Native state. No treaties with us—no official standing. Ruler's called the *mehtar*. He's a Mahommedan. Managed to keep Guahipore independent during the Sikh period. Helped us out a bit in the second Sikh war—maintains his own troops—undisciplined hillmen, but damn good fighters! Now that we've given Kashmir to Gulab Singh—damn silly decision, if I do say so—he's nervous. Doesn't like having Gulab next door. Can't say I blame him. Well!" He cleared his throat. "We need a man in the vicinity. Look after British interests and all that. More Europeans going that way, now that the Sikhs are down—more British travelers, surveyors —all that sort of thing. Wanted a resident in Kashmir, couldn't get Gulab to agree, but the mehtar of Guahipore has agreed to a British agent. No treaty, just a British officer livin' there, representin' our interests to the mehtar. That's you—if you want the post."

He gave Keith a sharp glance. "It won't be easy. Forty-seven varieties of heathen tribes, all trying to kill each other. Gulab Singh probably wanting to annex Guahipore. And the Russians sniffing about just over the border, as usual. Well?"

"I would be honored to take the assignment, sir." Colorless words for the excitement that was bubbling up in him. His first posting. The mountains. The tribespeople. His immediate superior would be the British resident in Lahore, many days' march away. This was a post where a man could have a chance at independent action, could really accomplish something. Brilliant pictures danced before Keith's eyes. If he could show the mehtar of Guahipore the advantages of friendship with the British, persuade him to make a formal treaty and invite a resident to stay there, what might not follow?

"How soon can you leave?"

"What?" The question interrupted Keith's glorious visions. "Oh! As soon as necessary."

Major Bouverie gave vent to a series of rumbling belches which Keith recognized as a laugh. "Good man. No hurry. Should take about a month by dak. You want to get there before August. Snows start any time after that. Give the women time to plan a wedding. They like that sort of thing, y'know. Hard on Lady Charlotte, havin' to go off to some godforsaken hill station first thing. Take y'r time. Now—let's get to work."

The major spread out a crackling, yellowed map of northwestern India that almost covered his desk. "You'll be here." His stubby finger covered a patch marked by little more than artistic renditions of mountains. "Not too well mapped. Some talk of a pass in the north—tribal territory. We're sending a fellow to map the area. Supposed to report to you when—if he gets back. Apart from that . . ."

For the next few hours Keith's attention was entirely taken up by the necessity of taking notes on the various subjects Major Bouverie thought worthy of his attention. He was unwillingly impressed. The man had a memory like an encyclopedia! Tribal customs, the last recorded visit of a Russian agent, the present mehtar's prediliction for building up a *zenana* to rival the great days of the Moghul empire—no detail was too small for his attention. And this was just one small part of the vast territory governed, administered or watched over by the British raj.

When he finally left the major's office, his head was

spinning and his pockets were crammed with hastily scribbled notes. And his respect for the men who governed British India had gone up several notches. Keith groaned. How had he ever thought to turn a modest talent for languages and a liking for the natives into a political career? He had so much to learn!

Keith was so deep in thought that Colonel Lanyer, seeing him emerge from the military secretary's office, had to call two or three times to get his attention. And then it took Keith a few minutes to switch his thoughts from the snowy hills where he was being sent to the present reality of Calcutta: hot, unsanitary and preparing for another cholera epidemic. But once he understood Colonel Lanyer's intention of sending his womenfolk into the hills, he heartily agreed that they should be gotten out of the city at once.

"Only . . . not Charlotte. I've a better plan." Keith hurriedly explained his new posting and got the colonel's approval for the somewhat unconventional course of action he proposed.

"Send m'wife into a tizzy, if packing for Simla ain't done it already," the colonel chuckled, "but what of it? Good for her. Keeps the blood circulating. All right, m'boy. I've a chuprassi waiting outside. You can send y'r chits by him. Leave the bishop to me. I'll have him waiting for you this evening."

Keith hastily scrawled two notes and gave them to the chuprassi with instructions to deliver one to Chowringhee, the other to Prinsep Ghat. Then he took his leave of the Colonel to hasten about his other preparations.

Bridget was aroused from a deep and satisfying, if somewhat confusing, dream in which she and Keith were floating down the Ganges River on the back of a crocodile wearing the bishop's second-best spectacles. Suddenly the crocodile dived under water and an adjutant-bird perched, screaming, on her shoulder. She raised a hand to bat it off and the bird turned into Agatha Lanyer.

"Charlotte? Do wake up!"

Bridget rubbed her eyes. Who was Charlotte?

Then she remembered. With a great effort she swung her legs over the side of the bed and stood up. Every movement was slow and difficult, as though she were pushing her way through air as liquid and heavy as water.

"Need to . . . see Keith," she articulated with an effort. "Is he . . . here?" In a minute she would remember what she had to see him about. All she knew now was that it was so terribly important that it had pursued her through all the dreams.

Aggie patted her hand. "Of course you shall see him, dear, but you must be properly dressed first. Is it not the most romantic thing? Mama was quite annoyed at first, because she wanted to have a big wedding with everyone in Calcutta, but when Papa told her that he had arranged for Bishop Gairdner to perform the ceremony, she felt better about it. And you'll never guess who is going to give you away! Lord Dalhousie himself! I tell you, nothing could reconcile Mama to anything faster than having the governor-general in the house! She has had the durzee busy all afternoon, letting out her old white silk gown with the Venice lace for you to wear."

Aggie's excited, shrill voice swept past Bridget with no more meaning than the screaming of the birds in her dream. Aggie seemed to be talking twice as fast as usual—or was it she who had slowed down? She put one hand to her head. "Dizzy," she announced. "Need to sit down." What was this about Lord Dalhousie giving her away? Had he known Lady Charlotte? What had he said?

She felt her way to a carved teakwood stool and sat there while the ayah sponged her face and hands with cool water. She could barely make out Aggie's white face and the ayah's white cotton clothes in the dimness of the room. "Why is it so dark? Is there a storm coming?"

"No, it is nearly evening," Aggie told her. "How you slept!" She giggled. "And here I am getting the story back to front, as usual. Keith sent a chit . . ."

Bridget sat passively while the ayah dressed her and Aggie rambled on. Slowly the fog of sleep cleared from her brain, and she began to understand the noises she had half heard while she slept.

The Lanyers were removing to Simla early, a month before the really hot weather started, for fear of the cholera. They had meant to take her with them, but Keith had a better plan. He had finally received his coveted posting, to some place very far away—Aggie was vague about its exact location—and he suggested that if they were married at once, they could leave together for his new post. Leaving at once would give them time to take the slow but comfortable river journey; it would be a sort of honeymoon.

"No!" Once Bridget grasped the plan, she was horrified. She jumped up and strode about the room while the ayah ran after her, chattering frantically, "Wait, missee sahib, no can do hooks!" and trying to do up her gown.

"I have to talk to Keith first."

"Charlotte, dear, it's bad luck to see the bridegroom on the day of your wedding." Aggie's firm little hands caught and held hers.

"'Twill be worse luck if I don't see him."

"You're nervous," Aggie said. "They say all brides are nervous on the day. I hope I find out someday." She called to the ayah to bring some more wine.

"Here," she said, giggling. "It's Papa's port. He doesn't know I drink it, but one must have something to get through this climate. And they say the hot weather hasn't started yet. Can you imagine! If we each have a little sip, no one will notice, and you'll feel ever so much better."

Aggie's "little sip" was a good-sized wineglass full. Bridget drank half and felt her head spinning again. "Could I just have some soda water?"

That set off the string of calls she had feared.

From the ayah to the bearer, "Tell them to bring soda water for the memsahib."

The bearer bawled down the stairs, "Oh khansamah, bring the European water for the ladies."

The khansamah called a further order, mercifully out of hearing.

In a little while the sequence of calls was repeated in the other direction, and not more than ten minutes or so after Bridget had made her request, the glass of water appeared.

She drank it down thirstily and reflected that in some ways it was easier not to be a lady. It might be more work to draw the water out of your own well, but at least you didn't have to negotiate with half a dozen people to get a glass of it when you wanted it.

"Tastes funny," she said, regarding the empty glass with puzzlement.

Aggie sniffed the glass and burst out laughing. "Oh, I think the khansamah smeared the glass with opium juice! Isn't that funny? He must think you are like one of the little native girls who has to be drugged because they are so afraid of being married!"

"I can't . . ." Bridget began, then put one hand to her head. There had been something very important she had to say. "I can't marry Keith. It's a mistake! I have to see him!"

"There, there, my girl."

Mrs. Lanyer sailed into the room, majestic in purple satin, and patted Bridget's hand. Her dry fingers closed around Bridget's wrist like a vise. "Let us not have any last-minute scenes. I have been working all day to make everything nice for your wedding. Did you know the bishop himself is here?"

"Yes," said Bridget wearily, "and Lord Dalhousie is to give me away. But he can't . . . I have to . . . I have to see Keith first."

Mrs. Lanyer beamed. "And so you shall, as soon as he gets here. Now calm down. We don't want any unseemly scenes, do we, dear Lady Charlotte?" Make a fuss, her firm tones said, and I'll make you sorry you were born, dear Lady Charlotte. Bridget was not so drugged that she could not recognize determination like Mrs. Lanyer's.

"It's not . . ." Why was it so hard to think? "Please, I need to talk to Keith. Alone!" She had to drag the words out one by one. Something very strange was happening to her mouth, it kept wanting to flow out of shape. The effort made her sound shrilly desperate.

Mrs. Lanyer looked around. "Aggie, go away!" When her daughter had retreated, she bent over Bridget. "You're not . . . worried about . . . your *marital duties,* are you, dear? Because . . ." She paused and looked round the empty room again. "Because it's . . ."

Her firm little mouth pursed. With an effort as great as Bridget's she pronounced, "It is over very soon, and you only have to be a good brave girl and think of something else for a little while."

Bridget laughed, and heard the note of hysteria creeping into her own voice. "Sure, and I know about that, ma'am! You don't understand . . ."

Mrs. Lanyer retreated a few paces and stood wiping her fingers on the edge of her skirt as though she had touched something dirty. "Know about it? Yes, I thought you did! Then why. . . ."

She recovered herself with a visible effort and resumed a soothing manner as false as the layers of white paint with which she was plastered. "Don't worry, dear Lady Charlotte. Everything is going to be all right."

A servant tapped at the door and Mrs. Lanyer rustled over for a whispered conference. She came back holding a bottle and a spoon in her hands.

"Lieutenant Powell is downstairs now," she announced. "Just be a good girl and take this, and you may go down and be with your Keith. You will like that, won't you?"

Obediently Bridget opened her mouth to accept the spoonful of medicine. It tasted sickly-sweet—like the wine she had had that morning.

"What was . . . that?" Her eyes focused on the waving silk fringe of a curtain and followed its lazy sway, in and out, in and out of the window.

"Just a little something for your nerves," Mrs. Lanyer said. The bottle had disappeared, and there were more people in the room—her ayah, and Aggie, urging her to stand.

"You'll be a lovely bride," Aggie said rapturously. "And it will be a lovely wedding. I'm almost as happy as if James and I—"

She shot a scared glance at her mother, but Mrs. Lanyer was too intent on her present plans to notice her daughter's blush.

Bridget stood very carefully and lifted the clinging white fabric of her borrowed dress an inch off the floor. Mustn't trip on her skirt in front of all these people. Something else she mustn't do, either, but she was having trouble keeping her thoughts straight.

"The medicine?" she asked.

Mrs. Lanyer flushed under her paint. "It is perfectly safe. Does not the least harm in the world. I've been taking it myself."

It was an effort to keep her eyes focused. Bridget gave up the effort and suddenly there were two Mrs. Lanyers, sliding sideways.

Then, without her knowing quite how, she was on the stairs. Well, that was good. She was going down to see Keith, as they promised. And then she could tell him . . . tell him . . .

Bridget frowned. It was going to be hard to explain. She was having trouble remembering things.

"Well, I won't be worrying about it now," she said aloud. "I'll just get myself safely down this divil of a staircase first, then I'll think."

At her elbow, Mrs. Lanyer encouraged her. "That's right, dear. Go carefully."

But it wasn't so hard after all. Halfway down the stairs became spongy, like she'd always imagined clouds to be. And she was in a white cloud herself, so it was easy to float down the stairs. It would have been entirely easy, except that Mrs. Lanyer was gripping her elbow.

She was still thirsty. "But it's so much trouble to get soda water," she said.

Then they were in the Lanyers' drawing room, and

Keith was standing at the far end, looking at her with a curious strained expression on his face. She started to go to him, to explain that she couldn't, must not marry him. But suddenly there were all these people in the way. Why, the drawing room was full of people! Why hadn't she noticed it before?

A tall, graying man in uniform offered her his arm. She was glad of the support and looked up to tell him so, but he hushed her. "Not while the bishop is speaking, my dear."

Now she was standing beside Keith. And yes—that was Bishop Gairdner, that funny old man, standing before them. He still didn't have his glasses. And he was making a speech of some sort, something long, with churchly words.

Bridget made an effort to concentrate, and the fog cleared just a little bit. Keith was looking worried; she smiled to reassure him, then frowned to concentrate on the bishop's words. The combination made her stomach lurch.

Something about the estate of holy matrimony.

The fog cleared a little more. Bridget glanced around the room. Holy Mother! Were all these people gathered to watch her being married to Keith Powell?

"Do you, Charlotte, take this man to be your lawful wedded husband?"

Bridget stared at the bishop while her mind raced, looking for alternatives. Could she say, "I'm not Charlotte?" Or how about "No?"

They were all watching her.

They were all watching Keith.

If she made a scene at the altar, it would be a worse scandal than anything that happened afterward. Wouldn't it?

Keith's smile was fading. He looked worried. And

there was a stir around the room, a rustling of ladies leaning to each other and preparing to whisper some malicious comment.

Bridget opened her mouth and took a deep breath. "I do," she said, loud and clear and defiant.

Then it was done, she was committed, and she let herself slip back into the cloud induced by wine and laudanum. But a small, cold awareness within her knew that she could never claim that she had been too drugged to know what she was doing.

Chapter Nine

THE SUNLIGHT FLICKERED IN THROUGH THE NARROW cracks in the split-cane blinds and danced over patterned chintz pillows, wicker furniture, white gauze mosquito nets. Bridget opened her eyes lazily and realized that she was still in a dream, for she felt as if the whole room were swaying gently from side to side. Such a dreamy, gentle, floating sensation! She wished it could go on forever and that she didn't have to wake up.

Floating.

She pushed back the gauze mosquito netting and stumbled across the rocking floor to the window. A cracked piece of bamboo left a chink in the blinds through which sunlight spilled onto the floor. She stooped to peer out. Instead of the broad verandah of the Lanyers' house and the compound walls beyond that, she saw muddy-brown river water, sandbanks in the distance and sparse clumps of trees.

The events of the previous night came back to her like disconnected fragments of a dream: the bustle and confusion at the Lanyers' house; herself standing with Keith before the bishop, insecurely laced into a borrowed white satin gown; then drinks and congratulations and Keith handing her into a carriage, saying something about the tide.

The boat rolled with a change in the wind; there were shouts and scurrying bare feet on deck, and Bridget lost her balance and sat down with a thump on the rattan sofa beside the window. She began to laugh. So much for good intentions! What was it Aggie had been saying? Something about Keith wanting them to take their honeymoon on a pinnace going up-river, as part of the journey to his new post. That must be what had happened.

She searched her memory, but could remember nothing after the beginning of the carriage ride last night. The wine and laudanum must have finally overcome her. But here she was, and no longer wearing the borrowed wedding dress. Bridget fingered the primly buttoned white muslin nightdress that covered her from neck to ankles and blushed. Someone had put her into this, and she was willing to bet it wasn't an ayah.

At the image of Keith's long, tanned hands moving over her body while she lay unconscious, she felt as embarrassed as though they had never exchanged anything more than a chaste handshake.

And in a way, they hadn't. Those brief moments in Gul Ram's house had happened to another girl, someone called Lady Charlotte Fitzgerald, who had been locked up in a strange place and, more frightened than she cared to admit, had turned to her old friend for comfort.

She was just Biddy Sullivan, maidservant from Bally-

111

crochan, on a pinnace bound up the Ganges. It wasn't her at all that Keith had made love to—it was that other girl, the one in his memory. And when she made her confession to him, lovemaking would be the farthest thing from his mind.

Convenient, she thought bleakly, that they were headed up-river. When Keith found out how she had deceived him, he would be only too willing to put her off at Berhampore and let her seek work as a governess to Mrs. Trenton's children.

On that discouraging note, Keith tapped lightly at the screen that covered the bedroom door and came in.

Bridget's heart twisted at the sight of him—the lean, tanned face with the lock of black hair that fell into his gray eyes, the long limbs that had known hers so intimately. He was looking at her with a blend of love and anxiety that hurt to see. In a moment, when she spoke, all that would be gone forever. Oh, if only she didn't have to tell him!

"Char?" he asked in a low voice. "Are you . . . feeling better?"

Bridget forced a smile, and saw Keith's face transformed. Why, he had been anxious lest she should be angry at him! Now he came across the narrow strip of matting that separated them and dropped to one knee, taking her hand and fondling it.

"I hope . . . I did not hurry you too much? There was so little time, you see. I wanted to be sure you were out of Calcutta before the cholera got even worse, and . . . and with this new post, I had to travel up-river anyway, and . . . well," he finished with a grin, "you did want to take a boat up the river, didn't you? And here we are!"

Bridget burst out laughing, less at the ironical way in which his promise to help her had come true than at the comically triumphant expression on his face. Keith stood up and pulled her to her feet, putting his arm around her waist to steady her against the occasional motion of the boat.

"You were . . . tired last night," he said. He looked down at the sprinkling of sunlight across the matting, and Bridget was surprised to see a warm color rising to his face. "I thought . . . maybe I hurried you too much?"

"No, Keith!" She could not let him go thinking that. Mary Mother, wasn't the trouble that she loved him too well? Else they'd not be in this tangle. "No, it was. . . ." She stopped and laughed uneasily. "It's drunk I was, and that's the plain truth of it," she said. "Drunk and drugged. Mrs. Lanyer gave me laudanum for my headache. And then Aggie thought I was nervous and made me drink a glass of port. And didn't even the khansamah himself get in on the act, and him rubbing opium juice on the glass of soda water when I called for it!" It was easier to laugh now. "Lucky we are I did not disgrace you before them all."

She stopped. Keith was frowning. She couldn't remember that well. "Ah . . . I didn't disgrace you, did I?"

"No, darling. You made your responses like the perfect lady you are."

Bridget clenched one hand in the fold of her nightgown. Oh, this was going to be hard—worse than ever she had imagined!

"And in the carriage, you simply put your head on my shoulder and went to sleep."

But he still looked unhappy.

."What is wrong, then?"

"Charlotte, I . . . you seemed quiet, but I did not know . . . I thought . . . I would not have rushed you

113

through a ceremony, if I thought you did not know what you were doing."

"Oh, I knew," said Bridget. Hard to keep her voice from quivering. It might have been easier to go through with her confession, if she could claim she had been too drugged to know what was happening. But it wasn't true, and she couldn't pretend it was; not when Keith was watching her so anxiously.

He sighed with relief. "Thank God. I think I would never have forgiven myself if my haste had forced you into something you would later regret."

Not her, Bridget thought. It was he would be regretting it, when she told him the truth.

He was still looking worried. She longed to reassure him. But how could she say she had no regrets when marrying her might have ruined his career? Ah, well, there was one thing she could say that was true enough. She slid one hand up his sleeve and stood before him, looking into his gray eyes and willing him to believe her. "It's entirely in love with you I am, Keith Powell," she said deliberately. "Will that be assurance enough for you, or will you want me to prove it?"

A wicked grin slanted across Keith's face, pulling up one corner of his mouth and setting small lights dancing in his eyes. "Ah, would you now, my love? In broad daylight, with the servants on deck?"

Both his arms about her, the warmth of his body striking inward through the thin nightdress; his lips on hers, conquering, plundering her reserve. She was drowning in his kiss.

"Keith!" she gasped. "I didn't mean . . ."

"Did you not, now?" he teased. "And will you not?" Between words, his fingers and lips roved over her body, setting her alight in spots she didn't even know about, teasing little gasps of surrender out of her. "And have you no pity?" A kiss on the side of her neck; the tongue flicking her earlobe. "On a poor lonely man?" One hand cupped her bottom through the thin muslin, fingers spread out, arrogantly claiming his territory. "Who undressed you last night and then slept on the mat beside the bed?" His leg between hers now, he bent her head back in a long, burning kiss that scorched her like a brushfire running over the naked land.

The sunlight dappled the white muslin nightgown and khaki shirt and trousers, thrown down together in mutual urgency. The mosquito curtains were pushed back from the bed where two bodies entwined, seeking the fulfillment of their love.

Bridget stroked Keith's lean flanks, marveling at the smooth working of muscle beneath the skin, the power and the beauty there in a man's body that she'd never guessed at. Her fingers lingered curiously over one long white scar that ran down his side in a jagged line; paused again on the sun-darkened chest with the two darker nipples and the line of body hair that ran down to his flat belly.

He guided her hand to the nest of darker hair between his thighs where his manhood sprang up strong and erect; sighed with pleasure as her fingers caressed the firm shaft. His own hand cupped her breast, thumb and forefinger teasing a response from the nipple. Quivering rays of pleasure radiated from that center through her body until she sighed and fell back against the pillows, eyes half-closed against the brilliance of the sun that spilled through the cracked blinds.

His body covered and penetrated hers like an extension of that golden warmth, a flood of sunlight that spilled between her thighs and warmed her with slow, caressing movements until she cried out and gripped him round the hips, caring for nothing but that he should drive fully into her and bring her to completion. Her body strained to meet his as if possessed by its own will. And then she was shaken, falling from a great height, floating, free, while deep within her she could feel the quivering of his own pleasure.

They lay in a close embrace on the tumbled bed. Bridget kissed Keith's shoulder and tasted the salty sweat that glistened on his body. There was a ridged scar there, too. Where had he been to get such scars, what had he done, this man whom India had brought to her?

She tilted her head to look at his face, and the heart turned over in her at the way he was looking at her, those gray eyes not hard now but dancing with promise, his whole face happy and relaxed as she'd not seen it before. Why, he could not be much older than she was herself, she thought with astonishment. The air of authority had deceived her; that, and the stories of the adventurous life he'd led. She'd thought of him—without really thinking about it—as a man in his thirties. But it was a boy who smiled down at her.

She did some quick reckoning on her fingers. Sixteen, Charlotte had been that spring when she went to Dublin; and Keith had been twenty-one. Five years. He would be twenty-six now.

Bridget's lips curved in a warm and unintentionally enticing smile.

"What's so funny, my Irish witch?" Keith asked.

"I thought you were older." Bridget clapped a hand over her mouth. "I mean, you looked older, here in India. Until now."

Keith stood up, laughed and stretched. Bridget watched unashamedly, glorying in the fine strong lines of his body, as he slipped a loose linen shirt over his head and fumbled on the floor for his trousers. "Maybe

I was . . . until I had you. This life ages a man." He
bent over the bed and kissed her on the mouth. "But
you make me young again."

His lips wandered, seeking out the soft curve between neck and shoulder, tracing the line up to the tip
of her breast. With one hand he caressed the other
breast, cupping her softness with an intimately protec-
tive gesture that made the breath catch in her throat.
"Do you know how happy you've made me?"

His face was young and grave and alight from within,
all the harsh lines of responsibility and solitude erased.
Bridget looked down at him and told herself that she
hadn't the heart to take that look from him just yet. Let
him be happy a little longer—let them both be happy!
Surely it would harm no one if she just enjoyed this
month on the river with him? There would be time
enough to tell him before they reached Guahipore.
Then she could turn back and leave him to complete his
journey alone.

She stroked his head and held it close to her breast.
"Not as happy as you have made me, Keith."

The slow days of their up-river journey passed too
quickly for Bridget. She soon learned her way about
the little pinnace with its three rooms of living quarters
and the broad deck where the crew and servants slept.
There was little work for her to do and that was
strange, but not so difficult as it would have been if she
hadn't had that week in Calcutta to practice being
waited on hand and foot. And she found more than
enough to occupy her time: viewing the strange and
exotic sights they passed, learning Urdu from Keith so
that she would be able to talk to the people in
Guahipore and, most of all, being with Keith. Talking
to him, sitting with him, watching his head bent over

the mass of official notes and correspondence he had to familiarize himself with—the daylight passed quickly enough.

And the nights were pure magic.

They usually anchored the boat around sunset, when it was growing too dark to make out obstructions in the riverbed. Sometimes they anchored near a temple or other scenic spot and went ashore for a while to explore; more often they were content with their own company on board the pinnace. The nights were heavy, damp, warm tropic air; strong scents of flowers and the faraway wailing of a temple conch; the red glow of a fire lighting up the faces and bronzed figures of the crew as they cooked their supper; and the moon hanging very low overhead.

And Keith.

Keith possessing her hungrily in the darkness with hands that roved everywhere and fastened on her as though she were his last hope of life; Keith drawing her with him to that spiraling dark delight that he knew so well how to rouse in her; Keith lying beside her, stroking her body with wondering hands, demanding to light a lamp so that he could enjoy her beauty with all his senses at once.

Often they lay awake until late at night, talking idly while the river lapped at the side of the boat and the crew snored in their cotton blankets. Those moonlit nights filled in many details of Keith's career for her. She learned that the aura of responsibility he carried had been no illusion. He had been the only British officer with the Mohammedan troops of the *Daud-patras* in the Sikh war, had held a fort against odds for days until relief came and with all this had still found time to study for the examinations every would-be staff officer must pass.

"Oh, but I am ignorant beside you!" she cried out, one of these nights.

Keith chuckled. "Don't say so. This is all I know, Charlotte—night marches and tribal wars and a few scraps of foreign dialects that would do me no good in the civilized world. I never learned French and German and to play the pianoforte and to dabble in watercolors."

Neither did she, Bridget thought, and sought for some way to turn the subject. "But all that is useless here," she said. "I want to know the things you know—how to talk to people, and what the birds and plants are, and, and . . ." She stopped, frustrated at her inability to express herself. "India is like a locked box," she said suddenly, "and I don't have the key."

Keith gathered her into his arms and held her there. "Yes, you do. I was lucky when I got you. I was afraid you would be one of these stiff memsahibs who feel only hatred and disgust for everything Indian. But you have the heart that cares for people and the eye that sees the beauty in the land, and you are learning the language. Not much like—"

He stopped in mid-sentence.

"Like what?"

Like Charlotte, he'd been going to say, but then lacked the courage.

"Oh, like most of the little girls who come out from home," he answered and then cursed his own cowardice. What a perfect opening that had been, to tell her he knew she was not Charlotte! And yet . . .

How much happier he would be, if she could bring herself to tell him voluntarily.

Well, no need to force her hand. He'd done enough of that with that sudden marriage in Calcutta and whisking her off up-country like this. In time she would tell him everything. She must know he loved her—whoever she was! And her responses to his lovemaking left him in no doubt about her own feelings. If only she could trust him enough to tell him the truth!

And Keith wondered uneasily exactly what she had done and who she had been, that she had been impelled to embark on this crazy masquerade. She must have been a passenger on the ship with the Fitzgeralds, must have talked with Charlotte enough to know that she was coming out to India to be married. But what had inspired her to take Charlotte's place, when she survived the shipwreck and Charlotte didn't? What could have seemed so desirable in Charlotte's life—or so frightening in her own?

What sort of woman would willingly give up her own identity to take on that of a stranger?

Keith smoothed his wife's long chestnut-brown hair, admired the white curves of her body in the moonlight and wondered if he would ever know more of her than these outward things.

Ten days after their departure from Calcutta they passed Berhampore, where this Mrs. Trenton lived. It was still early enough to be cool, and Bridget was leaning on the railing that went round the pinnace deck, watching the colorful scenes of life on the river as she had done for the last ten days: the women coming down to the ghats in their graceful bright drapery with huge earthenware pots on their shoulders, children splashing and playing in the shallows, shady mango groves and huge plane trees that shaded temples with curious stone carvings.

She was taken by surprise when the pinnace veered toward shore at a convenient landing ghat.

"Berhampore. That's where the silk for your yellow

gown came from," Keith said. "Want to anchor for a while? We could go into the bazaar and see if they have some more. One of the cook's helpers used to work for a durzee; he could sew up some dresses for you."

"No." Her hand gripped his arm convulsively for a moment, then relaxed. "No, my love, it's kindness itself you are, but I have clothes enough."

Keith laughed. "I never thought any woman would say that! Truly, you are a pearl among women, darling! Well, we'll just go ashore for a while and stretch our legs. I feel cramped sometimes on the pinnace."

But he noticed that she had gone quite white under the tan which she was beginning to acquire.

Berhampore . . . Did some part of the secret of her past lie there?

Impossible. He knew she was but newly arrived in India; dammit, he'd met the steamer himself!

"Are you feeling ill, my darling?" he asked. "Perhaps you should lie down for a while."

He was finding it harder and harder to call her "Charlotte."

"No," Bridget said. "No, we may as well . . . just look round."

It was in the nature of a gamble with fate. If she met Mrs. Trenton as Lady Charlotte, she could not go back there as a governess. Unless, of course, Mrs. Trenton proved to be a kind, understanding lady, the sort of person to whom one could confess everything. That would be good, would it not?

Bridget was hard put to it to account for her relief when Mrs. Trenton proved to be a hawk-faced woman whose mean, pinched manner of looking down her nose at the world accurately mirrored her attitude to all those less fortunate than she.

At first it had seemed that they would simply walk

round Berhampore and return to the pinnace, as Keith had suggested. Of course their stroll led them through the bazaar—there was hardly any other place to go—and inevitably Keith acquired piles of cloth for Bridget over her faint protests that he ought not to be spending so much money.

"Nonsense," he said cherrily. "Pater makes me quite a good allowance—oh, you didn't think I paid for all this out of my salary, did you? Good lord, they only pay us poor officers enough for drinks and dinner, if that. And I've heard the ladies say that these stuffs are amazingly cheap."

"Yes, but not if you buy out the bazaar!" Bridget protested. Never in her life had she imagined having as many dresses as could be made from the bolts of fabric Keith casually ordered sent to the boat: delicate pale embroidered muslins, quilted cotton, bright country cloth.

"Nonsense," Keith said again. "Only . . . I wish you would let me get you better things. I don't know much about this fashion nonsense, but I'm sure I've heard Aggie Lanyer say she wouldn't be caught dead in an Indian muslin."

"That's a queer kind of foolishness," Bridget said. "These are much more practical than silk for this climate. But these quilted stuffs are another matter. I don't know would I ever be able to use them with it so warm here."

Keith chuckled. "Oh, you will. Wait till we get into the high country. Guahipore itself—the city, I mean— is marked on the maps as being on a high plateau. The wind will come whistling down in winter. And from there the country runs north into the Himalayas . . . high hills where the snow never melts. Imagine, Char!" He squeezed her elbow. "From tropics to snow-covered mountains. What a country! What an adventure!"

"From barefoot servant girl to Lady Charlotte," Bridget thought uneasily. "I don't know how much adventure I can take."

"From prickly heat to frostbite," sniffed Mrs. Trenton.

Always alert to the bazaar rumors, she had heard of the presence of visiting Europeans and had sent her houseboy with a pressing invitation to tiffin while Keith and Bridget were still strolling round the bazaar. After the heavy meal of hot soup, curry and baked vegetables, they sat uneasily on a horsehair sofa and listened to Mrs. Trenton's peevish monologue about the difficulty of obtaining good servants, the dirtiness and laziness of all Indians and the prodigious sufferings she had undergone with the object of seeing her husband promoted to the coveted post of Collector of Revenue.

Her views on a wife's role were much the same as Mrs. Bouverie's, but lacking that lady's good humor.

"Take the Dalrymples now," Mrs. Trenton complained. "He may have seniority over my husband in the Civil List, but you may be assured that will not last long. Why, the ridiculous airs and graces of that Mrs. Dalrymple positively make me laugh! The other day I heard her claiming that she was so well served by her ayah, she could not even put on her own stockings! To listen to her common brogue, I will wager she had not even stockings to put on before she came to India. But these jumped-up Irish are the worst of the lot . . ." With an obvious start, she recollected who she was talking to and favored Bridget with a vinegary smile.

"I meant the common people, of course, Lady Charlotte. The true quality, Lady Charlotte, like you and I, are quite a different matter, of course." She tittered. "I am sure Lieutenant Powell need never fear lest marriage with *you* should retard his career!"

"Actually, Mrs. Trenton," Keith said, "Lieutenant Powell was not thinking about his career at the time." The nervous drumming of one finger on his knee told Bridget just how irritated he was becoming.

"No? But you will later—and then how grateful you will be to have a true lady like Lady Charlotte by your side. Why, some of our young men who have been too long away from home make the most dreadful mistakes. Did you ever know Mr. Grant, of the 104th? He says his wife is Portuguese, but there's no mistaking that touch of the . . ." Mrs. Trenton gave her brassy titter again. "Well, she is quite *dark complected,* if you know what I mean! And poor Grant wonders why he has been passed over for promotion so many times! And then . . ."

"Very interesting," Keith said, breaking in ruthlessly on the floodtide of malicious reminiscences. "But if you will forgive me, Mrs. Trenton, we really must be going. We have to . . ."

He paused, unable to think of any pressing errand which they could claim at this hour in a deserted country station.

Bridget had a flash of inspiration.

"Sure, and I'd never be forgiving Keith did he make us late!" she cried. "We've to meet some of his dearest friends for dinner tonight up the river, and I'm so looking forward to meeting them."

Mrs. Trenton goggled. "Up the . . . but, my dear Lady Charlotte, *no one* lives up the river from here, at least not until you reach Jungipur, and that is quite four days' sail."

It was Bridget's turn to glance at Keith for assistance.

"Actually, the river bank is very well populated,

Mrs. Trenton," he told her. "We intend to visit the *nawab* of Moorshedabad."

"The *nawab?*" Mrs. Trenton giggled. "Oh, dear Lieutenant Powell, now I know you are teasing me! Why the *nawab* is . . . he is a *black.*" She waved her hands feebly, apparently unable to express the social solecism the *nawab* had committed in being born an Indian.

"Yes, Mrs. Trenton, I'm afraid he is," Bridget said with a solemn countenance. "Quite, quite black."

"Been that way since birth, poor fellow," Keith added. "'Fraid it's too late to correct the condition."

He bowed, seized his wife's hand and towed her out of the house before she could explode in the fit of giggles that threatened to overtake her.

Chapter Ten

THEY MOORED THAT NIGHT IN A SHADY BEND OF THE RIVER near the ruins of an ancient palace.

"Unless you really want to dine with the nawab?" Keith teased.

Bridget giggled. "Is there really such a person?"

"Of course there is," Keith assured her, "didn't you hear Mrs. Trenton say so? I'm not acquainted with the gentleman, but he really does live along this stretch of the river. There is one of his pleasure boats now."

He pointed out to midstream where a light boat with its bow carved to resemble the neck and head of a peacock, richly gilt and painted, drifted down-river. As it passed, they could hear the plucked tones of a *sitar* and a woman's voice raised in song and could just glimpse the singing girl's red silk veil floating in the evening breeze.

Bridget sighed with contentment. "It seems like a fairy tale dream." Impulsively she turned to Keith and kissed him on the cheek. "Oh, Keith, how glad I am that I . . ."

That I met you, she'd been about to say. But that would never do, for hadn't Lady Charlotte known Keith since they were children?

"That we're here," she finished lamely.

Keith put his arm about her and bent his head to return the kiss. "I'm glad I met you, too, darling," he murmured.

Then he dropped his arm, as if embarrassed to be caught embracing his wife in full view of the crew. "I say! There's a fisherman! What do you say to fresh fish for dinner?" And he strode briskly to the stern of the pinnace. "Hi! *Mutchleewallah!* Show us your catch!" he shouted in Hindustani.

Bridget stared after him, one hand to her cheek. What an uncanny coincidence, that he should have used just the words she had forced back. She shook her head. Nothing—it meant nothing. Why, it was the commonest thing in the world for married people to say how lucky they were to have met one another. It was just a formula, like passing the time of day.

That evening they went ashore to explore the ruined palace by moonlight. The moon was full, and the brilliant white light pouring down on the stone ruins contrasted with the deep shadows of the encroaching jungle to make a brilliant picture of stark whites and deep pools of blackness. They wandered over a broken pavement in what had once been a wide courtyard, terminating in a roofless building that had been taken over by the trees. The feathery fronds of the palm trees waved above the roofless walls and thrust through the remains of windows.

Hand in hand, without speaking, they skirted the

buildings and came out by a black marble pavilion, built on a slight rise overlooking the river, with walls pierced by many small openings in an intricate pattern.

"This must have been a pleasure-house for the women of the palace," Keith suggested. "Can't you imagine how they would have sat here on a warm evening like this? Think of that girl we heard on the river, strumming her sitar. Perhaps a rajah would have come here to listen to the women play."

He drew Bridget after him through the arched doorway. Inside, the patterns of the carved windowscreens were repeated in the play of moonlight and shadow which covered the marble floor.

"No," Bridget whispered, "he had better music. Listen!"

From somewhere overhead came the piercing-sweet warble of a nightingale.

Bridget half closed her eyes to listen better. Now that the hot season was beginning, the night air was warm and balmy, damp with the promise of rain and sweet with jasmine. The gentle breeze brushed through her hair like a lover's caress, so softly and gently that she was not even startled when she felt her heavy braids loosened to fall around her face. Keith combed his fingers through the silken mass, setting it free until it hung loose like a curtain on either side of her face. When she put up one hand to push it back, he restrained her gently.

"No," he whispered under the sweet tones of the nightingale's song, so softly that she could scarcely hear him. "Don't you know that you are in the rajah's territory now? And the rajah must be obeyed."

Bridget stood with her hands at her sides, her face turned up to him. "Must he be?" she whispered.

Keith nodded silently. "His slightest whim."

His hands strayed down the front of her bodice, undoing without haste each of the tiny buttons that closed her in. As each button was released, he traced the vee of white skin thus exposed with one finger. Deeper and deeper his explorations went, until he was stopped by the white lace of the chemise that just covered her breasts.

When he would have slipped the bodice over her shoulders, Bridget gave a low, teasing laugh and backed away. "No," she whispered. "Let my lord rest, and his servant will endeavor to please him."

She bent her head and shook the clinging masses of her hair forward to cover her movements as she slipped out of the bodice with its long, tight sleeves. A moment later, and the skirt followed.

Keith had reclined on one of the long marble benches that lined the interior of the pavilion, resting on one elbow and playing the part of the rajah at ease among his dancing girls.

"Good! But come forward into the light, that I may see thee."

Bridget obeyed. She seemed to have lost all sense of shame in this clear, pure yet penetrating light. It dappled her shoulders and flanks with the window pattern, and she glanced down and saw that she was beautiful.

"Now the chemise." Keith's voice was low but firm. "Yes . . . turn . . . Ah! Come to me."

Her undergarments whispered to the floor in a froth of linen and lace. Naked to the cold white light, Bridget raised her arms and turned in the moonlight like a dancing girl, ending the movement with a slow sinking to one knee beside Keith's bench, her head bent so that her long hair brushed the marble floor.

"My lord is pleased?"

Keith laughed deep in his throat and stood up, drawing her to him and molding her against his male hardness. "More than pleased," he murmured in her ear. "Wild with desire . . . O Moon of my delight, thy beauty inflames me greatly!"

He loosened his clothing and sat back down on the bench. "Come . . ."

Obedient to the slight pressure of his palms, Bridget knelt astride him and slowly lowered herself onto his body. She could not repress the single cry of pleasure that broke from her as she was joined to him. Then, his hands clasped behind her back, he pulled her all the way down, and her hips were swaying in the oldest dance of all.

The tips of her bare breasts grazed against his loose shirt and stiffened from contact with the rough fabric. Bridget pressed herself down and against him and felt the tremors of ecstasy pass through both their bodies.

The sense of power intoxicated her. She played with her movements; now fast until the galloping excitement thudded unbearably through her pulse; now slow until Keith moaned with pleasure and his insistent hands on her buttocks speeded the pace.

So this is what men know, she thought. How to guide and lead the dance . . . how to bring such pleasure. . . .

Then all thoughts were lost as her body trembled and drove her onward to a fulfillment that pulsated through her in great crashing waves. She cried out again and fell limply forward on Keith's shoulder, only dimly aware of the spurting of his own pleasure deep within her.

That night and on other nights when Keith made love to her, it was easy for Bridget to put Mrs. Trenton's malicious gossip out of her mind. Sometimes she even thought that it might not be so bad when she confessed her deception to him. Maybe he would not quite hate her.

It was *her* he loved, Bridget thought, not Lady Charlotte. Even if he didn't know it. Lady Charlotte would have complained about every little problem on this expedition; she would have expected Keith to whisk away the insects with a wave of his hand, to lower the temperature for her benefit, and to tie up each night outside a cantonment station where she could dazzle local society with her gowns.

Keith would not have been happy with Lady Charlotte—not as he was with her. Bridget would lie awake long into the night, after Keith had fallen asleep with one arm flung possessively over her body, and wonder if he might not let her stay with him even after he found out who she was.

But in the merciless sun that blazed down on them in the day, it was a different story. Then the same light that revealed every crack in the floorboards and every smudge in the painted trim of the boat also revealed Bridget's own shortcomings to herself. How could she ever have thought to carry off the part of a lady! She who could neither sketch nor sing, do fine sewing nor speak French.

She remembered in glaring detail each of the slips or near slips she had made in her one week in Calcutta. Practically falling out of the sidesaddle. Missing Mrs. Lanyer's signal to retire from the dinner table, so that the Lanyers thought she wanted to remain with the men with their port and cigars. Offering to help Agatha's ayah move a heavy chair in the dressing room.

Here in the isolation of their pinnace on the river, Keith might be satisfied with her. But when they reached Guahipore—what then? If she had been unable to play the part of a young lady in Calcutta, how much less fitted was she to occupy the exalted position of the resident's wife in a hill station! Why, they—they would expect her to give dinner parties, and train servants and see that people were seated according to precedence—

Bridget's hands went up to her burning cheeks as she imagined in agonizing detail all the mistakes she would make and how the English ladies of Guahipore would laugh at her! Both Mrs. Trenton and Mrs. Bouverie had in their various ways stressed the importance to a political officer of being seen to have "the right sort of wife."

What was it Mrs. Trenton had said about Anne Dalrymple? "I suspect she had no stockings to put on before she came here." They would talk about her that way behind her back. "A lady! Not likely. She had the manner of a barelegged servant girl. Who would have thought that nice Lieutenant Powell would have lowered himself so?"

Yes, that was what it all came back to. She could bear whatever they said of her, but not what it must cost Keith. What did it matter if Keith forgave her? It would be the ruin of his career!

She looked at the dark head bent over his mass of papers and notes in the shaded sitting room and a tide of tenderness rushed over her that blurred her eyes and made everything, even that beloved head, dim and indistinct to her. She imagined him transferred from one minor post to another, forever wondering why he had been passed over for promotion, like "poor Grant" that Mrs. Trenton had mentioned. Or would he know why, and hate her for it?

She could not drag his life down to her level. Bridget's resolve hardened. She would travel with him until the river portion of their journey ended—no, perhaps she would go on overland with him just a little way—well, it did not matter, as long as she made her confession and turned back while they were still at least a day's march from Guahipore.

And her vision blurred once more, her eyes filling with tears, so that she did not even see the mass of pleasure boats and pinnaces and budgerows that clustered thick in the river.

So the long lazy days passed, gliding up the river from one small village to another. They passed the Hindu temples at Peer Point, and the red-brick fortifications of Monghyr. "Halfway from Calcutta," Keith said with satisfaction.

"Half my time with him over," Bridget thought with despair.

He wanted to pass the time by teaching her the Urdu she would need in Guahipore. Bridget thought it would be hard to concentrate on something she would never use, but after all it was not so difficult to imitate the sounds he made and repeat them. Her native gift for mimicry came to her aid. It was no harder to speak Urdu than it was to remember to speak like Lady Charlotte.

She flushed with pleasure when he praised her ear for languages. "Strange," he teased, "your governess was quite in despair over your French, but you do quite well with Urdu!"

Bridget tensed imperceptibly under his laughing glance. "I . . . never liked to learn from books," she countered. "Or to be shut up in a schoolroom. This is quite different."

"Yes, by Jove," Keith answered, leaning back comfortably. "Isn't it!"

They were passing a village on the left bank, little

more than a clump of bamboo huts covered with blue-flowered vines. A gigantic plane tree arched over the huts, and in its shade were two men weaving on a primitive loom built into the dirt, while in the distance a naked child shouted and waved a palm frond over his head to turn his herd of goats in the right direction.

"Yes," Keith repeated, "it's a far cry from cold, damp Ireland!"

His hand covered Bridget's for a moment and she looked down at him with a mixture of love and sadness. If only one could live in the moment, she thought, forget what was coming. . . .

The next day brought an unwelcome reminder, as they reached Dinapore.

"Cantonment town," Keith said briefly. "Before we left Calcutta, I directed our letters to be sent on here. The dak post only takes three and a half days, so there should be quite a lot of mail accumulated for us. Maybe even letters from home!"

He went for the letters while Bridget followed their cook through the market, purchasing eggs and chickens and fruit to supplement the supplies they had brought with them. Already she had learned that it was not always easy to get fresh food in the little villages along the river bank; one had to arrive on a market day or wait for a big town like Dinapore, else there was nothing to buy. And if she couldn't play the piano for Keith or sing French songs, at least she was a good judge of a plump frying chicken and had the wit to stock up on the grapes which proved to be a plentiful item in Dinapore this month.

"And that's more than Lady Charlotte could do, for all her fine airs," she thought scornfully. "At least he'll be well fed and cared for while he's with me!"

And the thought of the inevitable parting struck her

with renewed force, so that she had to turn aside and pretend to be examining some coarse linen towels and napkins while she blinked the tears back.

She was back at the pinnace before the noonday sun made the heat really unpleasant and found Keith returned before her, poring over a fresh stack of official correspondence under the awning that shaded their open "sitting room."

"Hullo, dear, have a good shopping trip?" he asked absently while scanning the open report in his hand. "Ha!" he exclaimed a moment later. "So Gulab Singh is up to tricks already! Oh, before I forget—letter for you from Aggie Lanyer. Nothing else, though." He tossed the packet at her and ripped open another bulky report.

"You remind me of the ladies in Calcutta," Bridget teased, "and them destroyed with eagerness to read the next installment of the serial story in *The Englishman.*"

Keith looked up at her with an unrepentant grin. "I'm a neglectful husband, aren't I, love? Shall I make it up to you by staying at Dinapore for a day or so? You could go shopping, or drink tea with the Colonel's wife or . . ." He ran out of suggestions. "Well . . . whatever ladies like to do. I know you must miss Calcutta society."

"No!" Bridget said. Mary Mother, that was all she needed—another searching inquisition by the curious English ladies in cantonments. "No, I don't miss it at all. Please, let us go on! There's nothing I'd like half so well as just be sailing quietly up the river with you."

The urgency in her tone flattered Keith. "All right," he said with a leer, "perhaps I can find some other way to make it up to you—tonight I promise you my undivided attention!"

Bridget felt weak in the knees with relief. "Yes, and I

135

promise not to scold you for spending all your time with those dreary old reports!"

"Not so dreary," said Keith. "You said I was like one of your ladyfriends waiting to finish a novel—let me tell you, this is as good as a novel! You wouldn't believe the amount of political intrigue and maneuvering that goes on in one of these small native states. Especially one like Guahipore, where the Russians are as eager as we are to get a foothold. I'll have to fill you in on the whole situation before we get there, else you won't know how to go on."

"Yes," Bridget said past the sudden lump in her throat. "Yes, you must certainly do that . . . before we get there." And she fled into the curtained privacy of the bedroom with her letter before Keith should notice anything wrong with her voice. The closer they got to the journey's end, the less she could bear these casual reminders. If only they could go on up the river forever!

Aggie's letter proved to be only a brief note folded round another enclosure. She missed Charlotte terribly, Mama was all in a flutter about going to Simla so early in the season, poor Papa had to stay behind and work so James M'Laughlin was going to escort them, on the eve of their departure this letter had come for Charlotte from Ireland and she remained Charlotte's devoted friend.

Bridget picked up the heavier enclosure as gingerly as if it contained a poisonous snake. Lady Charlotte Fitzgerald, the superscription said. She felt like a thief. Reading Charlotte's mail! She would just skim over it, she decided, to see if there was any news she really ought to have. She wouldn't pay any attention at all to the personal bits . . . if there were any personal bits.

The letter was from Father Geoghan, the priest at

Ballycrochan. He had just heard the news of the shipwreck and writing to condole with Charlotte on the loss of her aunt and uncle. Bridget scanned the close-written lines. Terrible loss, tragic, deep sorrow, God's comfort. Nothing personal there. But it gave her a creepy sensation all the same, reading this letter addressed to a girl whom only she knew to be dead. Poor Charlotte! Maybe she would have become a nicer person if she had lived to come out to India, had gotten away from the Fitzgerald family.

She turned the page, eager to get this business done, and her own name struck her like a blow in the pit of the stomach.

"The newspaper accounts of the shipwreck said that all the passengers were drowned, with the exception of yourself," Father Geoghan wrote. "I am hoping against hope that this may have been an exaggeration. Is there any possibility that your maid, Bridget Sullivan, may have been saved with you, and that the newspapers simply did not find this fact worthy of mention? I ask because I have recently received a communication from a distant cousin of hers who emigrated to America shortly before Bridget's parents died and she went to work for your family. Young Sullivan is apparently doing well for himself in America and has sent passage money for any of his relations who care to join him. I was reluctant to tell him that all but Biddy had perished in the famine, and she in a shipwreck, until I had direct confirmation from you."

Evidently Father Geoghan had not much faith in Charlotte's willingness to perform such an act of charity, for he added, "If I do not hear from you within the year, I shall simply assume that Bridget Sullivan is dead and I shall so inform her cousin."

Bridget's firm capable hands crumpled the paper

without her knowing it. She sat unmoving in the stuffy little bedchamber, holding the letter to her breast and mindlessly watching the antics of a fly buzzing in the sunlight.

"Bridget Sullivan is dead."

A creepy feeling, it was, to hear your own death announced like that. Bridget gave an uneasy laugh and dashed a tear from her eye. Dear Joe! In the years that had passed since he'd left for America, she'd never heard from him, had presumed him dead by now. But then Joe was never much of a hand at the writing.

"Bridget Sullivan is dead."

She could stop this farce now, by writing to Joe herself. But how would she do that? "Dear Joe, I am quite safe and well, but pray address your letters to Lady Charlotte Fitzgerald, or rather Powell, as—"

No. She could not bring herself to cut off this last link with her family by writing to confirm her own death. But she dared not reveal the secret of her masquerade to anyone. Especially not to her cousin Joe. She'd thought he was a bit sweet on her before he went to America. He would never understand.

Not that it mattered; not if she really meant to leave Keith within the month, before they came to Guahipore.

And she was quite resolved on that. Wasn't she?

Bridget unfolded the letter and scanned a few lines down, looking for more news of Joe. But the priest had finished, it seemed, with that subject and had gone on to other news of the estate. Let's see, he knew it must be painful for Lady Charlotte to hear of her family home passing into other hands, but thought she would be pleased to know that the distant cousin who had inherited was a complete gentleman and, more to the point, a good landlord. The only trouble since he took over had been with the factor, John Kelly. The accounting of the estate monies had revealed that Kelly had been embezzling small sums for years. The new landlord had turned him off; John Kelly had turned to drink and after some unpleasant weeks had enlisted in the army and left the area, much to everyone's relief.

Bridget put down the crumpled sheets on her knee, smoothing the paper over and over with a mechanical action and folding it into smaller and smaller squares.

So John Kelly was gone from Ballycrochan! She laughed again, but her heart was not in it. Fancy that, Ballycrochan safe for her to return to and her cousin in America offering her a home. Things were looking up for Bridget Sullivan. If she'd had this news at the time of the shipwreck, she might never have embarked on this perilous masquerade, and never, never . . .

"Never have met Keith," she whispered to herself. And then, aloud, "And I'm glad, do you hear, glad of it, in spite of everything!"

"Glad of what?" Keith asked as he stooped under the low doorframe to come into the room.

Bridget colored and dropped one hand to conceal the priest's letter in the folds of her skirts.

"Why, just that I'm glad to hear your friend James M'Laughlin is after escorting Agatha and Mrs. Lanyer to Simla," she improvised hastily. "I'm glad that they have this chance to be together, in spite of the fact that Mrs. Lanyer hopes to make a better match for her. See, here is Agatha's letter."

"Couldn't get a better young man than James for her," Keith said. "Is that all your news?"

"Yes," Bridget said. "That's all . . . that's worth telling." She rose so that Keith could store his new pile of official papers in the brassbound trunk on which she had been sitting, dropped a kiss on his forehead and glided out of the bedroom with one hand still concealed in her skirts.

Chapter Eleven

THE CURTAINED PALANQUIN SWAYED UP THE SIDE OF THE mountain to the monotonous, rhythmic chant of the bearers.

Bridget reclined inside, the only position possible in such a mode of travel. Her eyes were shut and her hands clenched tight at her sides as she reviewed her cowardice over the preceding days.

When they left the pinnace at Allahabad to continue their northward journey by palanquin dak—that was when she should have confessed her masquerade to Keith and turned back. But she had been unable to forgo the temptation of just one more day's traveling with him, then another, and another . . .

And then, there had never seemed to be a good time to make the confession! It was possible to travel round the clock by palanquin, if the bearers were arranged for ahead of time and if you could stand the constant movement. And Keith, feeling guilty about the lazy weeks sailing up the river with Bridget when he could have traveled much more quickly by steamer or dak, had pushed their pace so that they had very few rest stops. The few times that they had halted to rest in a dak bungalow, there had always been other travelers with whom Keith was eager to exchange news.

In other circumstances, Bridget would have reveled in the journey. The cool green hills that arose from the plain with their mighty forests of pine and cedar, the vistas of snowtopped mountains in the distance, the cries of unfamiliar forest birds, the rhythmic chant of the bearers who trotted along with the poles of her palanquin—all this new world was a constant delight to her. And the coolness of the hills was doubly welcome after the hot stuffy plains.

But it was all poisoned for her by the knowledge that soon—very soon now—any day, they must part.

She no longer felt sure that Keith would disown her. The love that had grown between them might be strong enough to override his inevitable anger at her deception. But in a way that only made it harder. Even if he still wanted her, how could she stay when she knew that the other English residents of Guahipore would laugh at him and that his career would be ruined if the truth ever came out?

Long ago, at the start of their journey, he had told her that the reason the British government was assigning a political officer to Guahipore was to look after the growing English community there. At the time this had seemed an insignificant detail; now Bridget saw it as the main bar to their happiness. Guahipore would have an English community as small, as isolated and as narrowminded as Berhampore. There was sure to be a malicious Mrs. Trenton there to watch "Lady Charlotte" and report her shortcomings.

A change in the regular motion of the palanquin brought her back to an awareness of her surroundings. The bearers' chant ceased abruptly and the palanquin was lowered to the ground. Bridget pulled the curtains back and looked out.

They had halted before a strange building, a massive stone ruin within which there rose a humble shed with mud walls and a rough plank ceiling.

Keith came over to her palanquin and offered her a hand up. "Well," he laughed, "how do you like our new dak bungalow? Sumptuous exterior, is it not?" He pointed out the carved arabesques that adorned the stone walls and the pierced turrets that rose at each corner.

"This must be one of the caravanserais built in the days of the emperor Shah Jehan," he explained. "I had heard that the buildings were sadly run down since the days of the empire, but this. . . .!" He raised one eyebrow at the mud hut occupying one corner of the once-elegant caravanserai. "Well, at least we can get tea and something to eat."

The tea had been flavored with salt instead of sugar, the "something to eat" turned out to be the remains of a very old sheep inadequately stewed and the interior of the mud guesthouse was dense with the smoke from the cooking fire. Coughing and choking, Bridget retreated to a stone bench along the outer wall of the serai. From this vantage point she could look down the plunging side of the mountain into an abyss filled with swirling mist through which the green-black pines rose like sentinels. In the distance on the other side of the abyss she could just make out a range of snow-covered mountains that seemed to float above the clouds.

What a beautiful land! Bridget felt a pang of regret that she was not to stay and know it better.

Keith came out of the hut carrying a bunch of grapes in his hat.

"They had fruit, anyway," he said, "and the water is clean enough and cold—they get it from melting snows. Will this do to be going on with, or should you like to unpack some of our tinned supplies and make a proper meal of it? We should be in Guahipore by evening. Not that I want to press you, of course."

Bridget could almost smile at his eagerness to get on to his new post. But the arrival that spelled a new life for him was the end of happiness for her. Now there were no more excuses, no more chance to delay. She must say what she had to say, get back into her palanquin and go back down the mountain, while Keith went on alone to Guahipore. He could make up some tale to explain his wife's absence better now, than if she arrived with him and then had to disappear.

She drew a brief, shaking breath. The cold clear air of the mountain pass was as heady as a draught of fine wine. Perhaps it would give her strength.

"Keith, there's something I have to tell you," she began.

Keith put one arm round her shoulders and drew her close to him on the bench. "Yes, my darling? There's something I have to tell you, too." He nibbled her ear. "Do you realize this is the first time we've been alone for two weeks—ever since we left the pinnace?"

Bridget slewed round involuntarily to look at the servants squatting in the shelter of the caravanserai wall. "Not counting sixteen bearers?"

"Well, yes. Not counting the servants." Keith laughed. "Do they make you nervous? I never thought of that. In India one gets so used to having them constantly around."

No. He wouldn't have noticed the servants. Bridget

sighed. "Keith, there's something I have to tell you about servants."

I used to be one. That could be her next sentence.

"Can't it wait, darling?" Now his lips were traveling over her cheek, advancing toward her own lips in tantalizing, nibbling caresses. "There's something I have to tell you too—about my wife. It occurs to me I haven't told her lately how much I love her."

"Yes . . . no . . . oh, Keith!" Bridget almost wailed as his arms tightened round her and his lips covered hers. Her mouth opened to the insistent pressure of his tongue, he pressed her backward on the bench and she could feel all her resolution melting away.

"Shall I send the bearers away?" he murmured into her ear. His breath was warm on her neck. "This is my confession." One hand ran along her thigh; she could not help the way she quivered under his touch through stout cotton skirts and petticoats, unbearably intimate, as if he were touching the bare flesh of her already. "I told them to stop here so I could have a little time alone with you before we have to get all official. That's the real reason I didn't want to bother with a meal."

He nuzzled at the opening of her bodice, warm soft touches of his lips and flickering of his tongue all along her neck. Bridget felt her resolution melting away. She put up one arm and clung round his neck, partly for balance, partly to prolong the contact. Perhaps they could find a sheltered spot inside the caravanserai.

After all, she told herself, this would be the last time. She would tell him afterward—

Behind them, an excited jabbering broke out from the corner where the bearers squatted. It grew louder and louder, mounting to a crescendo of panicky shouts and squeals.

"Oh, hell!" Keith raised his head and straightened his collar. *"Now* what?"

The bearers were pointing down the steep hill track that led to the plateau where the capital city of Guahipore lay. Keith strode over to the caravanserai gate, and after a moment to straighten her dress, Bridget followed him.

By straining her eyes, she could just make out shadowy figures in the mist that hung about the lower portion of the path. She heard bells tinkling and the clop-clop of horses' hooves.

In a moment the leading figures of the cavalcade burst through the mist and appeared clear and bright. Tall, dark men mounted on strong little hill horses, their clothes bright with colored velvets and gold embroidery, they made the horses caracole and rear as they galloped up the last stretch of the path. As they came on, they shot off their long rifles into the air and cried out in sharp, yipping sounds.

"Good God!" Keith muttered. He put one arm round Bridget and drew her to his side. "They must have walked their horses most of the way to save them for this gallop. But isn't it a fine effect? I wonder who they are?"

He didn't seem in the least frightened. Bridget surreptitiously wiped her clammy hands on her skirt and awaited the arrival of the riders, her head high and a smile on her face. At least she could match Keith's courage on the outside, even though her inside was clamoring with fear.

The leading rider galloped his horse almost to their feet before pulling the animal into a skidding stop. He leapt off and bowed before them. "Powell Sahib? I am Afzul-ul-Mulk, advisor to the mehtar of Guahipore, may he live forever. My lord sends you this poor escort in greeting and begs you to forgive the shabbiness of their costume and the small number of fighting men."

He spoke in a clear, unaccented Urdu that Bridget, to her relief, had no difficulty in following after Keith's lessons on the boat. Before he had finished his speech, the rest of the riders were around them, spurring their tired horses to make them prance, raising a cloud of dust through which Bridget made out tanned, fierce faces, beards dyed a violent red or black, hands that gripped reins or weapons with casual power.

Her eyes widened as she took in the grandeur of their costumes. Afzul's apology for their shabbiness must have been some courtly convention. The riders nearest her were dressed in flowing velvet coats covered with gold embroidery, beneath which could be seen silk shirts and trousers. Their stirrups and saddles flashed in the sunlight with the weight of silver decoration and their horses had raw turquoises braided into their manes and tails.

Further back were less gorgeously dressed men, whose loose coats were innocent of gold embroidery and whose turbans were only silk instead of cloth-of-gold. But the entire retinue made a dazzling picture, far grander than the English parties in Calcutta.

There was only one man who did not fit the general picture. His full beard was straggly and undyed, and he was dressed simply in a loose coat and trousers of brown homespun tucked into much-patched and dusty boots. It was to this man that Afzul-ul-Mulk beckoned when he and Keith had finished their flowery speeches of introduction.

"A countryman of yours," he said, "who begged to be allowed to join our escort to do your honor."

The shabby man pushed through the welcoming throng, seemingly undismayed by the horses prancing in his face and the muskets that were still being fired off at intervals.

"My God!" Keith exclaimed. "Henderson! Never tell me you're the mapmaker they sent up?"

The two men shook hands. Keith was laughing with pleasure. "My instructions are to give you every assistance. But from the looks of things, it'll be the other way round. Been here long?"

The man called Henderson pulled off his felt cap, allowing his shaggy mane of hair to fly loose. "I've been out *there* mostly." He jerked his chin back in the direction of the mountain ranges in the distance. "More to my taste than the mehtar's court. But when I heard they were sending an Englishman called Powell out, I thought I might just come back to the city a few days. To put you in the way of things. If you'll not mind?"

He spoke in a strange jerky manner, as if he had been long silent and was not yet quite used to speech. In the pauses, Bridget fancied she could hear the long silences of the mountains.

"Mind? *Mind?*" Keith was laughing again. He seized Henderson's hand and pumped it up and down. "Can't think of anyone I'd rather have, my dear fellow! Oh, I've been reading the Government reports"—he gestured toward the cone-shaped baskets, slung over poles, in which his papers had been carried—"but you know what that is. Never tells more than half the story."

"And often the wrong half at that," Henderson agreed. "Better talk to a living man than read a dead paper."

"That's what you always said in the Punjab. Remember the time . . ." And the two of them were off in their reminiscences, a spate of talk from Keith punctuated at intervals by two or three words from his friend.

While they talked, the men who had ridden out with Afzul-ul-Mulk rode round the caravanserai on their wild horses, smoked, shouted jokes at one another and inspected Keith's and Bridget's baggage. The bearers huddled into a little group in the corner, visibly afraid of these strange wild men who had appeared from nowhere. Bridget wished that she too could hide. But for Keith's sake, she stood straight, a little smile on her face, even when two of the men circled their horses round her with expressions of intent curiosity. Only, when one of them reached out with a lance to prod at the trailing hem of her skirt, she moved a little closer to Keith.

"Here, now, we're being rude to your good lady," exclaimed Henderson, breaking off in the middle of an account of his days leading a caravan over the Karakoram, disguised as a Tibetan trader.

"Don't be worried by the boys' high spirits, mistress," he said, bowing to Bridget. "They're curious about you, is all—never having seen a white faced woman before."

"Never!" Bridget exclaimed. "But I thought . . ."

Henderson regarded them both with a secretive smile. "Ah, so old Bouvier fed you that line about needing an agent here to look after the interests of the British community? Thought so. There's no English in Guahipore, Keith. Unless you count me, and I don't spend much time there. No, your real job is something different—and much stickier."

"Thought as much," Keith said, "from the reports I've seen. That Russian agent—"

Henderson cut him off with a gesture. "I'm sure you will find enough to occupy your time here. The mehtar is a fine old gentleman and Afzul here was schooled abroad. For all it pleased him to greet you in Urdu, he speaks French and English like a native."

Keith nodded to show he'd taken Henderson's warning.

With more yips and musket shots, the escort was reforming into a long column of men. Henderson turned to Bridget with another bow. "I trust you will not be too disappointed in the absence of English company here, Lady Charlotte."

"Why, no," Bridget said. She felt oddly breathless, as if the cold thin air of the mountains were not enough for her. The white jagged peaks beyond the valley seemed to be dancing up and down.

There was nothing now to prevent her going down into the valley of Guahipore.

No English to wonder at her ways and trip her up over ridiculous social details.

No one to laugh at Keith for having married such an unsuitable wife and wonder aloud about "Lady Charlotte" until his own doubts were stirred.

No need now for the confession she'd been about to make.

Bridget drew in a deep breath of the chilly mountain air, crisp with its hint of snowdrifts and pine trees. "No, Mr. Henderson, I am sure I shall find living in Guahipore an altogether delightful experience."

Henderson's smile in return warmed her like whiskey on a cold day. She realized that he must have had his own doubts about this socialite wife that Keith Powell insisted on bringing along to the back of beyond. "Good. I think our guard of honor is waiting. Ready to start protectin' my interests, Powell?"

Chapter Twelve

THE GAILY DRESSED CAVALCADE MOVED BACK DOWN THE hill with more shouting and firing of muskets. Extra horses, the finest in the mehtar's stables, had been brought for "Powell Sahib" and his wife; but of course, as there was not such a thing as a sidesaddle in all of Guahipore, Keith and Henderson both assumed it was impossible for a lady to ride. Bridget gritted her teeth and crawled back into the palanquin. There might be no English ladies in Guahipore, but there were still Keith's expectations to deal with.

But that was a small price to pay for this wonderful, unlooked-for gift of being able to stay with him. Bridget felt as if she had been reborn. She felt like shouting and singing in the palanquin, but a decent regard for the nerves of the bearers prevented her. She contented herself with pushing back the curtains to enjoy the view of the mountains as they went down.

She reveled in the sight of the white peaks in the distance, the dark green pines and cedars on the hillside below them and . . . a very steep cliff face dropping off rather steeply from the path.

Bridget tried to concentrate on the beauty of the color contrast, the harsh rocks softened by the little mountain flowers growing in every crevice. But the path was so close to that sheer drop!

She switched her attention to the other side. Here the rocks rose in jagged heaps, so close to the palanquin that she could have put out her hand and touched them. And there seemed to be more rocks ahead.

The bearers shouted in unison, heaved the palanquin round a ninety-degree turn and trotted down the impassable cliff face she had been looking at a moment ago.

Bridget's stomach lurched. She drew the curtains and concentrated on hanging onto the inside braces of the palanquin so that she shouldn't be catapulted from one side to the other.

She lost track of how long the journey down into the valley lasted. When she felt it safe to draw her curtains again, they were just going under a great arched stone gate, at least three times the height of a man and ornamented all over with arabesque carvings like those she'd seen on the ruined caravanserai.

Then they were threading through narrow streets where the stone buildings leaned overhead, almost shutting out the sky, and what light there was filtered through green vines that dripped down from the flat roofs of the buildings. Bridget pushed back palanquin curtains again and gazed about her with mounting excitement. So this was Guahipore—their new home!

The city seemed beautiful to her, but also dark and secretive. The stone houses were pierced with many narrow windows, most no wider than the palm of her hand, and even those openings were covered with ornamental grillwork. More ornamental metalwork covered the great wooden doors, which were additionally decorated with a pattern of iron studs sticking out several inches from the door.

"Elephants," said Keith when, the street having widened, he dropped back to ride beside her palanquin for a while.

Bridget stared. "Elephants? Here? But I don't see how . . ." She remembered the dizzying mountain pass. they had just come through.

"Well, Hannibal did take them over the Alps," Keith said, "so I suppose it's just possible."

Bridget wondered who this Hannibal was. Keith hadn't mentioned him when he was telling his stories of the Sikh wars. Maybe he was a relative? He talked as if she ought to know him.

"But I don't think they ever had them here," he went on. "But you see, in the plains you use elephants for fighting. Use them to break down doors, like we'd use a battering ram. And if you have whacking great iron spikes sticking out of your door, your elephant is reluctant to run his head against it. Ergo, iron spikes became the fashion—even in countries where they make about as much sense as crinolines," he finished with a laugh.

Bridget's ringing laugh seemed to bounce off the stone faces of the houses. She fancied she could see furtive movements behind the grilled windows. "Sure, and didn't I leave off me crinolines the day we started up into the mountains? You've nothing to tease me there with, Keith."

She felt exhilarated, almost drunk on the cool mountain air. And Keith was looking down at her from his high saddle with a wicked gleam in his eyes that she recognized of old. "I'm tempted to take you on to the real hills," he teased, "to see what more you'll leave off."

Bridget grinned and started to make a cheeky reply about the likelihood that she'd simply grease herself all over and wrap up in skins, and wouldn't he be sorry then! But halfway through she heard her own voice, too loud, too cheerful and too *common,* and subsided with a blush. When would she ever learn to act like a lady? The absence of other English wouldn't help her if Keith started wondering and making comparisons.

The street opened out into a wide square filled with people. It looked as if the entire population of Guahipore had gathered here to meet the *feringhis.* Ignoring the shouts and menacing gestures of the guard, they pushed close to the palanquin. Keith was largely ignored, but it seemed to Bridget that every inhabitant of Guahipore was bent on getting a feel of her dress or touching her white skin. The faces were friendly, laughing, innocently curious, with bright dark eyes and broad smiles. But there were so many of them! Cramped into the palanquin, unable to move, Bridget felt a moment of panic.

Then the crowds fell away and her palanquin was deposited on the stones of the square. Bridget made an ungraceful exit, shaking her skirts down and pushing strands of hair back from her face.

"I felt like a raree-show in a cage!" she exclaimed to Keith, who had dismounted to help her out.

"Hush," Keith murmured in her ear. "I think we're about to get the red carpet treatment. Semi-literally."

He directed her attention to the ground. Before them there stretched out a path made of many-colored fabrics. Most of the cloth that had been laid down was of simple muslin dyed in bright colors, but here and there was the glitter of brocade or the deep rich sheen of velvet.

"Felicitations on your arrival in the realm of the mehtar, may he live forever! These poor cloths are in the nature of a pathway to his hall. After you have passed over them, they will become the perquisites of your servants."

It was Afzul-ul-Mulk. Bridget whirled and found him standing practically at her elbow. This time he had spoken in English.

She felt a flicker of unease at his closeness. How much had he overheard? No, that wasn't it, she and Keith had only exchanged two sentences. But there was something that made her uncomfortable; perhaps the overly knowing look in his eyes as he examined her. She felt as if he knew everything about her—that she was tired, crumpled, dirty and in no mood to face a difficult reception; that she was a little afraid of this strange land, and more afraid of him.

Bridget shook her head. She was tired, that was all, and overwrought. And standing in a place she'd never expected to see. Some time tonight when she was rested, she would sort it all out. In the meantime—

"There is nothing to fear," said Afzul-ul-Mulk, this time softly, for her ears alone. "Even tired from travel, the moon of your beauty outshines the skies and will delight my master."

Something in his soft, insinuating tone annoyed Bridget unbearably. "As it happens," she snapped, "that is not my primary object in life!"

She placed one hand on Keith's arm and took her first steps on the path of muslin, of silk, of brocade and cloth of gold, that led to the reception hall of the mehtar (may he live forever) of Guahipore.

It turned out that the mehtar held his receptions in the open air, in a stone porch that ran round three sides of the walled courtyard outside which they had stopped. Just inside the gates, there were the nobility of Guahipore drawn up to meet them: another gaudy display of bright Chinese scarlet and blue silk, gold-embroidered coats and silver-mounted weapons, all topped by the lean, fierce faces of the mountain men.

As Keith and Bridget, hand in hand, entered the courtyard, the assembled dignitaries bowed as one man, while the mehtar remained erect, fixing Keith with his piercing and questioning eyes.

He was dressed like the other nobles and stood between two men who shared his hooked nose, bright eyes and black beard and mustache; but no one could have doubted who the ruler of Guahipore was. He wore his air of command like a royal cloak.

His full black beard fell to his waist, standing out in sharp contrast with his simply cut long tunic and breeches of green silk. Although he looked to be at least sixty, his back was straight and his eyes clear. He carried a gun slung over his shoulder and a long curving sword stuck in his sash. Altogether Bridget would not have been surprised to see him leap onto the back of a horse and gallop round the courtyard, firing a round of shots in their honor.

Two embroidered cushions were laid out in the courtyard, directly in front of the mehtar. At a gesture from Afzul-ul-Mulk, Keith sank down cross-legged on one of these cushions. Bridget followed his example, thanking Providence that she had left off wearing those fashionable crinolines for the journey. A pretty picture she would have made with her bell-shaped petticoats billowing out over the courtyard!

Directly they were seated, the Mehtar began a long formal oration in Urdu. Bridget was relieved to find that she could understand most of what he said, although the flowery circumlocutions he used sometimes defeated her.

The gist of the speech seemed to be that he wished to be friendly with the British government and hoped that they would make reciprocal gestures of friendship. He embroidered on this simple theme for nearly an hour, occasionally pausing and looking at Keith as though he expected some meaningful answer. Finally he sighed and clapped his hands three times.

In obedience to this signal, the assemblage of nobles filed out, leaving behind only the mehtar, Afzul-ul-Mulk and three men in their middle fifties.

"Afzul-ul-Mulk, my trusted advisor, you know already," said the mehtar. "These are three of my more important sons. They remain with us for the poor meal which I am pleased to offer you in token of my great friendship for the British raj." He clapped his hands again and servants began bearing in great round trays laden with rice and *pilau,* some kind of flat pancakes baked with green onions, and bowl after bowl of the fresh fruit of the valley, apricots and apples, peaches and cherries, all chilled with snow.

Those grizzled men were his sons! Bridget hastily revised her estimate of the mehtar's age upward.

"What did he mean—his 'more important' sons?" she whispered to Keith while the trays of food were being arranged before them. It seemed a strange way to talk about one's family.

"He probably has a few dozen more scattered around," he whispered back.

Afzul-ul-Mulk bowed and Bridget felt a flash of irritation that he had been so obviously eavesdropping. "The mehtar—may he live forever!—is blessed with thirty-two sons . . . and several girl-children."

"Thirty-three! Thirty-three!" the mehtar corrected Afzul. "The one coming will be a boy—by the favor of Allah. How many sons do you have, *ferenghi?*"

"None, Your Highness," Keith answered. "My wife and I are but recently married."

"Send your wife to visit mine," the mehtar directed. "My junior wife, Aziza, knows many charms for fertility." He rolled up a flat pancake full of chopped meat and began chewing on it. "Too many girls, though," he complained. "Aziza's charms make too many girl-children."

Bridget sat rigid, her cheeks flaming. Children! Why had she never thought of that? What would she do if she found herself with child by Keith?

"You could never leave him then," suggested the voice of temptation.

Keith's hand covered hers. "Don't be embarrassed," he whispered. "It is . . . he is not used to taking account of women."

Bridget returned the pressure of his hand with gratitude. Dear Keith! He thought she was embarrassed by the mehtar's frank talk. It was no worse than she'd heard at home many a time. She'd had a hard time of it when she was coming out with Aggie Lanyer, learning what subjects would put Aggie to the blush. But she could hardly explain to him what was really troubling her.

She was almost relieved when the mehtar returned to the subject of his opening speech. Now that most of his audience was gone, he was somewhat more blunt about

158

his expectations. "If the British Queen is my friend, then she will send me guns to fight Gulab Singh."

"The Queen desires friendship with both you and Gulab Singh," Keith said.

"Impossible!" the mehtar exclaimed. "My enemy's friend is my enemy. Now tell me the truth. The British raj has made Gulab Singh great. With open hands it has given away to him the territory gained in fighting the Sikhs."

"Gulab Singh helped us during the Sikh war!" Keith returned. "Where were your men then? Raiding the caravans at Leh or hunting in the hills? I did not see the men of Guahipore at Multan."

The mehtar's face darkened with a rush of blood to his temples and he drew himself erect, looking down scornfully on his European visitors.

"Now I see the truth," he said. "You have been sent here by the British raj to spy on me in the interests of Gulab Singh. I invited you into my country in a spirit of true friendship, but now you mock at me because I am not rich and powerful as Gulab Singh is—with his hands full of the wealth of Kashmir! Confess that you came as a spy! Confess! Confess!"

With his long beard and exotic robes, the mehtar looked like an Old Testament prophet hurling down curses and brandishing his stick. He was a terrifying figure, yet Bridget felt there was something artificial about this sudden rage.

Keith was rising to his feet now, ready to answer the mehtar's accusations with angry words of his own. Bridget glanced at Afzul-ul-Mulk. Surely, as the mehtar's trusted advisor, he would not wish to let this continue!

He was laughing.

Bridget saw the secret smile, the sleeve raised to hide his evident pleasure. Why did he want Keith and the mehtar to quarrel?

Without giving herself time to think, she scrambled to her feet in time to stand before the mehtar with Keith. She smiled on him as though she had not understood a word of his angry speech and slowly spread out her skirts and sank back to the ground in the full court curtsey that Aggie Lanyer had taught her.

As she had hoped, the mehtar broke off his speech in surprise.

"Wah! What new trick is this?"

Bridget kept her head demurely lowered and answered him in careful Urdu.

"It is the way in which ladies of our country show their respect, Your Highness."

The mehtar laughed. "So . . . so! A new form of salaam. So, you have respect, though your husband has none?" He walked round her, admiring her spreading skirts. "Get up," he commanded peremptorily, "and let me see it again."

Bridget rose as commanded, but when she was standing she looked the mehtar in the eye. "Neither my husband nor myself is lacking in respect, Your Highness. Perhaps our imperfect command of your language has caused misunderstandings. My husband has brought many gifts for you from our queen in token of her desire for friendship."

The mehtar turned on Keith. "Why did you not tell me this?"

"Since you refused our friendship, I did not wish to insult Your Highness," Keith replied. "Please forgive my wife for having the insolence to speak to you of so small a matter. The gifts are insignificant and not worthy of your attention—especially since you do not trust us."

"Not trust you! I was but testing you," the mehtar said. "Ya Mahmoud! Let the gifts of the *feringhi* be brought."

The youngest of his three sons bowed and left the courtyard.

Afzul-ul-Mulk stepped up to Bridget's elbow. He was so close that she could smell the spices in which his velvet coat had been packed and the rosewater on his hands. A man shouldn't smell like that, she thought crossly. It was . . . upsetting.

"A beautiful woman is a treasure which is displayed for men to envy, but a clever one is as a secret which brings in more treasure," he murmured. "Your husband is twice rich in you." His eyes frankly appraised the outline of her figure in the tight-fitting cotton basque.

Bridget felt her cheeks warming, but she smiled back at him and refused to let her eyes drop. Their eyes met like enemies rushing to combat. Bridget thought of men wrestling, naked, entwined—No! This was someone else's fantasy in her mind.

The entrance of the mehtar's servants, bearing the gifts Keith had transported from the plains, saved her. Afzul-ul-Mulk broke his hypnotic stare for a moment to look at the train of gifts, and Bridget took the opportunity to curtsey again and to move closer to Keith.

The mehtar was delighted with the presents, which consisted of such diverse items as jeweled looking glasses, nested silver cups and gold cloths from Benares. "Never know what these hill fellows will like," the resident in Lahore had advised them. "Anything bright and shiny. But no weapons, mind!"

If the mehtar still resented the absence of guns, he did not say so again, and soon Keith and Bridget were able to take their departure in a reasonably friendly spirit.

"You will come again to visit my ladies," the mehtar told Bridget. "You will come tomorrow . . . I will that you teach them this new way of doing salaam!"

"Whew!" Keith exclaimed when they emerged from the courtyard into the public square. He slipped an arm round Bridget's waist. "That was good thinking. You distracted him just in time. And it's quite an honor to be invited to visit the zenana. You know, it could come in handy, that. You might pick up some good gossip if you keep your eyes and ears open."

The crowd that had greeted their arrival was gone now; the presence of an armed man standing at each of the entrances to the square suggested that this was not quite by accident. Only the hillmen who had carried them and their baggage remained, with a dusty, ragged figure in the brown cloth of the hills guarding the baggage: the explorer Henderson.

"I'll show you to your house," he said and nodded in response to Bridget's half-checked exclamation of surprise. "Oh, yes. You've been assigned living quarters. The mehtar sees to everything, as you'll be learning."

Once again his tone indicated that it was unwise to discuss the matter further. He shouted an order to the bearers and they rose and took up the baggage, now considerably lightened since Keith had disposed of his gifts to the mehtar.

Bridget was relieved to find it was not far to the house that had been chosen for them. But even though the distance was not great, the twists and turns they took had her so confused that she doubted whether she would ever find her way back.

162

"It's not so difficult when you've the way of it," said Henderson. "Go by the street of the Great Mosque, turn at the charcoal-seller's, take a short cut through Ali Ali's back porch and here we are."

"Here" was a stone house of two stories, with a miniscule walled courtyard in which a cherry tree bloomed. Bridget gave an exclamation of pleasure as she saw the little courtyard and bit back the gasp of dismay at her first sight of the interior of the house.

In the dimming light of a cold evening, it was a dismal sight: floor of beaten earth, no fire or light and the one room that filled the lower story strewn with rubbish.

Keith's arm was about her again, warming and supporting her. "Tomorrow we'll hire servants," he promised. "They'll set this place to rights in no time."

"Servants nothing," said Bridget, "I'll have it cleared in less time than that."

After all, it was no worse than the hut where she'd grown up outside Ballycrochan. Better, with these good stone walls and no doubt a good solid roof above them. Had she been aping a lady for so long that she'd forgotten how to care for herself and her man? Bridget rummaged through the baggage for a cloth to tie round her hair and told Keith and Henderson they could have a smoke in the courtyard until she called them in.

Before night had fallen over the city, the lower floor was swept clean of the debris which had cluttered it, a good fire was snapping and crackling in the corner, the cushions of their palanquins were arranged for improvised beds and the two hillmen who admitted to knowing something of the city had been sent to a cookshop and had returned with an anonymous pot of rice and spiced vegetables which they all three dipped into, sitting before the fire.

Bridget had prudently decided to leave the upper floor for the next day. Investigation up the shaky ladder which served as a staircase had revealed a number of spider webs and the nests of some larger pests.

"Wise," Henderson agreed. "And a cozy wee place you've made of it, mistress. I'll tell you now that I had my doubts when I heard Keith had married a lady born, and her fresh from home. But you've done well for yourself, Keith."

"Aye," Keith drawled in imitation of Henderson's Scots accent, "I think I'll keep her."

He had settled against the wall, where he could lean back and watch the dying flames and support Bridget against his shoulder.

"Our first home," Bridget thought. "The first real one, for I don't count the boat."

She blinked back tears at the thought that it would also be their last home. Someday Keith would be transferred from Guahipore to a larger and more important station where there were other English, and then she would have to go away. But she would not think of that now. She would simply enjoy this unexpected reprieve, this dear time of being with him, however long it might last.

She sniffled and told herself how perfectly happy she was, just to be leaning on Keith's shoulder in their own home and maybe to get to stay with him for months, even years more. If only Henderson would go away and they could be alone together again.

Keith moved slightly to support his wife's head as it drooped down onto his shoulder. He smoothed her brown hair and wondered once again what went on under those smooth braids, that white forehead, those wide innocent eyes. But why torture himself with these questions? Whatever was in her past, she herself was true and honest—he would stake his life on that.

Meanwhile, he was perfectly happy just to be here with her, on the brink of beginning his real career.

If only Henderson would stop explaining the politics of Guahipore to him and leave them alone together!

Chapter Thirteen

THE FIRST MONTHS IN GUAHIPORE PASSED BY SO SWIFTLY and easily that later, looking back, Bridget was tempted to think she must have been living in a dream. After Henderson's departure, she and Keith were left entirely on their own. With no British residents to look after, Keith found his duties consisted of nothing more onerous than courtesy visits to the mehtar and his advisors. During these visits he regularly suggested the benefits to the state of Guahipore of making firm treaties with the British, and the mehtar regularly smiled, nodded and agreed to consider the matter.

"Why does it matter whether we have treaties with Guahipore?" Bridget asked when Keith came back frustrated from one of these meetings.

Then he knelt down on the freshly raked sand of the garden path and drew maps for her. "Kashmir is here; the mountains of the Hindu Kush, here. And beyond those mountains Russia is moving ever closer to us. If the native tales of a pass through the mountains are true, it is a road through which Russia can strike at India. They could bring men through the pass, little by little, and station them here in Guahipore until they had a great force built up. There are Sikh leaders enough who would ally with them to take back the Punjab. And from there, they could take India."

Bridget nodded and Keith scuffed over the scribbled map with the heel of his shoe as the gardener approached. "Let's go upstairs."

"Upstairs" meant a scramble up the ladder which still formed their only staircase to a wide second-floor room which Bridget had divided into study and bedroom by the simple expedient of hanging curtains. A Guahi carpenter had knocked up a desk and chair for Keith, their bed was a string charpoy piled high with quilted silk *rezais,* and the only other furniture was the wicker baskets they had traveled with, now put to use as storage chests and seats. But Bridget had made the rooms bright with lengths of embroidered cloth and cheap hammered-tin ornaments from the bazaars and Mirza, the cook's daughter, swept and polished them daily to spotless cleanliness.

Keith dropped onto the charpoy and stretched luxuriously. "So now you know why I'm really here . . . Not that I'm doing much good! But I don't suppose it matters too much, one way or another, until Henderson reports back. When was the last message we had from him?"

"Three weeks ago," Bridget said. She was as concerned as Keith when the intervals between messages became too long. She had grown to like the old explorer during the week he'd stayed with them before setting out for the high mountains.

"You know, it's not like the post office," she reminded Keith. "He has to depend on caravans coming this way. And if he's deep in the mountains, he might not encounter any other travelers."

"I know," Keith concurred. "It's too early to worry yet."

But as spring gave way to summer, as the white waves of blossoming fruit trees in the valley gave way to the green and gold of peaches ripening among glossy leaves and then to the red-gold hues of fruit piled on every flat roof for drying, they had no more word of Henderson.

Time seemed to be standing still that summer. Keith made friends with the mehtar's oldest son and went hunting with him. Bridget learned enough Urdu to gossip with her neighbors and shop for food. For the most part, people were friendly and willing to accept her, once they got over the novelty of her white face and peculiar garments. She didn't like the continual stares, but she could handle them.

The one person who still could make her feel uncomfortable was Afzul-ul-Mulk. He had formed the habit of dropping by their house at odd intervals, ostensibly to see Keith; but when Keith was not at home he would remain to talk with Bridget, making frequent admiring remarks about her beauty, her difference from the ignorant women of Guahipore and the wisdom of the English in letting their women go unveiled so that all could enjoy their beauty.

He never said anything rude or threatening, but something in the way he looked at her made Bridget uneasy. Then, too, he never went away of his own accord; he always waited until she excused herself to deal with some household task. And when he took his departure with more flowing compliments, she wondered just what she would do if he ever refused to leave.

One day when Keith had been on a three-day hunting expedition and the rain had prevented Bridget from going out to visit her neighbors, she found that she did not quite want Afzul to leave.

After that she formed the habit of keeping Mirza by her whenever Keith was out of the house.

Mirza was a tall, cheerful girl who was always singing one of the high-pitched, quavering native songs as she went about her tasks. In many ways she reminded Bridget of herself when Lord and Lady Fitzgerald first took her, orphaned, into service at the Great House: strong, willing and capable of making a mistake a minute if somebody didn't stand over her!

"Never mind, Mirza," she said one day in her slow, careful Urdu, finding the girl in tears over a pile of Keith's papers that had cascaded over the floor while she was attacking his study with vigorous strokes of a twig broom. "You have to go more slowly is all. Think before you start a task!"

It was advice she might well have taken herself, she thought. How much thought had she given this mad impersonation when she'd embarked on it? Never had she expected to find herself so thoroughly caught up in the part of "Lady Charlotte"—even married to Lady Charlotte's fiancé and instructing servants! It was the mercy of God she hadn't got into worse trouble than any Mirza could imagine, so it was. But now they were in Guahipore, things were going smoother . . .

Leaning against the desk, Bridget allowed herself to imagine a future in which the government, responding to Keith's talent for working in the remote places of the earth, sent him to one mountain kingdom after another where there was no English community to catch her out in mistakes. After years of such service, he would be knighted, and when they retired in Ireland—

An ink bottle crashed to the floor, and Bridget's thoughts came down with it in a heap as Mirza wailed her distress. Ireland. Keith might not wait for retirement; he might want to go home on leave when his work in Guahipore was done. And how long would she last *there,* pretending to be Lady Charlotte, and the whole country full of people who'd known her? Better to keep to the present. The present was all right, as long as you didn't worry.

"Never mind, Mirza," she said again. Her gown, one of the few they had brought from India, was splotched from hem to knee with the gritty, brown-black ink that was all Keith could find in the bazaars. "That is enough cleaning for today. Why do you not come with me to the bazaar and help me buy fabric for another dress?"

Soon she would need something warmer anyway. This was the height of the hot season in the plains, but here in Guahipore she was grateful for the warmth of Keith's Kashmir shawl in the evenings. In winter, they said, the snow blocked doorways and the icy wind off the mountains howled down the narrow streets.

Bridget usually took Mirza with her to the bazaar. Her Urdu, though passably fluent, was not yet up to dealing with the native shopkeepers, whose speech was heavily laced with words from their tribal dialects. And she was still embarrassed by the way people ran to stare at her whenever she went outside.

"Don't let it trouble you," said Keith when she mentioned the matter to him. "They have never seen a European woman before, that is all. When they tire of the novelty, they will leave you alone. And when you learn to speak the language better, that will help, too.

Have you made friends with any of the mehtar's women yet? They could help you."

Bridget sighed. "I could move myself bag and baggage into the zenana and not be knowing Habiba any better than to be saying 'Please,' and 'Thank you,' and 'If Allah wills it!' "

Her visits had all taken the same depressing pattern. Whenever Keith went to talk with the mehtar, Bridget would accompany him. While the men talked, she was shown through several courtyards to the locked gate where the zenana gardens began. Escorted through the gardens by a slave girl, she heard suppressed titterings and whispers on either side of her, but saw no one else.

The mehtar's senior wife, Habiba, received her in a long room lined on both sides with pillars. Habiba reclined on cushions while a single, rickety, straight-backed chair was brought in for Bridget, emphasizing her foreignness.

Their conversation consisted of a series of polite statements and questions on Bridget's part and monosyllabic answers from Habiba. Every once in a while there would be a burst of giggling and the sound of scuffling feet outside one of the windows of pierced stone. And once when Bridget was being escorted back out through the zenana gardens, she had seen the silver swing that hung from the biggest tree still swaying as though a girl had just been pushing herself back and forth in it. But the life of the zenana was still a closed book to her.

All that was to change as a result of this day's impulsive shopping expedition.

With Mirza at her side to interpret and bargain, Bridget wandered through the bazaar. The goods here were brought in by caravan, and mostly there was not so good a selection as she had seen in India. But there was one stall where the merchant specialized in brilliant red and blue Chinese brocades such as she had seen some of the nobles wearing. Today she was in luck; a caravan had recently arrived from Leh, and the merchant had a fine selection including some yards of a turquoise blue silk that she had never seen before. Blue and green by turns, it shimmered like a jewel in the sunlight.

"We call this color 'Peacock's Tail,'" the merchant told her.

Bridget was enchanted and promptly bought up all he had to add to her more prosaic purchases of country wool and wadded cotton. The extra material, added to what Mirza was already carrying, made a stack beyond what either she or Bridget could manage with ease.

"Oh, how stupid I was not to bring Daud with us!" Bridget exclaimed. Their gatekeeper/gardener could easily have managed the whole load with one hand.

To add to her annoyance, a brisk wind came whisking through the bazaar, lifting clouds of dust and slipping under her skirts with an insinuating knife-edge of cold mountain air. The impish gusts flicked up her skirts, first at one side and then the other, and Bridget had to drop her parcels to hold her skirts down decently. Even when she stood with both arms pressed to her sides, the wind whipped her skirt up around her knees. The bazaar loafers laughed and pointed and a crowd began to form to enjoy this latest tale of the *feringhi* woman.

Bridget was about to beg the stallkeeper for shelter until the freakish wind storm passed, when a hand tapped her on the shoulder. She turned and looked into the concerned face of the palace servant who had escorted her to the zenana on each visit. In an undertone he explained that he had been on an errand buying sweetmeats for his mistress, and anticipating that he might find new trinkets to amuse her in the load from the latest caravan, had brought along a *jampon* to carry his purchases. He would be happy to convey her home if she did not disdain so humble a vehicle.

The Guahipore *jampon* was their version of the palanquin of the plains, a squarish platform in which one could not recline, but sat cross-legged like a tailor. Bridget was grateful to see that the one offered her was curtained. She scrambled in and directed Mirza to pile the purchases around her. As soon as she let down the curtains, the bearers picked up the poles and they were off, swaying through the crowded bazaar.

Bridget was surprised to open the curtains a few minutes later and find herself outside the zenana gardens instead of in her own courtyard.

"There is a mistake," she told the servant. "I was not supposed to visit the mehtar's ladies today."

"No mistake! No mistake!" he repeated, grinning. The door in the high wall swung open and a smiling girl beckoned Bridget inside. She had no recourse but to go in. The girl picked up her bolts of cloth and, staggering slightly under the weight, followed her and kicked the door shut with one foot.

They went by a path that was unfamiliar to Bridget, ending at a little pavilion whose walls of latticework and carved top made it look like a white iced cake against the greenness of the garden. There was laughter inside and the sound of a stringed instrument being lazily plucked.

Bridget hesitated with one foot on the step. She remembered the deserted pavilion of black marble that she and Keith had discovered on their journey up-river, and his speculation that the rajah might have used it as a pleasure room where he was entertained by his dancing girls. What sort of scene might she be breaking in on?

The girl staggered forward under the load of Bridget's bolts of cloth. "Go on!" she said.

At the sound of her voice, a panel in the latticework slid open and a woman's face—young, laughing, painted—looked out. "Ya Allah!" she screeched. "It is the *feringhi* woman come to visit us at last!"

The next moment the panel slammed shut, a door opened and the young woman ran down the steps to put her arms around Bridget, hugging and kissing her and laughing as if her dearest friend had suddenly appeared.

"I am Aziza, the junior wife of the mehtar, may he live forever!" she announced. "And I have been waiting a long time to meet you. Old Habiba wants to keep all the fun for herself because she is my lord's senior wife and because she has more sons than I do, but this time I am cleverer than she is." She beamed and kissed Bridget once more.

Bridget smiled back at this first display of warmth in the zenana. It would be hard, she thought, not to smile at Aziza. Her animated little face, though not strictly beautiful, was intriguing with its wide, black-rimmed eyes and delicate features. She wore her hair loose, in quantities of black curls glossy with oil and jasmine, and peeped coquettishly out from behind the wide, gauzy veil that half covered her head and set off her silk tunic and trousers.

Aziza took Bridget's hand and pulled her into the pavilion. The interior was white also, a stark white that served as background for piles of silken cushions in glowing colors. Aziza disposed herself on a blue cushion with a graceful movement that showed off all the beauty of her fine-boned wrists and ankles, further accentuated by heavy gold bracelets. "Now we can talk comfortably," she announced.

From Aziza's excited chatter Bridget learned that whenever she and Keith made an official visit to the mehtar, Habiba ordered the younger wives and the slave girls to stay clear of her chambers, saying that the *feringhi* woman was proud and shy and did not want to be bothered with all of them at once.

"But my slave Laila who goes to the bazaar for me says that you go there also, and that you are young like me and not proud at all, and I think maybe you want to have a friend here. So I tell her next time she sees you in the bazaar she must run, run, and tell old Abdul the gatekeeper to bring a *jampon* and carry you to me."

Aziza giggled at the success of her plot, and Bridget laughed too. In a few minutes they were both seated on the silken cushions of the pavilion, chatting like old friends. Aziza told Bridget that the reason Habiba never said more than "Yes" or "No" or "If Allah wills it" was because she did not speak very good Urdu.

"Well," Bridget confessed, "neither do I."

"Yes, but you talk better than old Habiba!" said Aziza. "But Habiba comes from Bashiri tribe, up in the mountains. She doesn't like to live in Guahipore. Of course I did not like it either when the mehtar, may he live forever, brought me here from Delhi, but I got used to it." She looked pensive. "I cried all the time at first though. It is very sad to go to a strange country and to be far away from your mother. Did your mother cry when you came over the water?"

Bridget shook her head. "My mother is dead."

Aziza patted her hand. "That is *very* sad. Did someone poison her? Habiba has tried to poison me, three times already, but I am cleverer than she is!"

Bridget was fascinated by this glimpse of life in the harem. "No," she said. It had been a long time since she thought about those days before she went into service at the Great House. "No, my mother and father died because they did not have enough to eat." The bitterness of the memory was still strong within her.

Aziza's slim brown hand covered hers. Her large dark eyes were liquid with sorrow. "We have famines in India, too. Not here, but in the plains where I come from. But in our famines, only the poor die. The mehtar told me that your parents were princes in their country."

Bridget supposed that was how he had translated Lady Charlotte's title. "Well, not exactly," she began, searching her limited Urdu vocabulary for an explanation.

Then she stopped. She was tired of explaining and equivocating and plain outright lying. And Aziza was the first woman who had touched her in friendship since Aggie Lanyer—dear Aggie, so far away now! Bridget felt the tears filling her eyes.

"No," she said. "My parents were not princes. They were peasants and they died in a famine, just as your poor people do." She looked at Aziza with her pretty, graceful hands, her delicate features surrounded by black ringlets drenched in jasmine oil. Nothing more foreign to Ballycrochan could be imagined, and yet Aziza's impulsive warmth had made Bridget feel truly at home for the first time since she left Ireland. How she had longed for a friend to confide in!

Prudence fought a brief, doomed struggle with the desire to tell someone—anyone—the simple truth, just for once. Bridget drew a deep breath. "Aziza, can you keep a secret?"

And before she knew it, she was spilling out the whole story that had burned within her so long. Even told in the simple words that were all she knew in Urdu, reduced to storybook flatness, it was a relief to let it out to someone.

"There was a great famine in my land, and the people were dying. My brother went away to look for work in a foreign land, and we thought we should never see him again. Then my father and mother died, and I had no place to go. There was a wicked man who was the . . . the . . ." How did you translate John Kelly's position? Did they have such a thing as an estate factor here?

"He was the advisor to the lord who owned our land. He fed me when I was sick, but when I was well he wanted to use me for his pleasure. I ran away from him, and I found grace with Lord Fitzgerald and he allowed me to remain in his house as a serving maid."

Aziza's eyes were fixed on her with unblinking interest. "It is like a romance from the *Alf-Laila-u-Laila*, the Thousand and One Nights!" she exclaimed. "And then you met Powell Sahib, while you were serving in the house, and he married you and brought you away from the wicked man!"

"Well . . . no," Bridget said. "Not exactly. Powell Sahib was already here in India. He was to marry the lord's niece, whom I served as . . . as an ayah."

Looking down at her hands, she told Aziza something of her life in the Fitzgeralds' house. Lady Charlotte had not been a kind mistress, but Bridget served her because as long as she worked in the Great House, John Kelly didn't bother her. And there were compensations. She and Lady Charlotte were much of a height, and even had the same coloring; sometimes she inherited one of Charlotte's old dresses. And her natural talent for mimicry found ample material to work on in the Fitzgerald family.

"I used to imitate her disdainful way of speaking to amuse the other servants. I suppose it was not very nice of me, but then Lady Charlotte was not very nice either." Reflexively, Bridget's hand went up to rub the thin white scar on her temple where Charlotte had once hurled a silver-backed brush at her.

When the Fitzgeralds suddenly announced that they were escorting Charlotte to India to marry Keith Powell and that the house was to be shut up until they returned, Bridget had been afraid. John Kelly cornered her one day and told her that as soon as the Fitzgeralds were not there to protect her, he intended to have her—and he would make her pay for the years she'd held him off.

The invitation to accompany Charlotte on the voyage as her personal maid had been a godsend. And when the ship was wrecked off Malta and all the other passengers drowned, Bridget had recovered from the terror of near-drowning only to face the fear of being sent back to Ballycrochan.

"But when I came round, the doctor addressed me as Lady Charlotte. I had been wearing one of her cast-off dresses, you see. And there was no one in Malta who knew her. I decided I would pretend to be her. Just until I got to India. Then I meant to slip away and find work."

"And instead you met Powell Sahib and he fell in love with you in spite of your humble origin and married you instead of Lady Charlotte!" Aziza finished rapturously. Her eyes were shining. "It is *better* than the *Alf-Laila-u-Laila.*"

"No." Bridget studied her fingers with intense concentration. The nails were cut short and the burn she'd had from the cooking pot when she was thirteen still showed as a reddish blush on the side of her index finger. Not a lady's hands.

"No, that's not exactly the way it was." She drew a deep breath. "Powell Sahib . . . still thinks I am Lady Charlotte."

Then the tears she had been holding back burst out and flooded over and she was crying, first into her square capable hands, and then somehow she was sobbing on Aziza's shoulder while two slender brown arms encircled her. Aziza was crying too; Bridget could feel the sympathetic sobs shaking her delicate frame while her lustrous jasmine-scented black hair mingled with Bridget's own brown curls.

The confession and the tears released something in her. When she and Aziza finally drew away from one another, Bridget felt calmer than she had been in a long while.

"Now," said Aziza, squatting back on her heels in the midst of the silken cushions, "now my slaves shall make tea for us, and we will talk of ordinary little things for a while, because it is not good for the heart to dwell on great matters for too long." Her eyes were full of sympathy. "Wherefore . . . wherefore, we shall talk of such important matters as the teething of my new babe and the design of dresses. Laila tells me you had a little trouble with the wind today. You should dress as we do! Will your husband beat you if you come home in tunic and trousers?" She burst out laughing and embraced Bridget again, and Bridget found herself laughing too.

"Show me what you have bought at the bazaar," Aziza commanded, and Bridget spread out the yards of fabric for her new friend's inspection. Aziza passed by the sober country cloth and quilted cotton without

179

interest, but she lingered over the "peacock's tail" silk, stroking it with loving fingers.

"This is very lovely. I wish that I could go to the bazaar myself to pick out such things, but it is not proper for a woman in my position. And by the time this stupid one goes," she complained, aiming a mock blow at Laila, "all the best stuffs are gone already."

"It would give me pleasure if you would accept this as a gift," Bridget said.

Aziza's eyes brightened. "Really? Oh, beautiful!" She unfolded the lustrous length of cloth and wrapped it around herself, turning this way and that and holding out an arm draped in shimmering folds of silk to admire herself. "Look, Laila! Will not the mehtar be driven mad with the passion of youth when he beholds my beauty in this?"

"May he live forever," muttered Laila with a reproving glance.

Aziza looked down. "Yes, of course," she murmured.

But a moment later her spirits were high as ever. She declared that it would be shame to her to let Bridget depart without a gift also, sent Laila to fetch a wooden carved casket and rooted around in its depths till she found what she wanted.

"Here!" Proudly she held up a gold embossed forehead ornament studded with emeralds. The round-cut stones did not have the faceted fire of Western gems, but their deep true color was finer than anything Bridget had seen in Calcutta.

"How green they are!" she murmured in admiration. Her hand went out as if of its own volition to touch the central stone, its shimmering depths lit with green light. "As green as the fields at home. But I cannot take it," she added regretfully, knowing that British government regulations prohibited the political officers from accepting anything so valuable for themselves.

Aziza pressed the ornament on her and refused to hear any denials, even when Bridget explained that according to regulations Keith would have to sell it and place the money in the Government treasury.

"No!" she decreed, stamping her foot with a clash of heavy gold ankle bracelets. "No, he will *not* sell it, and you *will* take it! I will lose honor if I take from you and give nothing, not even one little trinket that I do not like anyway!" Her eyes sparkled with indignation.

But Bridget had to stand firm. It would be worse to have Aziza hear later that the jewel had been sold than to face her temper now.

"Then you will take something else from me," Aziza said.

"What?" Bridget asked apprehensively.

Aziza shook her head. "I do not know yet. But it is in our stars. Perhaps my astrologer will know what it is you truly want. And now we are friends again?" She collapsed backward onto the cushions with a fluid movement and raised her hand without looking to accept a glass of tea from Laila.

By the time Bridget took her departure, she felt that she had gained a friend indeed. Her impulsive confession had cemented the friendship as nothing else could have done. Though the rest of the afternoon passed in idle chatter, as Aziza had promised, the consciousness of having a new friend warmed Bridget's heart.

She gave Keith an edited version of the day's events that evening when they were dressing for dinner. It seemed foolish to Bridget to go through this ritual of clambering up the ladder into their bedroom, changing into evening dress and climbing down again only to partake of the inevitable mutton pilau and bowl of fruit

181

in their mud-floored common room. But Keith insisted that it was a way of preserving a sense of civilization.

"I'm not surprised," Keith said when Bridget told him that Aziza seemed really to like her company and to want her to visit again.

"No?" Bridget felt unaccountably dashed. She knew that making a friend in the zenana did not compare with the important talks Keith was having with the mehtar and his advisors, but he had said it would be helpful to him. She had expected more reaction.

"No." Keith bent over in the midst of fastening his shirt studs and dropped a kiss on Bridget's forehead. "Darling, you make people love you wherever you go. Look at little Aggie Lanyer. Look at me for that matter. You know, when you came out I was not exactly happy about the arrangement. Thought your people were pushing the marriage too hard."

"I know," Bridget said. "You . . . made that clear." It still hurt, just a little, to recall those early days in Calcutta when Keith had seemed to dislike her so much.

"I was a damned rude, prejudiced young puppy," Keith corrected her. "But I couldn't help loving you, even before I found out—"

He stopped abruptly and his ears turned crimson. He dropped a shirt stud on the floor and dived under the bed after it.

"Found out what?" Bridget asked. Her heart always seemed to beat faster when people used words like *found out, discovered, caught.*

"Ah . . . found out how sweet and good you really are," Keith improvised as he crawled out from under the bed. He dropped another kiss on her forehead and almost regretted the impulse which had led him to change his words. Someday, before they went back to the plains, they would have to have it out. But not now—not when he had unpleasant news to break to her in a moment.

Keith sighed to himself and wished that somehow his lovely, lovable wife would find it in her heart to tell him who she really was. Until she trusted him that much, he found it hard to believe she really loved him. Still, there were times . . .

Keith's sigh changed to a reminiscent grin as he pondered those times. She was so sweet then, so warm and yielding! He pictured her naked body on the bed and felt desire stirring in his loins.

"How long do we have before dinner?" he asked Bridget.

"Oh, perhaps half an hour. Why?"

By way of answer, Keith ran his hand over her shoulders, bared by the low-cut evening dress, and watched her tremor of response. "Long enough." His hands went to the tiny hooks at the back of the bodice, peeling apart the fabric to reveal the creamy skin beneath.

Bridget caught her breath at the light, teasing touch that always awakened her desires. Did he mean . . . surely not . . . yes! She felt the cool air on her bared back, then Keith's lips warm against her skin. The bodice first, then the skirt, shivered to the floor in a whisper of silk. Keith's hands followed the skirt as it slipped down, caressing her legs through the petticoat of soft washed linen, then back up under the linen, hard now against her naked thighs, parting them, gently forcing her backward onto the bed.

Her knees were trembling uncontrollably. She fell back, half-sitting on the edge of the bed, supported by her hands behind her on the quilted silk coverlet. The silk was cold and slippery against the backs of her thighs; the linen petticoats were warm by contrast, rough against her skin as Keith pushed the ruffles up out of his way.

His lips grazed upward along the sensitive skin on the inside of her thighs, teasing and nibbling with sharp touches of teeth and tongue that set her afire. Bridget's arms could no longer support her; she sank back onto the quilt and felt him lifting her legs, supporting her even as his tongue continued its darting forays of exploration. She cried out with pleasure as he probed her most sensitive secret places, his tongue flickering over her moist center and rousing her to uncontrollable shaking joy.

Then he was over her, leaning on his arms, thrusting himself into her with quick sure strokes that would not let the passion he had inflamed die. Bridget cried out again and pulled him close to her, digging her nails into his back and wrapping her legs about him. For uncountable ages they were one, moving back and forth in a place beyond time, while the desires he had roused burned unchecked between them. Bridget felt the pulsation of their fulfillment rocking through her until it seemed she could bear no more.

Then there was the silk under her damp with sweat and the ruffled petticoat crushed between them and her breasts still pressed upward by the corset that he had not had time to remove. She twisted from under him and sat up.

"Angry?" Keith asked with an undertone of laughter in his voice.

Bridget smoothed the damp hair back from his forehead. "No . . . my corset. It wasn't built for lying down in."

"I can fix that." Keith pulled at the ribbons until her breasts sprang free of their tight confinement. He loosened the tie of her chemise at the neck and pulled it down until he could bury his face between her breasts. "Mmm. Why didn't I do this before?" More gentle, insistent tugs, and the chemise was about her hips. She stood and let the underclothes spill down onto the floor. A sliver of wind knifed through the room from the ill-fitting shutters and raised goosebumps on her white skin.

"Cold!" Bridget jumped back into the bed and wrapped the silk *rezai* tightly around her.

"Selfish!" Keith discarded his shirt and pulled at the coverlet until she let him crawl under it with her.

His hands were cool and demanding where her flesh was beginning to warm under the covers.

"Hungry?"

"Mmm. Not very." Bridget snuggled into the curve of his arm and laid her head on his chest.

"Why don't we . . ."

". . . skip dinner. Yes." She let her own hand stray, caressing his flat stomach with teasing light fingertips until he gasped and directed her hand farther down.

And so it was morning before Keith broke his news to her, and they had no time for discussing it at all.

Chapter Fourteen

IN THE MORNING BRIDGET WOKE TO THE SOUND OF bundles being moved and men shouting in the courtyard. She slipped on a wrapper and scrambled down the ladder to find Keith, fully dressed, supervising packing operations.

"Where are you going?" she demanded. The dirt floor was littered with baskets and blanket rolls, and Keith was consulting a faded map which seemed to consist mostly of blank spaces.

"Mountains," Keith mumbled, looking away from her. "Tribal territory."

"Why?" She could not imagine what emergency had necessitated this sudden departure.

Keith took her arm and drew her aside. "Now, look, darling, there's no need to get upset. I'll only be away a few days—well, maybe a couple of weeks. Can't tell yet. Depends on the situation up there. Why don't you

186

sit down and relax?" He indicated a fully packed basket with a nice flat top.

"I am not upset," Bridget said. She took care to speak slowly and clearly. She folded her arms to emphasize how calm she was. "I only want to know what this situation is. Then I will decide whether or not I am upset."

Keith turned away and pretended to be consulting his map. "Henderson's dead."

"What!"

Bridget sat down rather more suddenly than she had planned.

"Knew I shouldn't have told you," Keith said.

In a few sentences he explained the rest of the situation to her. He wasn't the only one who had been worried when the messages coming back from Henderson's mapping expedition had suddenly stopped. He had been getting messages from the resident in Lahore, demanding more and more information about a situation which Keith knew no more of than did the resident. Yesterday, two things had happened that greatly increased the urgency he felt.

The first was that the resident's latest message had explained why he was putting so much pressure on Keith. The commander of the regiment quartered in Lahore had begun talking of sending soldiers over the border to search for Henderson. Such a rash move would inflame relations between Guahipore and the British and might put Keith in danger or force his recall. But the resident had no direct power to control the movements of the army; all he could do was advise.

"You said two things," said Bridget when Keith finished this explanation and turned away to see to his packing.

"Yes. Well . . . you were in the bazaar yesterday, weren't you? You know that caravan that just came in from Leh?"

Bridget nodded. Keith rummaged in a half-packed basket and brought out two things which he showed to Bridget.

Balanced on his open palms, gleaming in the pale light from the open door, were a dented tin box and a compass.

"Henderson's drug box and his compass." Keith's voice was rough with suppressed emotion. "Can you imagine him casually tossing either of these items aside? Neither can I. They were offered for sale in the bazaar; Afzul recognized them and brought them to me. The leader of the caravan said he bought them from some Bashiri tribesmen in the mountains between here and Leh.

"Henderson must have been murdered for the few things in his pack. If I report this to Lahore, the army will march in. They'll take it as a God-given excuse to take Guahipore by force. And I know the mehtar. Any treaties he signs under duress won't be worth the paper they're written on—and I wouldn't blame him! These people deserve better than that of us. They need schools, they need clinics, they need a few years of peace. They don't need to be annexed by force, and they'll die fighting us if we try."

His hands, warm and calloused and strong, encased Bridget's cold palms. "Do you understand, darling? Henderson's death is a tragedy. But I can't let that tragedy destroy all I've worked for here. These people deserve better from us than that."

"What can you do?" Bridget whispered. But she had already guessed the answer.

"I'm going up to Bashiri country. I'm going to see the

elders of the tribe and tell them they have to pay reparations for Henderson's death and hand over the men who did it. If I can report that his murderers are under Guahipore justice, then maybe I can keep the army out of this."

"And maybe you can get yourself killed the same way."

Keith gave an unconvincing laugh. "Don't be silly, darling. I'm a British officer. They wouldn't dare attack me."

Bridget withdrew her cold hands from his grasp and called for Mirza. "Bring the large basket and my warmest dresses."

Keith was watching her warily, balanced on the balls of his feet as if ready to spring. "And just what do you think you're doing?"

"Thank you, Mirza. Now my toilet things." Bridget knelt on the floor, packing her breakables between folds of the dresses. The basket was half full before she deigned to answer Keith's question. "What does it look like I'm doing? I'm going with you."

"You're not, you know." Keith rocked back and forth on the balls of his feet, a half-smile on his face. She had seen him stand so when anticipating the attack of an enemy . . . that day in Calcutta when he was expecting the cholera riots so long ago.

"And my warm shawl, please, Mirza, and the small box of tea and the sugar canister and two brass cups." Bridget packed the last articles firmly down into the basket, tightened the leather straps over the top and rose to face her husband.

Systematically, she demolished his arguments one by one. There was no need for a litter: she would ride like him.

"Astride. Remember my telling you about my problem with the wind in the bazaar? Aziza suggested that I make some of my full dresses into divided skirts. I had Mirza working on them last night."

She held up the dress she meant to wear on the trip in front of Keith. The full skirt had been cut into two full trouser legs, gathered in tight at the ankle.

"That's indecent!" Keith said.

"Less indecent than having the wind, not to mention every lounger in the bazaar, up my petticoats." Bridget folded the dress over her arm and prepared to ascend the ladder to change clothes.

"It's too dangerous for you," Keith tried next.

"What about staying here alone? You think that's safe?"

"A lot safer than chasing about after wild Bashiri tribesmen who'd as soon kill you as look at you!" Keith shouted. He grasped Bridget by her shoulders and forced her to face him.

"Not two minutes ago you were ready to swear on the holy saints there was nothing safer!" Bridget bawled back at him. "You can't have it both ways. If there's no danger in it, you've no reasonable objection to my company. If it's dangerous, I'm not having you go up there without me."

"Look who's having it both ways!" Keith's fingers tightened on her shoulders and he shook her till her teeth rattled. "I—am—not—taking—you!" he stated, punctuating each word with another shake.

"W-well . . . I'm . . . g-going!" Bridget got out through chattering teeth.

A shadow fell across the doorway and startled both of them into silence.

Afzul-ul-Mulk was leaning against the doorpost, elegant as ever in his high boots of soft leather and tight-fitting blue velvet coat. The single sapphire pendant that he always wore flashed at his throat between the stiff blue edges of the coat collar.

He smoothed the folds of his turban with one hand and smiled at them both.

"Pray forgive me for interrupting, O my brother," he said in liquid Urdu. "If you are concerned for the safety of your woman, I will be happy to guard your household during your absence." He smiled at Keith while his eyes slid toward Bridget.

Suddenly she was intensely aware of the flimsy material of her morning wrapper and the way it clung to her body, revealing all too clearly that she wore no corsets. She put her hand to the neck of the wrapper and pulled it closed. She could feel the heat starting in her cheeks as Afzul's dark almond-shaped eyes held hers in his compelling, almost hypnotic gaze.

Keith stepped between them. "No problem," he said. "My wife accompanies me."

"Do you think that wise?" Afzul murmured. "To expose her to the dangers of the road?"

"The city also has its dangers," Keith said.

Afzul smiled and shifted his position in the doorway so that he could see Bridget again. She knelt beside the basket and pretended to be fussing with the leather straps that held the lid closed. She would not go up the ladder with Afzul's mocking, burning gaze upon her. She could feel his eyes on her now and his will, his desire that she should look up at him. She kept her head lowered over the basket.

"I would not that you should be concerned for your woman upon such a journey," Afzul said. "For your peace of mind, O my brother, I will even take your woman into my own household. She shall reside among my wives, and you shall have the surety of knowing that she is under my protection until your return."

At this Bridget looked up, ready to cry a denial.

"I thank you," Keith repeated steadily. "My wife travels with me."

Afzul shrugged and turned away. "As you will," he said. "It is written as it is written."

They were at the gates of the city, mounted, with the bearers behind them carrying the baskets slung on long poles, when Afzul-ul-Mulk joined them again.

In contrast with Keith's and Bridget's serviceable, plain costumes, he glittered as brightly as the blue sapphire at his throat. He had changed his embroidered velvet coat for one of leather inlaid and tooled in various patterns, but as it was left open to reveal an under-tunic of bright green silk and deep green velvet breeches, all caught up with a wide Chinese braided belt of silver and gold cords, the overall effect was not diminished in the least. The saddle and headstall of his horse glittered with silver and turquoise, and the gray falcon that perched on his arm had its legs banded with silver.

"I will ride a little way to set you on your road," he announced.

"I thank you, but that will not be necessary," Keith replied. "I have hired good guides."

"The road can be . . . treacherous, even in summer," Afzul murmured. "Pray allow me to accompany you on the first stages."

Keith could hardly demur further without outright discourtesy, and so the oddly-assorted cavalcade set forth. For the first half-day's ride Afzul rode between Keith and Bridget, entertaining them with a flow of light conversation about the people and scenes they were about to visit and flying his falcon for amusement at whatever small game they started. Bridget and Keith exchanged wary glances behind his back, but remembering his fluency in English, did not risk any conversation beyond casual comments on the road and the scenery.

They rode steadily upward, on a broad path leading toward the first of the passes into the snow country. When the path leveled off in a meadow, they stopped for a few minutes to rest the horses. Afzul sighted a rabbit bounding through the grass and sent his falcon after it with a swing of his arm.

"In spring this meadow would have been full of flowers," he told them while waiting for the falcon to return. "It is called the Golden Meadow, because it turns yellow with the thousands of wildflowers that bloom then."

As the falcon hovered, the rabbit froze in the long grass. Bridget held her breath, feeling its fear as if it were her own. The bird swooped down and seized the struggling prey in its talons.

"*Shabash!*" Afzul exclaimed. He turned his disquieting smile on Bridget. "Then, I could have offered you flowers. Now I have only the fruits of my morning's hunting to offer."

The falcon came to his arm. He took the rabbit, its eyes bright with fear, and slit its throat with a single motion of his hunting knife. He held out the bloody corpse to Bridget.

"Fortunately," he said in an undertone that only she could hear, "I am invariably successful in my hunting."

When they rode on, Bridget thought that Afzul was talking louder than usual. The path led downward through a rocky defile where they had to go single file and the horses' hooves clattered on rounded stones that gave very poor footing.

"I will go first," said Afzul loudly, "to make sure the way is safe. The mehtar—may he live forever—would be ill pleased if you met with harm so near to his capital city. I too would be most displeased!" He spurred his horse forward and rode the length of the defile ahead of Keith.

Although it was scarcely three hours past noon, the sun had already dropped behind the crags to the west, leaving the narrow pass in shadow. Bridget shivered as she rode through it, less from cold than from the sinister appearance of the pass. The very rocks above them seemed brooding and hostile. She breathed a sigh of relief when they reached the end of the narrow stretch and the path opened out again among the cedar forests of the high hills.

"Here I will leave you," said Afzul, turning his horse's head. He reached out for Keith's hand. "Good hunting, my brother, and may thy way be safe!"

When the echo of his horse's hooves returning up the pass had died away, Bridget turned to Keith. "I have a feeling there is more going on here than I expected."

"I too," said Keith in an undertone. "But I don't think this is a healthy place to discuss it. Wait till we make camp tonight."

Two hours later they camped in an upland meadow like the one where they had paused earlier, except that this one was nearer the snow line and colder than the first. But with their little tent up, a smoke-blackened kettle swinging over the crackling fire of cedar twigs and rough woolen blankets unfolded for a sleeping place, Bridget felt as comfortable as at home.

"Indeed, and at least it is cleaner than me real home was!" she thought, with a recurrence of the brogue that she had almost conquered after months of practice. "But it would never do to be telling that to Keith, so it wouldn't."

Instead she asked him if he could explain Afzul-ul-Mulk's strange behavior on the trail.

"Not entirely," Keith replied. He moved closer to Bridget and put his arm round her. "Put your head on my shoulder . . . there . . . now laugh!"

Bridget obeyed, and he kissed her, but for once there was no passion in the touch of his lips.

"Now no one will wonder why we are speaking low," he said.

"The bearers don't speak English anyway, do they?"

"Who knows? Afzul recommended at least two of my servants."

Bridget glanced at the men squatting round their own fire, apparently absorbed in recounting stories and eating their dinner of flat bread and vegetables.

"As for Afzul's behavior," Keith went on, "I think you have as much of the key as I do. Why didn't you tell me he was making up to you?"

"I wasn't sure," Bridget said. "I'd no wish to be troubling you over little things. A man can look at a woman, and she to complain, everybody would laugh at her to be troubled over such foolishness."

Keith's arm tightened round her momentarily. "I had wondered why he was so eager to get me out of the city. He brought me Henderson's things, it was his idea that I should go and talk to the Bashiri elders. Now, well, it would have been mighty convenient for him to have me away, and you staying in his zenana, wouldn't it?"

Bridget felt a coldness that had nothing to do with the night air. "I don't think I would ever have got out," she said quietly.

"No," Keith agreed. "I don't think you would." He paused. "Because I might never have come back. I think he had an ambush planned for that first pass, and when you decided to come along with me he knew no way to stop it but to ride along with us. I may owe you my life, darling."

Here in this peaceful meadow it was hard to contemplate the thought of an ambush. Bridget laughed uneasily. "Remember that next time we have a fight! . . . Keith?"

"Mm?" He was relaxing now, leaning back against a baggage roll and pulling her down against him.

"Forgive me that I was shouting at you." She couldn't think what had come over her. All her life she'd been trained in the importance of giving polite answers to the gentry, no matter what your real feelings were. And here she'd been yelling at Keith as if—why, as if he were really her husband!

Bridget smiled and snuggled into the curve of his arm. Why not? Here on the edge of the mountains, the gulf between them did not seem so great. All their little party seemed so small and insignificant beside the great peaks towering above them and the stars sprinkling the sky above that.

Keith stroked her hair almost absently and stared off past the campfires. "I wish I could be sure that was his only reason for wanting me out of the way," he muttered, almost to himself.

At midday on the second day they reached the point where the horses had to be sent back.

They had been marching along the deep gorge cut by a river, first on a narrow path chipped out of the hillside, then on the naked rock that slanted perilously out and downward. Finally they came to a broad ledge where they were to cross the river.

Bridget looked around in some perplexity when

Keith told her they would have to dismount and cross the bridge on foot.

"What bridge?" She could see nothing but some twisted ropes stretched across the canyon. But the path came to an abrupt and unquestionable end here, the ledge broke off sharply and the cliff plunged down a dizzying drop to the river that foamed beneath them.

"That is the bridge," Keith said with a tight-lipped smile. Henderson had described such contrivances to him, but until now he had not really understood how fragile and perilous the rope bridges were. He bit his lip as he looked at his wife.

What a fool he'd been, to let her come along on this expedition as lightheartedly as though they were going on a picnic! Surely there must have been some place in Guahipore where she would be safe. She could have stayed with her friend Aziza in the mehtar's palace. Why hadn't he thought of that? The truth was, for all his protestations, he was a blind, selfish fool who'd secretly wanted her to come with him.

Bridget saw Keith's worried expression. She forced herself to smile as she studied the bridge. One thick rope for the feet, two above to serve as handholds. "Sure, and it's a lucky thing I ripped up me skirts!" she said. "Wouldn't I look the grand fool indeed, balancing across that thing in a crinoline!"

Her laugh sounded weak and shaky, even in her own ears, but Keith smiled as though he believed it.

"I'll go first," he said. "Then you come, and then two of the men can take the baggage over. The rest will camp here with the horses until we return." He paused with one foot on the bottom rope. "Remember, now. Whatever you do, don't look down!"

Then he was out over the river, and Bridget bit back

a scream as she saw how the bridge swayed under his weight. She forgot to breathe until she saw him put a firm foot on the other side. Then he waved, a tiny stick figure waving his hat in the air, and it was her turn, and there was a roaring in her ears that surely could not be the river, and the ropes swaying under her the way it would make a person sick, and once her foot slipped and she balanced for a sickening moment on one foot but didn't look down, never look down, one foot after the other, count steps, one hundred and you'll be across, ten, twenty—

Keith's arms about her, and blessed, beautiful solid rock under her feet.

"I never *appreciated* rocks before," Bridget said fervently, "but sure, I feel as if I could just kneel and kiss this one!"

Three days later Bridget was beginning to wonder just what she had found so remarkable about that particular bridge. After all, it had all three ropes in good condition, was firmly anchored on either side of the gorge it crossed, and was sheltered from high winds. Several of the bridges they had encountered since then were lacking in some or all of these desirable qualities.

After three days' marching through the hills, Bridget was sunburned, her dress was torn and her legs ached with weariness at every step she took.

She could not remember ever being so happy.

There had been three days of aching climbs, sobbing for breath, to summits where new mountain vistas opened before them; of breathtaking descents into tiny green valleys where every square inch of cultivable land was used and where shy children stared solemnly at them before running to hide with their herds of goats; above all, three days of Keith's uninterrupted companionship. By turns friend, lover, guide, he and the mountains were all she desired.

Now they were approaching the Bashiri fort.

It was not one fort, but a conglomeration of squarish buildings, the same color as the rocks and soil of the mountainside and seeming to grow right out of the mountain. The crenellated buildings, windowless but for round holes a little bigger than a musket barrel, spilled down the side of the mountain to the very brim of the river.

Bridget stopped and caught Keith's hand when they got their first sight of the fort. They stood in silence for a minute, imagining the grim warrior culture that had created such a structure here in the middle of nowhere. "I wish—"

Bridget bit the words off. Wish what? That this march through the wilderness could go on forever? That they didn't have to go down and argue and deal with the Bashiris? What was the point?

"Don't worry, darling," Keith said. "They're not such fools as to attack a representative of the British raj."

Bridget nodded and followed Keith down the narrow path that led to the river's edge and the inevitable rope bridge. Where did it come from—this self-confidence that allowed Keith to walk into situations of danger without even turning his head to look behind him? Perhaps it was something that came of being born gentry.

Halfway down the path, their way was barred by an ancient tribesman with a scarred forehead who sprang out from a grove of cherry trees, thrusting his long silver-mounted musket at their breasts. When Keith explained who he was and repeated several times that he came in friendship, the man shouldered his musket and marched down the path before them, shouting to alert his fellows in the fort.

Before they had reached the rope bridge the fort was alive with curious heads peering over the parapets of the flat roofs, and Bridget heard the shrill babble of women. She realized that hundreds of eyes must have been watching their progress from those blank, dark holes in the walls. Now that they had been identified and judged as not dangerous, the women were scrambling back up to the rooftops to get a better view of the visitors.

When they reached the rope bridge their guard motioned them back with his musket, shouting some words in a language Bridget did not understand.

"Fascinating!" Keith exclaimed. "I think Bashiri may actually have retained some words of the classical Greek. By Jove, I wish I had my lexicon with me. You know, darling, there is a legend that Alexander once passed this way."

"I didn't know any of your friends besides Henderson had been fools enough to come here," snapped Bridget. An instant later she regretted her cross words. It was just that she was tired and worried about their reception. But Keith was laughing as though she had made an excellent joke, so she decided not to apologize. Men! You never knew what would set them off.

Evidently they were not to approach any nearer the fort than this bank of the river. A few minutes after they had settled on the stone outcroppings that made natural benches, the tribal elders appeared and made their way across the rope bridge. Although their long white beards and wrinkled faces proclaimed them to be men in their sixties or seventies, they crossed the bridge as calmly as though they were walking down the middle of a street in Dublin.

Keith spread out the blankets from their baggage rolls when he saw the elders coming. A boy who followed the men balanced a basket on his head that proved to be full of dried fruit. The headmen seated themselves cross-legged on the blankets, fruit was ceremoniously handed round and both sides murmured polite nothings in whatever language came handiest.

Bridget looked curiously at the tribesmen. Their coarse woolen garments lacked the elegance of Afzul-ul-Mulk's gilded city clothes, but the flash of silver and precious stones on their weapons showed that the Bashiris were not lacking in wealth. The men's faces fascinated her: fierce, wild, untamed, they seemed to represent the very essence of that mountain spirit that the Bashiris in the city only hinted at. Several of them wore their turbans pushed up high enough that she could see a repetition of the line of crosslike scars that had marked the forehead of the guard. A tribal sign? But conveniently covered, when the turban was worn low as was done in the city. So, she thought, a man could conceal his allegiance until the moment came to reveal himself.

After an interval of munching and nodding, the individual with the best command of Urdu among the Bashiris launched into a speech of welcome. Keith countered his speech with a flowery description of the power and wealth of the British raj and the desire of his queen to make friends with the Bashiris, whose fame as fighting men had spread even across the great ocean to come to her ears.

Another round of dried peaches and apricots was passed out at the conclusion of the speeches, and then the serious discussions began.

Keith wanted to know if another *feringhi* had recently passed this way; the Bashiri spokesman wanted to know if the great queen across the waters felt like giving guns to her friends the Bashiri, who badly needed them to keep the Guahis in their places.

Keith passed out the gifts he had brought across the mountains. The engraved silver goblets and lengths of Berhampore silk were well received, but the case of scented soap gave rise to a slight misunderstanding when one of the elders who spoke only Bashiri bit into a cake and began foaming at the mouth.

Once he convinced the Bashiris that the soap was not an attempt to poison them, Keith inquired more specifically after Henderson, saying that he knew he had come this way and that the queen over the water would be very angry with her friends the Bashiris if she found that they were protecting the misguided persons who had harmed her friend Henderson.

The tribal elders smiled into their beards and folded their hands.

"If Henderson has been harmed, the queen will be very angry," Keith repeated. "But if you give up the men who harmed him to me, and I take them back to prison in Guahipore, the queen's wrath will be appeased and justice will be done."

"Our men live by freedom," responded the spokesman. "If you take them to prison, they will die. Is that justice? If the queen is angry, let her pronounce blood-feud and send the men of her family to fight our men."

"That is what she will do," Keith told them. "She will send not one man or two, but thousands of the redcoats. I see that two of you are carrying arms of the queen's army. If you saw service with our army, then tell your fellows how numberless are the men of the queen and how powerful in battle."

The interpreter translated these words. The elders sat impassive as if considering; then one man who had not previously spoken said a few words. There was a snicker from somewhere in the back of the group.

"Ismail Khan says that we should be honored by the presence of the queen's men, but he fears that our country is rather a difficult one for your army."

With that pronouncement, the conference was over. The elders rose and nodded to Keith and returned over the rope bridge. The last statement was, "We shall return when we have considered your words."

Chapter Fifteen

"I DON'T *THINK* THAT WAS A THREAT," KEITH SAID. HE SAT cross-legged, balancing his pipe on one knee, and watched the elders threading their way back across the bridge.

"What do we do now?" Bridget asked.

"We wait."

They had not long to wait. Before the sun had crept into the valley to warm the ledge on which they sat, the Bashiri elders returned. This time a new figure crossed the bridge first of all—a man with shaggy hair stuffed under a woolen cap, wearing a coat and trousers of rough country homespun faded with age and much patched.

Keith started and dropped his pipe when the man was halfway across the bridge.

"Henderson, by all that's holy!"

By the time Henderson had crossed the bridge, Keith

had recovered his composure. He rose and greeted his friend with a handshake.

"And what brings you here?" Henderson asked.

"You do! You're supposed to be dead, old fellow."

"Yes, that's what the Bashiris told me you said," Henderson drawled. "Though I don't know where you got such an idea. Didn't you get my letter?"

"Nothing since—" Keith counted on his fingers. "Since May."

"The devil you say!" For the first time Henderson looked startled. He turned to the tribal elders and harangued them vigorously in Bashiri mixed with a few Scottish curses.

Bridget tugged at Keith's sleeve. "What is he saying?" she whispered.

"Beats me. All I can understand is—"

Bridget nodded. "Yes. I can understand that part too."

"Well, you shouldn't." Keith withdrew his sleeve from her grasp and turned to face Henderson as he concluded his harangue.

"I sent my maps back by one of the Bashiris," Henderson said, more quietly now. "Last month. With a letter to tell you that I would not be back for some while. The bastard charged me for it, too. I had to give him my medicine box and my compass."

"How did you think you were going to make maps without a compass?" Keith asked.

Henderson folded his arms and smiled. "I don't need a compass anymore. I've found it—the pass. It's up there." He pointed in the direction of the snowy ranges beyond the fort. "It's all in my maps." His expression changed. "My maps! The black bastard lost my maps! God damn it, I didn't mind if he drowned his own useless carcass in one of the river gorges, but he lost my maps too!"

"I don't think he did," Keith said. "Your medicine box and compass turned up in the bazaar at Guahipore—or so I was told. I think I know who has your maps. The same man who brought me your other things."

"And who might that be?"

Keith answered with another question. "Do you happen to know whether Afzul-ul-Mulk has any Bashiri connections?"

"His mother was tribal." Henderson clutched at his beard and moaned. "I warned you not to trust him!"

"Trust," Keith said, "has very little to do with it. I suspect that all your messages to me passed through his hands first. The last one he evidently decided to stop altogether. Until . . . now why should your things turn up in the bazaar just now?" He pounded one fist into the palm of his other hand.

"How soon can you be ready to march, Henderson? I don't know what Afzul's game is, but I think we'd better get back to Guahipore as fast as possible."

"Aye," Henderson said slowly and with marked emphasis. "That you had."

"You'll have to come with us. The rumor of your death is Afzul's making—I need you to confront him."

"You can tell him I'm alive and healthy. I stay here."

"You're mad!" Keith sprang at Henderson and caught him by the greasy front of his homespun coat. At once half a dozen muskets were leveled at Keith's head. He dropped the coat and fell back a pace.

"No, lad," Henderson said. "I'm sane. And I don't much count on getting my maps back from Afzul. There's only two places in the world where the knowledge of that pass exists in a manner that can be

206

interpreted by a civilized man. One is on my maps and the other is here."

He tapped his head and grinned. "If I go back to Guahipore, Afzul may just think that he'd benefit by reducing the number of places by one. And as I prefer my head in its present condition, I think I'll just stay here with my friends the Bashiris until things in Guahipore are sorted out."

"You just told me that Afzul's a Bashiri too," Keith reminded him. "If he could stop your messages getting to me, aren't you afraid he could get to you here?"

Henderson grinned. "These folk set good store by hospitality. I've eaten salt with them. More than that, I'm an honorary Bashiri."

With a dramatic gesture, he pulled off his dirty woolen hat to reveal a puckered line of crisscross scars across his forehead. Bridget felt sick at the sight of the half-healed incisions.

"Good God, man!" Keith exclaimed. "How could you do that? What kind of a game are you playing?"

The grin left Henderson's face. "No game, Powell. I respect these people, and they respect me. This is where I belong. No . . . I'll trust in my friends' hospitality. And if you've got any sense, you'll do the same. What odds is it if Afzul is the next mehtar?"

"Not much to you, maybe," said Keith. "Something to me. I like the mehtar, and I like these people. They deserve better than whatever Afzul's cooking up." He took Bridget's hand, squeezing it so fiercely that she almost cried out. "Come on, my love. We've a long march to make before night."

Keith set a punishing pace on the return, intent on getting back to Guahipore as quickly as possible. There were no more halts to admire a striking vista or to rest in one of the infrequent mountain meadows. They marched until dark and halted only when they could no longer see the path before them.

Bridget was almost too tired to eat the unappetizing mess of boiled grain and salty butter which was all they had, since Keith had been moving too fast to hunt game for the evening pot. She took the bowl and choked down a few mouthfuls, then set it aside. She felt like one solid ache from neck to toes, too tired even to rest. She leaned back against a blanket roll and tried to relax, but could not find a comfortable position for her aching muscles.

Keith put his arm about her shoulders and pulled her close to him. "Lean on me."

"You're not much softer than the ground," Bridget teased. "All bone and muscle."

"Yes, but I appreciate you more than the ground does." He rubbed the back of her neck in long, soothing circles. "I'm a lucky man. Not many women would have managed such a long march at all, let alone without whining."

"Oh, I whine," Bridget said. "I just don't open my mouth when I do it!"

Keith burst out laughing. She felt invigorated by his praise, eager to earn more and to prove herself in some new way. Even her aches seemed to be less now. She took up the bowl of porridge and finished off the cold scraps with a good appetite.

"Sometimes I feel guilty, though," Keith said. "After all, you had a comfortable life in Ireland. And because of coming out to me, first you lost your aunt and uncle, then I dragged you off to the edge of the world to play hide-and-go-seek with Bashiri tribesmen. It's not much of a life for a gently bred young lady. Do you ever think about your life before you came to India?"

Bridget glanced at him, uneasy at something in his tone. His eyes were gleaming in the moonlight and he was rocking back and forth slightly as he awaited her answer.

"Never," she said firmly. "You are my life now."

"But you must miss the dear old days in Ballycrochan and Dublin," Keith pressed.

The clear, cold moonlight gave his face almost a sinister cast. Why was he looking at her with that expectancy? Bridget glanced around her for some distraction. The cold white light illumined every crack and crevice of the cliff by which they were resting. She had the feeling it was showing the doubt and fear on her face just as clearly.

Moonlight!

"Look, Keith." She pointed down the path, now a white streak clearly outlined against the black shadows of the cliffs. "The moon has risen. I believe we can make another stage tonight."

Keith nodded and slowly rose to his feet. "Yes . . . yes, of course, we must move on."

Thank God, there was no chance for conversation on the trail. They had to go in single file and give all their attention to where they were stepping. After a mile Bridget's weariness returned, but not for worlds would she have given in now. Not when Keith had praised her for going on as she had—and not when he was in such an inconvenient, reminiscing mood! She could only hope that by the time they camped for the night he would be too tired for conversation. It made her nervous when he wanted to talk about Ireland.

Two hours later Bridget was so tired she could only

think of putting one foot in front of the other. She plodded along with her head down, watching the hypnotic movement of her own legs in the dusty folds of her divided skirt. Keith's outstretched arm stopped her without warning.

"Look!" He drew her close to him and pointed out across the river gorge.

They had been traversing a half-circle round an outcropping hill, so that the path here faced almost back the way they had come. The white peaks of the Hindu Kush rose in the distance, gleaming pale and unattainable above the clouds. At their feet, the moon-light shining on mist and spray from the river created a series of ghostly rainbows, shimmering webs of pale color. And just ahead, the torches of the bearers setting up camp were a cluster of firefly points of light shining through the mist.

Bridget turned her face up to Keith's, speechless with the beauty of the moment. Now she felt that she could meet his eyes. The mountains made them all equal.

And now, too, he no longer had that strange half-smile on his lips, that almost hostile look. She saw nothing now in his eyes but love for her and the mountains, so mingled that she hardly knew which was which.

She pressed her lips gently to his cheek. His arms tightened about her and she felt the hardness of his limbs against her.

"The tent is ready," he murmured in her ear.

Hand in hand they moved over the last steps of rough ground to the single-poled tent that the bearers had erected.

Inside there was barely room to stand at the center. Bridget stripped off her travel-worn clothes and crawled between the blankets, shivering at the cold touch of the fabric on her naked skin. When Keith joined her, she huddled gratefully into his warmth.

"So tired," she protested when his hands began roving over her body, exploring the peaks and valleys that he knew best of all.

"Mmm. I won't do anything you don't want," he promised, slipping one arm about her waist. His free hand caressed the swell of her buttocks, lingering for tantalizing moments in the hollow of her thighs and then passing on down her legs. "Do your legs ache? Shall I rub them for you?"

Bridget sighed with contentment and rolled over on her stomach. Keith's hands passed up and down her legs, kneading the aching muscles into peace and arousing flickering nerve endings that she had thought too tired to respond. As his hands moved higher, pressing more intimately, she let her thighs open for his caresses. He moved on, stroking her bottom and back, and she whimpered an involuntary protest.

"Ah!" Keith's soft, exultant laugh was a cry of conquest. He shifted his weight, knelt between her parted thighs and pulled the blanket over them both with one hand. His other hand was darting between her thighs now, opening her where she was moist and ready to receive him; then she felt the warmth of his body all up and down her back and his hardness against her. She tried to turn over but he held her down, very gently, stroking her and murmuring love words into her ear.

Then his hand was under her, urging her up, half onto her knees, and he slid into the opening thus offered and his hand in front added its pressure against her most sensitive parts as he plunged into her from behind and her world exploded in a shower of lights and warmth flooding her and she cried out under him and felt his thrusts deep inside her. He collapsed over her, warming her body with his own, and they fell asleep still entwined, sharing warmth and love in a unity too deep for speech.

Keith was up and moving again before it was light. Bridget ached all over when she moved, but she crawled out of the nest of blankets and helped him to roll them up again by feel. She hurried into her stiff, dirty clothes in the dark, feeling colder than before at the touch of the night-chilled fabric against her skin.

In the gray chill just before dawn they shared hot unsweetened tea in brass cups and shivered before the winds that came down from the high peaks where snow lies year-long.

They were only half a day's march from the place where the horses waited; perhaps less. Back in Guahipore, there'd be no time to talk. Bridget watched the first light illuminating the mountains. They seemed to glow with their own light, while here where they sat—though still high above the river—the world was still and dark.

Now, she thought. Now, if ever, she could find the courage to make her confession; in this world apart from the world, with the memory of his loving still warm about her. Here there seemed nothing intrinsically wrong in her impersonation of Charlotte. It was merely the road she had had to take that led to Keith.

She set down her empty brass cup, carefully, on the stone ledge. She turned to Keith, her lips opening on the confession that would have to change everything between them.

Before she could utter the first word, he had taken her hands and begun talking. And then she no longer wished to tell him.

"You wondered why I was angry at Henderson yesterday," he said. "I couldn't tell you then. I was . . . it hurt too much, seeing what he'd done. Now I think I understand, and I want to make you understand."

Keith stood up and paced a few steps on the mountain ledge, staring out across the gorge at the pink- and rose-tinged glory of the Hindu Kush. "It's not just that he won't help me in Guahipore. It's that . . . oh, hell! He was my friend . . . I trusted that man. And now he's gone crazy. Look at him! Wandering around in the mountains without his compass, getting his forehead tattooed and pretending to be a Bashiri chief."

He rubbed his own forehead with a bemused look. "How can he do that? You can't simply throw away your breeding, your whole culture and put on fancy-dress and live in somebody else's world. I don't care if he gets himself tattooed and scarified from neck to ankles, he is not one of them and never will be. Can't he see that? What the hell does he think he's doing?"

Bridget released her hands and picked up her brass cup from the ledge. The cup made a tiny metallic clink against the stone.

Not one of them—and never would be. Well, there was her answer, and she hadn't even had to ask the question.

"I suppose he is doing what he must," she said. "Like all of us. Have you finished your tea? The bearers are ready."

Once in Guahipore, there was no time to talk, and Bridget was glad of it.

By hard marching and some harder riding, they reached the city just before night. This time there was no procession of warriors to greet them, no formal reception at the mehtar's palace. The city was like a pot boiling over with people shouting and chanting in the streets. They went unchallenged at the gate; there was no one guarding the walls.

Bridget was astonished to hear familiar accents in the noise of the crowd. If she hadn't known better, she would have thought someone was shouting in a thick Irish brogue.

She peered through the mob of figures and saw two redcoated soldiers, half unbuttoned, swaggering down the street with their arms round dancing girls in flimsy gauze.

"Look, Keith!" She pointed.

"I see," Keith muttered. "Redcoats. Damn!" His hand clenched round the reins of his horse. "I need to get to the mehtar—find out what's been happening."

He glanced at Bridget, and his thoughts were as clear as if he'd spoken them aloud. He regretted having brought her with him, regretted her presence at this moment and the necessity of escorting her home before he could go to request an audience with the mehtar.

She spoke before he could. "Go on. I can find my own way to the compound."

"Are you sure? I don't like to—"

"Go on." She gave him a playful push. "The crowd's in a good mood—can't you see? Don't I go to the bazaar with only Mirza beside me? What harm can I come to with eight bearers, two baggage rolls, a tent and three wicker baskets around me?"

Keith laughed unwillingly. "All right . . . if you're sure?"

But he had turned his horse's head even before she nodded.

At the time, Bridget was sure enough. The shouting, merrymaking crowd might be a little rough around the edges, but she'd seen worse at the fair in Ireland many a year. One thing you had to say for Moslems, she thought, forcing her reluctant horse through the crowd. They didn't drink.

Two streets further on and she was beginning to regret her certainty. The mob might be mostly good-humored, but they were excitable, and they were beginning to take sides. Bridget saw fights breaking out here and there, and almost always one of the fighters was a Bashiri with the distinctive line of forehead tattoos, and the other was a Guahi.

She had become separated from the bearers almost at once; a horse cleared a better space than a man on foot could manage, and the men had been inexorably pushed back from her by an ever-widening stream of revelers. Bridget clamped her knees against the horse's sides and thanked all the saints she'd talked Keith into letting her ride without a sidesaddle. She would never have managed the beast in all this crowd if she'd been perched up at an angle like a lady.

At the opening to the next alley, a stream of redcoats poured into the main street and pushed her and the horse against the wall. The horse jibbed and rolled its eyes nervously, and Bridget realized that she didn't have so much control over the animal even now. Also, Moslems might not drink, but English soldiers certainly did. Where had they found the stuff? The fumes of raw liquor were so strong about them that they made her dizzy.

One of the soldiers lunged for her bridle. His other hand clawed at her skirt. He was shouting something, his words all but lost in the noise of the crowd. Bridget screamed as the horse reared and came down with its front hooves square in the man's face; screamed again as it went up again and she felt herself sliding back, losing her balance in the air.

"Infidel dogs! Back!"

The words were accompanied with the crack of a whiplash. Bridget's horse came down again with a hand cruelly yanking its headstall, and stood passive, shivering and sweating. The soldiers scrambled out of the way, and two Bashiris dragged the fallen man back into the alley.

Afzul-ul-Mulk, mounted on his gray stallion, released her horse's head.

"I will escort you to your compound," he announced.

"Wait!" But they were already moving on down the street. Bridget peered behind her. "We can't just ride off like that."

"We cannot stay," Afzul corrected her. "The streets are not safe for you today."

Bashiri riders closed in behind her, cutting off her view of the alley.

"But that man—"

"My servants will take care of him." Afzul shot her a glance. "Strange, that he should have attacked you so. Did you by any chance hear what he was shouting?"

"No," Bridget lied. "I . . . suppose he was drunk."

"I suppose so," Afzul agreed.

"I was surprised to see you back in Guahipore so soon," he went on, pacing his stallion beside her as though they were riding down a quiet country lane. The crowd parted without difficulty to let them through. "I am also surprised to see that your husband permits you to ride through the streets alone at a time like this.

Perhaps there are some flaws with the way the British treat their women?"

His smile did not quite reach his eyes.

He was elegant as ever, today in flowing blue cloak and gray velvet tunic and breeches, with the blue sapphire glittering at his throat in its setting of gold. Beside him, Bridget felt even more dirty and disheveled than she surely was.

"I am grateful for your help," she said finally.

Afzul made an airy gesture with his free hand. "Oh . . . the soldiers? Think nothing of it. My nation deals differently with both women and soldiers than does yours. But there is really nothing to it."

His eyes were fastened on her face, seeming to penetrate to the very core of her being. "It is merely a question of knowing when to apply the whip."

They were at the gate to the compound. Bridget slid off her horse unaided and called for Daud to stable the animal. She held up one hand to Afzul. "Thank you again," she said. "I will not keep you. I am sure you have pressing duties elsewhere."

Afzul's hand captured hers and slid up to her wrist. He held her arm lightly, but with enough strength that she knew she could not break his grip. He turned his hand a fraction of an inch, and she was forced to step closer to his side. The gray stallion stood perfectly still even when she was so close that her breast touched its side.

"Perfect!" Afzul murmured, looking down from his saddle. "Quite perfect! The training is all."

Bridget stared back up, willing herself not to drop her eyes before his burning gaze.

"As it happens," Afzul said, "for today you are correct. Your husband's sudden return might possibly

. . . inconvenience me. But I am sure that these details can be adjusted. When my 'pressing duties' permit, I will call on you again. In the meantime . . ."

He felt in his tunic and pulled out the sapphire pendant, a gleaming blue eye set in a teardrop of gold.

"In the meantime, you may wear this for me."

He tossed the jewel in a glittering arc through the air. It fell on Bridget's neck, slipped coldly down across her skin and under the neckline of her dress and came to rest between her breasts.

Chapter Sixteen

KEITH'S ATTEMPTS TO FIND OUT WHAT WAS HAPPENING IN Guahipore kept him away longer than he had planned.

First there was the frustration of finding out that the mehtar had secluded himself in his palace and refused to see him.

"He thinks you are responsible for the soldiers' coming," Hamed, the Mehtar's oldest son, told him.

"And you?"

Hamed gave Keith a level, penetrating look. "If I believed that, you would not have lived to reenter the city . . . no. You are my friend and the friend of Guahipore. I know who brought the redcoats here."

"Afzul?"

Hamed's face shuttered. "Go talk to your English colonel."

The army was encamped on the plain just south of Guahipore. By the time Keith had ridden there, it was dark. He frowned at the disorderly appearance of the camp, with tents half-pitched, draught animals staked randomly among the tents and many soldiers obviously drunk around their campfires.

With this as prelude, he was not surprised when the commanding officer turned out to be Colonel Faraday. He remembered the colonel from his service in the Sikh wars. Faraday had been only a major then, but he had managed to lose more men in reconnoitering expeditions than other officers had lost in pitched battle. Clearly the colonel's military skills had not improved in the meantime.

His interview with Colonel Faraday did nothing to soothe his ruffled temper.

"Punitive expedition, m'boy." Faraday leaned back on his folding campchair and lit a cheroot. "Damned natives can't go murdering our explorers and get away with it, can they now?"

"Henderson's alive." Keith was barely able to hold his anger in check. How dared this blustering career officer march in and destroy the good relations he had worked so hard to build up! "I spoke with him myself not two days ago."

"Ah. Bring him back with you, did you?"

Keith shook his head. "No. He was . . . concerned about the maps and letters he sent to me, which seem to have miscarried. He wanted to retrace his steps back to the pass."

They argued around this point for some time, Colonel Faraday demanding firm evidence that Henderson was alive and Keith responding that his word as an officer and a gentleman should be enough.

"*Political* officer," Faraday said. "Not meaning to insult you, old boy, but it's not quite the same thing is it, know what I mean?"

With detachment, Keith noted that he was gripping

the front of Faraday's traveling writing table with one hand so hard that the knuckles turned white. "No, Colonel Faraday, I do not know what you mean. I have not resigned my commission with the 16th Lancers. I expect you to accept my word as you would that of any other gentleman in the queen's service."

"Now, now," the colonel soothed between puffs of smoke, "nobody's impugnin' y'r word, m'boy. Just tryin' to get the facts straight. Just look at it from our side."

Faraday leaned forward and took the cheroot out of his mouth, stabbing it forward like a pointer to emphasize his statements. "We hear from a reliable source that Henderson's dead. We send a detachment up here and find that the mehtar can't keep order in his own capital city. Our clear duty is to restore order. Interests of British government require a strong leader on the throne here."

"There was no disorder before your troops arrived," Keith protested. "And you've no business here in the first place. Dammit, I've told you Henderson's alive!"

The colonel leaned back again and laced his fingers over his stomach, giving Keith a benign smile. "So you have, m'boy. So you have. And I'll include that in m'report."

"You will?"

"To be sure." The colonel's smile never faltered. "I'll report that the only person who claims to've seen Henderson alive is a young political officer who's obviously going native."

Faraday waved his cheroot at Keith's travel-stained clothes of native wool, which he had not paused to change before riding out to the camp. "First step," he said. "Seen it often. Start dressing like the natives, thinkin' like them. Next thing you know, the poor chap's taking the native's side against the white man—maybe even concealing evidence. Seen it many a time. No one blames you, m'boy. Sure you do think you saw Henderson. Sunstroke. Mountain fever. Hallucinating. Don't worry about a thing. I'll recommend you for a nice long recuperation in Simla. You'll like that, eh?"

His bland smile infuriated Keith past the point of reasoning. "You're the one who's mad," he said shortly, and made for the tent-flap.

"No, m'boy," the colonel called after him. "I'm the one who's got the army. You think it over."

Keith had ample time to do just that on his cold dark ride back to the city.

"I did everything wrong," he confessed to Bridget that evening.

"I don't see what else you could have done." Bridget called to Mirza to bring up another can of hot water. Having spent two hours soaking the accumulated grime of the journey off herself, she was now ready to start on Keith.

"Faraday hinted that someone from Guahipore has been in correspondence with him. Probably Afzul, but I should have found out for sure."

"It is," Bridget said without thinking. "He told me as much this afternoon."

Keith's head came up so sharply that he almost cracked her on the chin as she was pouring the fresh hot water into the tin bath. "Has he been bothering you?"

"He . . . helped me get home." Bridget's eyes slid to the bed. She had concealed Afzul's sapphire between two folds of a summer dress in a wicker basket under the bed. The secret weighed heavily on her. Should she tell Keith? No. What good would it do for him to get into a fight with Afzul over her? He had enough to worry about now.

And so did she. Afzul's attentions were a minor problem compared to the one that had faced her just before his arrival. Bridget closed her eyes for a moment and prayed for guidance.

Afzul had believed her, when she said she did not hear what the soldier was shouting. And she thought he had not heard, or had not been able to make any sense out of it. So that put the problem off for a little while. Dear God, how long? How badly had the man been hurt when her horse reared? She realized that she was praying he might die of his injuries. She crossed herself and hastily converted her prayer into the general wish for guidance with which she had started.

But she couldn't think of any other solution.

Keith was ready to get out of the bath. Bridget handed him a towel. "Did Colonel Faraday say anything else?"

"Nothing worth repeating." Keith saw how pale and worried his wife looked and forced himself to smile. He hadn't meant to load all his troubles on her shoulders. "But he brought letters with him! Nothing for you, I'm afraid, but I have a good long screed from home. I mean to neglect you shamelessly and indulge myself by reading it tonight."

"Yes," Bridget said. She was relieved that she would not have to make conversation any longer that evening. "Yes, you do that."

She scooped up the damp towels and made her escape down the ladder on the pretext of giving them to Mirza to launder.

Alone in his curtain-partitioned "study," Keith frowned over the lengthy missive he had received from Ireland.

The letter was from his older brother, Neill, heir to

the Powell estates. Neill wrote that he was now completely recovered and there was nothing for Keith to worry about.

"Recovered!" Keith muttered. It was the first he'd heard of any illness.

He scanned the crossed sheet for an explanation.

It seemed that Neill had taken the typhus last year, when he insisted on personally visiting all of their tenants during the epidemic. Typhus had been succeeded by a relapsing brain fever and for some months he had not been expected to live.

"Lord Fitzgerald, whom our father consulted, advised against writing to you then," Neill wrote. "He told Father that he meant to go to India himself, with his family, and that it would be better if he broke the news to you personally. I did not recover my senses until after the Fitzgeralds sailed, and naturally I did not tell Father of my concerns, but I hope this letter reaches you in time. You know how Lady Fitzgerald and Mama were always clucking about the chance of joining our families by getting one of us to marry that poisonous little Charlotte Fitzgerald? I suspect their sudden trip to India is planned to hustle you into marriage on some pretext or other, as when I was so very sick they thought I must die and you would be the next heir. They would be well served if their plan succeeded and they found they'd tied Charlotte to a younger son with no prospects, but I shouldn't like you to have to put up with her—even though it would get her off my back! So watch out, if the Fitzgeralds track you down . . ."

Neill went on to give news of the estate and the crops, news months out of date by now. Keith sat turning the flimsy sheets of paper between his fingers. The letter had come a long and circuitous way to find him. Neill had addressed it to his old regiment in the

Punjab, and from there, to judge by the stained envelope, it must have traveled round half India—arriving far too late.

Too late? Keith laughed. He had needed no words of Neill's to put him on guard against Charlotte Fitzgerald. And no words of Neill's could poison him against the lovely girl he'd found in Charlotte's place . . .

He frowned. Often he'd wondered what could have motivated his wife to masquerade as Charlotte Fitzgerald. Neill's letter provided an unwelcome answer.

The brown-haired girl in the next room had been the only passenger saved from the wreck. But instead of keeping her own identity, she had elected to travel on as Lady Charlotte; facing distance, danger and the perils of a masquerade. Why?

That was the question he had been asking himself ever since it became clear to him that this girl was not Charlotte.

Now he might have an answer, and it was one he hated.

Had she become friends with Charlotte on the steamer, gossiped with her and learned of Charlotte's expectation of marriage to a young man who was the heir to vast estates?

It had already become clear to Keith that his wife, whoever she might be, did not come of the same class as his family and Charlotte's. In itself this mattered little to him, but now he wondered if she had been driven by poverty to this masquerade.

Had she cynically seized the chance offered by the shipwreck to take on Charlotte's identity and Charlotte's expectations?

Keith groaned and fell back into the chair, leaning forward on the rickety wooden table with the letter still crushed in his fist.

A rustling of the curtain behind him warned him that he was no longer alone. He swung round to see his wife standing there, looking the picture of innocence in her long white nightgown with her hair bound into two thick plaits that lay over her breasts.

"Keith, it is late," she said, and there was an undertone of pleading in her voice. "Are you not coming to bed?"

He studied her face. She looked the same as always: wide clear brow, dark eyes, wide generous mouth, firm chin. If he'd seen her on the street, he would have said that this woman was incapable of telling a lie. But as he'd learned to his cost, she was entirely capable of living one.

When he first trapped her into giving him false answers, he was so happy to be sure she really was not Charlotte Fitzgerald that it didn't matter to him who she was or where she'd been. But then he'd thought she really loved him. He'd thought himself the luckiest fellow alive, that such a glorious woman should want him, a mere lieutenant, at the beginning of his career, a second son with no prospects.

And night after night she'd shown just how much she loved him. Her trembling responses, the pliant submission of her body in his arms, the fire with which she returned his caresses—could those be lies?

He pushed the chair back once again, crossed the few feet of space which separated them with two strides and crushed her against him. He could feel the generous curves of her body through the thin nightgown. They inflamed him as they had that first night in Gul Ram's house, when she had been so sweet, so innocently seductive.

That first night. Why had she been waiting there alone? Gul Ram had said she was ill. She wasn't ill. She said she was frightened, she threw herself into his arms, she was wearing next to no underclothing, she had been irresistible.

Had it been chance that brought them together, or a desperate plot made up by her after their quarrel? She must have been taken aback to realize what good reason he had to dislike and distrust Lady Charlotte. Here she'd taken on this impersonation only to discover that Charlotte Fitzgerald was the last woman on earth that Keith Powell would ever marry.

And that very night, they had been thrown together in circumstances that made it all but impossible for him, as a man of honor, to do anything but marry her.

Keith's arms slackened, releasing the beautiful, false creature he called his wife. Tonight he could not assuage his doubts by making love to her.

"Go to bed," he said.

He had not called her "Charlotte" for a long time, and now he could not bring himself to use the love-words he had been in the habit of substituting for her name.

Chapter Seventeen

FOR THE NEXT FEW WEEKS IT SEEMED TO BRIDGET THAT time stood still again, but not as it had in the pleasant days on the pinnace. Now, as the short Guahipore summer faded into a cold autumn with the threat of snow heavy on the air from the mountains, it seemed to her that she and Keith and all those around her had frozen into attitudes of mistrust and waiting.

After the disastrous first days of the army's presence in Guahipore, the mehtar had acted as decisively as he could. He had not the power to force the English soldiers out of his land entirely, but he made it clear that they were not welcome, and requested Colonel Faraday to keep the men out of the city. The Guahis who knew Bridget remained friendly, but a number of the lower sort in the city resented her and Keith and blamed them for the coming of the soldiers. Bridget gave up going to the bazaar altogether, sending Mirza to do the daily shopping for her, and she only visited the zenana when Aziza sent servants with a jampon for her.

Those visits to the zenana were the only bright spots in her long lonely days. Keith had never explained his sudden coldness toward her. During the day he spent most of his time at the mehtar's palace or at the army camp, trying to find some means of reconciling the two sides.

Of his work she knew only that the presence of the army had turned the mehtar against the British, so that he swore he would have no treaty with them nor allow a resident. Only his personal regard for Keith made it possible for Keith to continue his visits. On the other side, Colonel Faraday, having evidently become convinced of the impossibility of a punitive expedition against the Bashiris, had settled down on the plains outside Guahipore with the intention of staying there until the mehtar agreed to his demands for reparations for Henderson's "death" and for permanent treaties.

For Keith, caught between the two sides, it must be an agonizing time. But why should that cause him to turn against her? Bridget wept over his coldness in secret but was afraid to ask him the cause of it. "Afraid of what I might hear," she admitted to Aziza. "What if he has found out what I am and despises me and wants me to go away? I couldn't bear that."

Aziza enveloped her in a scented embrace. "No one could despise you. But I think you ought to tell him. It is not good to lie to a husband—except in small things, which is always necessary!"

"I do not lie to Keith in small things," Bridget said. "Only in this. And I cannot tell him while he is so cold and far away, Aziza! I can't!"

"Wait until he comes to your bed," Amina suggested with a smile. "That is the best time to tell a man anything he may not want to hear—afterward, when he is feeling good—you know?" She brought out a small bottle of gold studded with rubies, and twisted the cap open to release a heavy, cloying jasmine scent. "Here, take some of my perfume and rub it well into your skin, all over. Then he will be unable to resist you."

Bridget took the perfume but could not bring herself to tell even Aziza how little chance she would have to use it. Only once since their return from the hills had Keith shared her bed. That was the night of their return from the mountains, when he sat up late over his letters and came to bed only when she should have been long asleep. And when she put her hand on his shoulder, he gently replaced it, rolled to the far side of the bed and lay rigid and perfectly still until morning.

The next day he had set up a campbed in his study, saying that he expected to be working late until this matter of the army was resolved and that he did not wish to disturb her by coming to bed at odd hours.

The one thing Bridget had cause to be glad of in this period was that the city was closed to English soldiers, except the few who were allowed to come in and buy supplies from the bazaar and the few who sneaked past the guards to buy illegal liquor.

She wondered daily what had become of the man who had accosted her and had been trampled by her horse, but as the weeks dragged past and she heard no more of the incident, she began to believe that he had died of his injuries, or perhaps had concluded that he was mistaken. In the daytime that theory served her well enough, particularly when she reasoned that the city was closed to soldiers and that Colonel Faraday might march his men away soon and there would be no reason to fear another encounter.

But in the nights she started from sleep, crying out in fear as she relived the moments when she had looked down from horseback on a horribly familiar face and had heard John Kelly's drink-coarsened voice shouting, "Biddy! Biddy Sullivan from Ballycrochan!"

It was almost a relief when she heard the hoarse whisper from a sheltered corner of the compound garden. At last it was really upon her, the fate that had been pursuing her in her dreams.

It was a cold gray evening. The fruit trees in the garden had long since dropped their leaves, and the flowering creepers that covered the stone wall were bare, brown stems. There had been nothing to tempt Bridget outside except her own restlessness and loneliness. How had he known she would come?

He was crouching behind a pile of the garden rubbish that had accumulated ever since old Daud, their gate-keeper, had left saying he was afraid to work any longer for the hated feringhis. Bridget lifted her skirts and went to the compound wall to talk with him. She noted in some detached corner of her brain that her hands were icy cold, though she was not conscious of any fear until the moment when she saw his face. Then she started back, feeling sick and frightened.

One eye was gone, the empty socket half-covered by a flap of crudely stitched flesh. The line of stitching extended down his cheek, pulling together the edges of what must have been a ghastly wound—the sort of wound caused by the slashing hooves of a horse. A ragged cloak of native wool half-covered the wounded head and concealed the red soldier's tunic beneath.

"John . . . John Kelly?" she stammered. She'd not

have known him but for the Irish brogue to his voice, and the fact that there was but one man in India who would call her by that name.

The scarred features twisted into a grin. "That's me. John Kelly, factor of Ballycrochan—or what's left of him, once you got done with him! Well, 'Lady Charlotte'? D'you like your work?"

Bridget put up her hands to shield her from the sight. But his voice followed her, merciless, penetrating.

"Wasn't it enough to have me turned off the estate? But no, you had to follow me to India too. You trampled me with your horse, me high and mighty lady, and what your mare's hooves didn't do, your nigger lover and his servants finished. Crippled for life I am."

One clawed hand caught at her skirt, drawing her close to him. Half paralysed with horror, Bridget was powerless to fight him.

"No . . . I didn't . . ." she whispered. How could she communicate with his twisted brain? He blamed her for all his misfortunes. And he had her here, at his mercy.

Looking at his hunched figure, she almost accepted the guilt he wanted to lay on her. Tears misted her eyes. She'd hated and feared John Kelly, the factor of Ballycrochan, for the power he held over her and her family. But he'd been a fine, strong figure of a man in those days, and more than one of her neighbors had told her she was the fool not to take him. Now—

"There was a time when I was so mad for you, I might even ha' married you," came the hoarse whisper, as if he read her thoughts. "And thought I was lowering meself to do it. Now look at us! You're playing the fine lady in silks and satins, and I'm the cripple on the street. But what if I turned it around, eh? What if I turned it around?"

"W-what do you mean?" Bridget stammered. But already she knew and would not admit the knowledge to her heart.

"Your fine officer husband—I'll wager he would pay a pretty penny to know who his wife really is, and where she comes from. And then he'd pay more to stop me spreading the word. Then we'll see! He'll turn you out, Biddy Sullivan, and then I'll be rich, and you'll be on the streets!"

The malicious whisper trailed away into a paroxysm of dry coughs that blended in with the scraping of the bare branches in the wind.

"Rich . . . rich," he whispered in between coughs. And then, holding out one hand, "Give me a drink. Me throat's dry. Give me a drink!"

When Bridget did not answer, he fell to alternately cursing and pleading. She looked at the crippled body and mutilated face that had once housed John Kelly of Ballycrochan, and for all the repulsion and pity she felt, her brain cleared and she knew what to do.

"You want money," she said. "Very well. There's no need for you to be going to my husband. I will pay you."

She felt cold all over now, not just her hands, but her whole body turning to ice so that she could not be hurt by this creature at all, could not even be touched by him. She would do what was necessary, and he would go away, and she would not think about it ever again, she promised herself.

He waited in the garden while she went inside. Mirza was cleaning in the bedroom, and she had to make an excuse to send her away while she got the housekeeping money out of the locked chest where they kept their valuables. She put aside a few rupees for immediate expenses, closed and locked the chest with meticulous care and went back into the winter-dark garden where John Kelly was waiting for her with his brain full of hate and drink.

"This is all the money I have." She raised the bag of rupees so that he could hear them chink. He snatched at it greedily.

"Not enough, not enough!" he complained. "You can do better than that, me fine lady."

Bridget shook her head. "My husband keeps the money. I have only enough for housekeeping." She prayed it might be enough.

"Not enough," Kelly grumbled again. But he stuffed the bag into his coat pocket and patted it two or three times. "You'd best have more . . . next time. Sleep well, 'Lady Charlotte!'"

He hobbled away into the darkness, laughing as he went.

But Bridget did not sleep well—that night, or the next, or the next.

There could never have been a worse time to make her confession to Keith. He was being punctiliously correct, polite, yet always somehow distant from her. After a few very polite repulses, she had learned not to touch him. They managed their life in the large downstairs room and the curtain-partitioned upstairs so that she never brushed against him, even accidentally, never needed his hand to steady her on the ladder, never undressed before him.

And yet, there were times when she felt a burning sensation and looked up to find his eyes on her with a longing, questioning look that melted all the anger she felt at his sudden, unjust coldness.

She wondered if he was remembering more things about the Charlotte Fitzgerald he had known in Ireland. Perhaps those letters home had reminded him of that Charlotte; perhaps he was thinking it had been a mistake ever to marry her.

Sometimes in the evenings, when he was staring into the fire, she wanted to kneel beside him, her head on his lap, and tell him the whole story. She bitterly regretted that she had not done so earlier, when he seemed to love her. Now it would be a thousand times harder. The way he retreated whenever she made a gesture toward him stopped her from confiding anything at all.

Or perhaps it wasn't that that stopped her, but the memory of his anger at Henderson. "He's not one of them and he never will be. How can he delude himself like that?"

Bridget remembered the scorn in his voice. Would he feel that way about her too? She wasn't one of his kind, for all they'd been born of the same race and in the same land. Not one of them, and never would be. She didn't dare risk hearing that from him. Better to wait out this unhappy time. After all, what was bothering him might have nothing at all to do with her. He had enough other things to worry about, goodness knows!

When the whispers began again, she bitterly regretted that she hadn't told him the truth.

For several days after John Kelly's visit she had avoided the garden because of the unpleasant memories it contained. But eventually boredom and inactivity drove her out to walk again. And on the second evening, she heard the whisper.

"Biddy Sullivan! Biddy Sullivan!"

He looked even worse, if possible, than the last time she had seen him.

"The pain from me wounds is somethin' cruel," he

whispered. "I need a drink, Biddy, I need the drink, and these beggars charge more than I can give them out o' me pay."

"Of course they do," Bridget said. The calm of hopelessness settled on her. "Isn't it against the mehtar's laws to make or sell alcohol? Of course they charge you the high price for it, and them risking to have the hands chopped from their arms if they're caught."

John Kelly gave a hacking, dry laugh. "Was there ever a worse country for a man with me besettin' sin? God's truth, Biddy, if I could see ould Ireland once more, I'd die happy."

Hope flashed before Bridget, as bright as the jewel Afzul had once given her. She forced herself to speak slowly. "You'd never desert from the army?"

"Wouldn't I just?" The cripple laughed again. "An' what has the army given me, but flogging and exile? I'd desert me own mother for a chance to get out of this devil-dry land again."

The remains of John Kelly gave a ghostly chuckle. "Your money would have lasted longer, Biddy Sullivan, but the whore as bought the drink for me did me a rare favor. Stole the rest of the money when I was drunk and dumped me back in the camp. Forty lashes for breakin' bounds! And forty more for drunkenness." He ripped off his shirt and showed her the black clots on his back.

Bridget closed her eyes, sickened by the sight. Her head was whirling. If only she could sit down for a moment! She held onto a branch of a tree, clutching it so hard that the sharp stubs on the branch dug into her hands and the pain helped her concentrate. "If I get you money, will you go?"

Kelly nodded.

"I don't believe it. You'll drink it up again." She closed her eyes again and tried to think. "I will hire a jampon and bearers for you. I will give the bearer some money for you—you may see it—but I'll tell him not to let you have it until you are in the plains. Then it will be up to you. You can drink yourself to death there, or you can get home to Ireland."

"All one to you, eh?" He cackled obscenely.

"You are perfectly right." Bridget felt that coldness stealing through her veins again. It steadied her and helped her to think. "It's nothing to me what happens to you, so you leave me in peace. But if you don't take the fine chance when it's before you, don't be thinking you'll live to spread tales to my man. I have friends here in the city. Do you understand?"

Kelly nodded. "Yes. I heard about you takin' up with the black as had me beaten. Bazaar says he's wanted you for a long time. You pay him good for his services?" He spat in the dust at her feet. "And how do I know you've got the money for me, eh? Maybe you're just puttin' me off so you can have me killed. You told me that sack of rupees was all you had. Maybe I ought to go to your man now."

"He'll pay you nothing," Bridget said. She folded her hands. "It's the free choice I'm offering you, John Kelly, and nothing more. Which do you want more—revenge, or your passage home?"

There was a silence broken only by the harsh cry of migrating birds overhead. "Show me the color of your money," Kelly said at last. "Then I'll wait—maybe!" He cackled. "And maybe not. Do you good, my fine lady, to wait and wonder every day until you've got me safe out of here."

"Wait here," Bridget said.

She hurried into the house and scrambled up the ladder to her bedroom. There was one thing left to her with which to bargain for her life. The sapphire Afzul-ul-Mulk had given her the day they returned from the mountains.

He had not visited the house since then, and she had managed to forget the veiled promises and threats of that day. The sapphire had been tucked away where she need not see it, waiting for a good chance to tell Keith—a chance that had never come, now that he was so cold and distant.

Keith was in the study, bent over his reports as usual. She knelt beside the bed and reached under, feeling with shaking fingers for the hard lump that was the sapphire hidden among her summer dresses. There! It seemed to burn her palm. She closed her fingers over it and started down the ladder before Keith could come out and ask her what she was doing. As her feet touched the dirt floor of the bottom room, she heard his chair scrape overhead. Mary Mother, let him not take a notion to come and take a turn in the garden now!

But she knew he would not—not so long as she was there. It was a bitter knowledge that gave her safety.

Kelly was still crouched in the corner. She stood a few paces away from him and opened her hand. "There. Now do you believe I can get the money?"

Kelly sucked in his breath at the sight of the glittering jewel. "Let me see that!"

He made a grab for it. Bridget closed her hand and jumped away, but not before his hand caught the trailing fringe of her overskirt. He jerked her back with a mad strength that caused her to lose her balance and fall against him in a parody of an embrace. His free hand fumbled against her body until he caught her hand, closed over the sapphire. He twisted her wrist until shooting pains stabbed up her arm. Her numbed fingers opened and the sapphire fell to the ground. Kelly pressed her against the garden wall with his body while he stooped and picked it up.

"Just like old times, eh, Biddy?" he whispered. "Give us a kiss for old times' sake?"

Cripple though he was, he was still a large, powerful man. She was crushed between him and the wall. The smell of him, unwashed and stale with drink, filled her nostrils.

When the pressure relaxed and Kelly fell backward away from her, she stared uncomprehending at Keith's face.

With one hand in Kelly's collar, Keith threw him to the ground. He sprawled full-length on the garden path and the sapphire fell from his hands, bouncing across the sand in a glittering blue arc. Keith snatched it up before Kelly could catch it.

"So!" His voice was cold with disgust. "Afzul-ul-Mulk's sapphire." He threw the pendant back onto the ground as though it were a thing of no consequence. "Take this back to your master," he told Kelly. He drew back his foot as if to speed him on his way with a kick, and Kelly scrambled away into the shadows, the pendant dangling from his fist by its chain.

He turned to Bridget. "At least I am spared the final humiliation of trying to guess who your lover is. Do you feel such great fondness for him, that you embrace the messenger too?"

His face was hard as though cast in bronze, his eyes colder than the snow on the mountains. He spoke almost mechanically, as though the effort of dragging the words out was too much for him. Bridget could sense the agony of betrayal he must be suffering.

"But why?" she whispered, putting up her hands as if to ward off a blow that never came. Why should he be so quick to assume that she had betrayed him? But she realized that all the circumstances were against her. "Keith, it's not . . . not what it seems."

Keith folded his arms. "All right. Tell me what it is."

He waited. Bridget's eyes darted from one corner to another of the garden. Now she realized what a trap she'd gotten herself into. How could she tell him the truth?

What else could she tell him?

"That man . . . is one of the British soldiers," she began. "You remember the crowd that was in the streets the day we came back? You left me to go to the mehtar's palace, and I came home alone."

"My first mistake," Keith said. "Yes, I remember. You even told me how Afzul had escorted you home. Was that when it started?"

"No!" Bridget cried out. "It's not that at all, Keith. Keith, you must listen to me, I'm beggin' you!" Her hands went out of their own volition to clasp him. He removed them like poisonous insects and stepped back, separating himself from her. A fine sleeting rain began, ignored by both of them.

"That man—he was drunk—he frightened my horse and made her rear. She trampled him. Afzul came along then and helped me get home safely, so I never knew what happened to the soldier. Then he came here, begging. I felt sorry for him, and it was my horse that injured him, so I wanted to give him something."

There, all that was true enough. Bridget waited,

hearing only the fine needles of the rain falling against the back of her dress.

"And you just happened to have a valuable sapphire pendant of Afzul-ul-Mulk's to give him." Keith's voice was light, mocking, with an undercurrent of intolerable anguish. "Go on. You are so good at making up stories—I am sure you can explain why you never mentioned a little thing like Afzul's having given you his sapphire."

Bridget felt a betraying flush spread over her face and neck. "Maybe I never mentioned it because I was afraid you would be feeling this way," she said. "As it happens he gave it to me on the day we returned from the mountains."

"Oh—the same day this soldier is supposed to have attacked you," Keith mocked. "My, you certainly have an interesting life the moment I take my eyes off you, don't you?"

A thunderclap and a flash of lightning heralded the onset of the real downpour. The rain thundered about them, drumming on the roof and the garden path, beating Bridget's hair into a damp mass plastered about her neck and cheeks. Keith caught her arm in a bruising grip. "Come along inside, *wife*," he shouted over the rain. "I can see that if I want to keep you, I'll have to build a zenana like the mehtar's, with locked gates and eunuchs standing guard. But until I can manage that little construction project, our bedroom will have to do."

He dragged her inside, stumbling over the sandy path, and pushed her up the ladder ahead of him. Drenched and shivering, Bridget faced him in the bedroom.

"Take those things off," Keith said. His voice was

gentler, and he reached out to brush the wet curls away from her face. "You'll catch cold."

Bridget stripped off her wet garments and rubbed herself dry with the coarse towel that Keith handed to her. But when she reached for a wrapper, his hand fell on her arm and restrained her.

"No," he said. "I might as well see what Afzul is buying." His own clothes were still dripping wet, and his dark hair was plastered to his forehead by the rain, and the hands on her were cold and wet.

Bridget stared at the wall behind his head as his eyes scorched every inch of her.

"Yes," he said finally. "Well worth a sapphire."

"Keith." Bridget had to try again. "Keith, please believe me. You are making a mistake. There is nothing between Afzul and me."

"No?" Keith seemed almost amused. "Do you really think I haven't noticed the way he looks at you? He's wanted you since the day we came to Guahipore. But until now, I thought my *virtuous* wife had resisted his advances." His hands gripped her shoulders, forcing her back and down onto the bed. Still fully clothed and soaked from the rainstorm, he leaned over her like an avenging figure out of her nightmares.

"Go on," he invited her. "Tell me again that Afzul has never touched you."

Bridget remembered the day when Afzul had thrown the sapphire between her breasts. His hand about her arm, drawing her to stand beside his horse; his eyes stripping her. She felt herself condemned by her own blushes, her own silence. She began to shiver with cold, but she could not move to cover herself.

Keith lifted a coarse gray blanket from the pile at the foot of the bed and put it round Bridget's shoulders with an unexpectedly tender gesture. She remembered the day he had put the Kashmiri shawl round her the same way, in the Lanyers' garden in Calcutta. That was how it had begun. And was this the ending? Tears streaked down her face.

"I thought you loved me," Keith said. His voice was quiet, almost reminiscent. "I thought myself the luckiest fellow in the world—couldn't understand what you saw in me. Then Neill's letter came."

Bridget looked at him with blank surprise. "Who the divil may Neill be?" she demanded. "Another of these lovers you're after inventin' for me?"

Keith grasped her shoulders and shook her until the blanket slid down about her waist. "You know perfectly well who Neill is!" he shouted.

"The divil I do!" Bridget shouted back. She clawed at his face. Keith caught her wrists and forced her hands together, holding them with one hand and pushing her backward onto the bed.

"My older brother, Neill," he informed her between clenched teeth. "*That* Neill. The one who was like to die of the typhus last year. Only Lord and Lady Fitzgerald thought they could bring their niece out to India and get her married to me, quick, before I found out I was the new heir to the estate."

His body, still clothed in the dripping wet uniform, pressed into hers, branding her with the imprint of stiff fabric and cold metal buttons.

"It didn't work," he said. "Neill's going to live. So you haven't married money, my dear. You've only tied yourself to a poor devil of a junior political officer. There'll be no rich lands at home, no linen tablecloth and Waterford glasses and milady's carriage. Only a series of posts like this one, off in the back of beyond with a mud-floored house."

"Keith," Bridget gasped. His weight was crushing

her. "Keith, I don't understand. This is all I want! What are you going on about crystal and linen for?" Perhaps he was going mad. His face seemed awfully red. Fearful, she tried to wriggle out from under him, but his hand crushed her wrists together and his body held her prisoner against the bed.

"All you want?" Keith laughed. "No doubt that explains why you were so quick to console yourself with Afzul-ul-Mulk."

"Keith, I didn't!" Bridget almost shrieked. "Please, please believe me—"

His hand tightened about her wrists until she gave an involuntary squeak of pain. Mary Mother, but the bones would be crushed for sure!

He let her go and swung away from the bed. Trembling with fear and outrage, Bridget sat up again, pulling the coarse blanket up over her breasts.

"I hurt you." Keith's voice was muffled. Head down, he leaned against the wall and pounded the window frame with one fist. "I never meant to do that. But how can I believe you, when you've been lying to me all along?"

Bridget tucked the blanket under her arms and tiptoed across the floor to him. "I never meant to hurt you, either, Keith," she whispered. Now she would have to tell him everything, right from the beginning. At least let him hate her for the right thing, instead of torturing himself with these stories about Afzul and God knew who else.

He turned and took her in his arms, and Bridget gasped at the look of agony imprinted on his face. "Keith, I have to tell you—"

"No!" His arms tightened about her. "No more words. We hurt each other too much with words. Whatever you've done, I don't want to know about it."

His kisses were burning hot against her cold lips. Bridget kissed him back with all the hunger and desire and fear that was in her. At least in this they could still be together—his hands on her, her body pressed to his. She reached up and put her arms around his neck and the blanket slipped to the floor between them.

Chapter Eighteen

KEITH ROSE EARLY, DRESSED AND LEFT THE HOUSE THE next morning before his wife was awake, with no particular object except that of avoiding talking with her. He felt the need to be alone until he could sort out his feelings. He felt he had been unjust to her, leaping to conclusions the way he had. Evidence or no evidence, he would swear she had always been true to him.

But then—wouldn't he swear to her truth in anything? And he knew for a fact she was lying to him about her identity.

Moody, confused, Keith was in no spirits to try to sort things out right then. But it did occur to him, as he climbed quietly down the ladder that connected their bedroom with the ground floor of the house, that she might be just a little bit annoyed with him for the way he'd assumed her infidelity. And one thing he did know about this woman he'd married. She was not one to sit passively by and let things happen to her. Look at the way she'd run away, that time in Calcutta!

Keith chuckled at the memory. Setting out with a Kashmir shawl, an old Hindustani grammar and a conch shell, to make her own way in India! Only his luck and her ignorance of the land, which had forced her to Gul Ram for help, had enabled him to get her back that time. If she took it into her head to pull the same trick today, there was no telling where he'd find her! The mehtar's zenana, most likely.

It would be a severe embarrassment, to say the least, to have to petition the mehtar for the return of his wife. Keith considered the problem, then took steps to make sure that he would not have to worry about his wife's whereabouts until he was ready to talk with her. Mirza and the cook watched with approbation. At last the feringhi was treating his wife as a proper man ought to!

Keith felt a little better after he had solved his immediate problem. Perhaps a good ride in the morning air would clear his head and help him find the way to approach Charlotte. He had his horse brought round and went out of the city by the south gate for a good gallop on the plain between the city walls and the army camp. As he rode, the problem came back to him in its full force. Could he really trust his instincts? He knew so little, really, about her!

She had been lying to him since they met; that lie he had excused all these months, but didn't it show how little regard she had for the truth and how little she was to be trusted? And hard on the heels of an explanation for that lie—while he was still trying to convince himself she had not married him for his inheritance—he had surprised her in a secret tryst with a man who bore Afzul's token. Keith's hands tightened about the reins at the memory.

Against his anger, the memory of her face filled his eyes. Every instinct told him that she was true and honest. Only the facts told him the opposite. He would have to be rational, forget his instincts, forget the way she'd followed him uncomplainingly into this strange and frightening land—

Keith's fist crashed down upon the pommel of his saddle, startling the horse beneath him. "No, by God, I won't!" he exclaimed.

He could not condemn her unheard. He would talk to her tonight. It was time all the lies were out; he would tell her all that he knew or guessed and let her tell him the rest. The woman he had known and loved all these months *could not* be the scheming female of his imagination. There had to be another side to the story. And if he could only get her to listen to him, assure her of his forgiveness no matter what she had done in that past life she was trying so desperately to conceal, perhaps she would finally trust him enough to tell him her side.

Keith turned his horse's head back toward the city. But in that very moment a shout split the air.

"Powell! Come to mess with us?"

It was Dan Weaver, Colonel Faraday's aide-de-camp, also out for a morning ride. In a matter of moments he was at Keith's side, telling him the latest gossip of the camp and issuing a pressing invitation to breakfast with him and the colonel.

One word in the stream of gossip caught Keith's ear. "Afzul-ul-Mulk? What of him?"

"Why, you know the colonel has been treating with Afzul," Dan said. "He thinks, since the mehtar remains obdurate, it is time to replace him and Afzul is the logical candidate. Wouldn't you agree?"

Keith's lips tightened. "Translation," he said, "Afzul

has scared Faraday into thinking the Russians mean to march over that pass Henderson has discovered and cozened him into thinking that he will be true to British interests in that eventuality."

"What pass?"

Keith drew rein sharply and half-turned in his saddle to stare at Dan. "You mean Afzul hasn't mentioned Henderson's maps?"

"What maps?"

Keith felt the smooth motion of the horse under him speeding up in response to his tightened knees. All at once he felt gloriously alive. The whole plot was unfolding before him, and he was in the right place to stop it with a word. "Dan, I think I'll accept that invitation to breakfast. I have something to say to Colonel Faraday."

The horse sprang forward at a touch, and Keith felt a sense of limitless, intoxicating power in the few minutes of the smooth gallop across the plain.

He should have known that he would have no effect.

"Interestin' story, m'boy." Colonel Faraday leaned back in his grossly overburdened camp chair, still holding the leg of cold chicken on which he had been gnawing while Keith poured out his theory. If Afzul had not mentioned the maps, didn't that prove his double-dealing? He must have been corresponding with the Russians at the same time, ready to sell the maps to the pass to whichever side helped put him on the mehtar's throne.

"No evidence." The Colonel belched and held out his empty glass for the refill that was silently provided by a white-robed servant in a corner of the mess tent.

Keith stared. "What do you mean, no evidence? His failure to produce the maps is proof enough!"

"Ah, yes. These maps. Ever seen them, boy?"

"No, sir. But Henderson told me . . ." Keith broke off, seeing too late where the conversation was leading.

"Exactly." Colonel Faraday waved the chicken leg in the same way he usually gestured with the cheroot. Keith wondered wildly if he would put it in his mouth and try to light it in a minute. "You want me to withdraw my support from Afzul-ul-Mulk—who, by the way, looks to me like the only friend the British people have in this corner of the earth, a damn sight better friend than some young smart-ass political officer who's halfway to going native—you want me to withdraw support from this fine gentleman because of the non-appearance of some maps that you heard about in a conversation you hallucinated having with a dead man. Eh?"

The Colonel gnawed the last bit of meat off the chicken leg, chewed, swallowed and wiped the back of his hand across his mustache. "Tell you what. You show me something—maps, Russian letters to Afzul, a real Russian if you can find one—you show me one solid piece of evidence, and maybe I'll take your allegations seriously. Until then, my official view is that you've let your first political appointment go to your head and have forgotten whose interests you're supposed to be serving here."

With a satisfied belch, he stuck the end of the chicken leg in his mouth and struck a light. Keith snorted and left without waiting for permission.

The only immediate effect of Keith's accusations took place not in the mess tent but in a private house in the city.

"So," Afzul-ul-Mulk mused after receiving the report from his spy in the camp. "So. Powell Sahib becomes a nuisance . . . and his wife is still very beautiful." His smile did nothing to soften the hard lines of his face. "I have always preferred economy of action."

And sitting at his writing desk, he inscribed a brief letter which he handed to his chuprassi before informing the other servants that they might shut up the house and depart to visit their relatives, as he was going on a prolonged hunting trip in the mountains and would not require their services for at least a month.

While Keith was breakfasting with Colonel Faraday, Bridget woke, alone and confused. The events of the previous night had so mixed themselves with nightmares while she slept that she thought at first it had all been one long dream. But the sense of loss in her heart did not go away, and when she saw the heap of rain-soaked garments on the floor and the faint bruises encircling one wrist, she could no longer put memory away from her.

Keith hated her, as she had always known he would one day. And not even for the truth—for some fancied betrayal he had made up out of his own head! But what did that matter? She could not convince him of her innocence without telling him all the truth. And after last night, she no longer believed that his love for her was strong enough to pardon her lies.

Something like panic seized her at the thought of facing his accusations again. And after that panic, her way became simple and very clear. Their marriage was at an end. There was no need to go through the mockery of confessing her deception to him, giving him one more thing to hate her for. She would simply go away—now—this day. And this time he would not come after her as he had before. There would be no last-minute salvation. Doubtless he would be glad to see her go.

Bridget scrambled out of bed and threw on the first
clothes that came to hand in a feverish haste to be gone
before Keith came back. Where she would go, she had
no idea. Perhaps Aziza would give her shelter for a few
days, until she decided what to do.

She went to the square hole in the floor and knelt to
descend the ladder.

No ladder.

Bridget felt around the edges of the hole, unwilling
to believe the evidence of her eyes.

No ladder.

She lay on her stomach and stuck her head through
the hole. The ladder must have slipped loose somehow.
In that case it should have fallen on the dirt floor just
below—though she couldn't imagine why she hadn't
heard it.

No ladder.

"Mirza!" she called.

After a few more shouts, Mirza appeared in the
square which was all she could see of the floor below.

No, Mirza told her, the ladder wasn't in that room at
all. Powell Sahib had taken it away and locked it in the
stable.

"That's despicable!"

Mirza's half-concealed grin suggested she did not find
the situation as strange as Bridget did. Further conversation established that removing the ladder was a
common method, among Guahis, of ensuring that their
women kept *purdah*.

"Only rich men can do it," Mirza assured her
mistress. "Poor men have to let their women go to
work, go to market—like me. You're rich, lucky, you
can stay in the house all day. What's so bad? Powell
Sahib will let you out when he is ready."

She disappeared, grinning, and Bridget sat back on

her heels and fumed. "Only rich men." Wouldn't you just know it! Being a lady was as complicated in Guahipore as it had been in Calcutta.

But she couldn't let Keith get away with this.

"Next thing, he'll be flingin' one of them heathen veils over me head and puttin' ankle bracelets on me legs to ring their bells when I walk," she muttered. "What next? Nose rings?"

Then she remembered that there wouldn't be any next thing, because she was never going to speak to Keith again after the way he'd accused her last night.

It would have been a rare comfort to sit on the floor and bawl as if her heart was breaking, which indeed it was. But she'd no mind to be caught by Keith in a puddle of tears, acting the penitent wife. He'd likely take it as one more evidence of her guilt.

"Where there's a will, there's a way," Bridget told herself. She looked about the bedroom for a substitute ladder. The charpoy? No good, it was light enough but too wide by half to go through that narrow hole, and it would take an axe, which she didn't have, to enlarge the hole. But there were the mosquito nets that billowed above the bed. Her nail scissors might make some impression on those.

It took quite a long time to hack through the nets with her scissors and even longer to knot them into a rope and brace the charpoy against the hole. But once she'd done, the finished product didn't look that much worse than the rope bridges she'd crossed in the mountains. It was only to slide down a few feet instead of balancing over a gorge for hundreds of feet.

She dropped her shoes through first. Then she crossed herself and inched backward through the hole, gripping the improvised rope with hands and feet.

It worked fine while she had her feet round the

mosquito nets and her elbows supported by the floor of the upper room. But as soon as she let herself slide entirely through the hole, the weight of her body on the rope dragged the charpoy up against the hole with a sharp jerk.

The knotted mosquito nets above her made a tearing sound and sagged.

Bridget realized that in her hurry to be free, she had forgotten to do any stress testing on her new creation.

She wriggled cautiously down a few inches. Each movement of her body made the rope spin and rock crazily. There was another tearing sound and a whole section of mosquito netting gave way, letting her drop a foot all at once. That shock did for the rest of the rope. She watched helplessly as the sections slid apart, one by one. How far to the floor? She was afraid to look. There went the last bit . . .

She shut her eyes and dropped into a man's arms.

"Ouf!" Keith staggered backward, nearly lost his balance and recovered only by half-dropping her. His arms still about her, he squeezed her to his chest. She wasn't sure if he intended to embrace her or merely break a couple of ribs.

"What the hell do you think you're doing?" he shouted. "You could have been killed!"

"There's no need to be shouting as if you'd drink taken," Bridget said. "My hearing is perfectly good." As Keith's arms slackened, she stepped backward, away from him.

Keith rubbed his forehead with the heel of one hand. "Yes. It's your brain that's going, evidently."

Bridget shrugged. "And wouldn't it have worked if the mosquito nets hadn't been rotten, bad cess to them?"

Keith spread out his hands helplessly and stared at her. Suddenly, without warning, he burst out laughing.

"Mosquito nets . . . rotten . . . oh, Lor'!" he gasped between laughs. "My fault. Should have known better than to try such a fool trick as that. Forgot about the time you nearly burned up Gul Ram's roof."

He advanced toward her. "Darling . . . about last night . . ."

Bridget felt a sinking in the pit of her stomach. "Please, Keith," she implored, clasping her hands before her. "Please don't ask me about that again!"

Keith stroked her cheek with one hand. "I don't need to," he said, repressing the doubts that still coiled within him. "You wouldn't have anything to do with Afzul. I know that."

But did he? He couldn't bring himself to question her now. Instead he put his other hand on her shoulder and drew her up against his body, pressing his lips to hers in a long kiss that should have melted away all the distrust between them.

"Powell Sahib?"

It was Mirza, holding in one hand a red silk bag richly embroidered in gold.

Keith glanced at the seal that fastened the golden cords round the mouth of the bag. Then, in spite of himself, he looked at his wife.

"It is Afzul's seal."

She folded her arms. "Open it. I've no more notion than you what he will be writing about."

Keith opened the bag and unfolded a sheet of paper decorated with flowers and bordered with very finely hammered gold wire. He puzzled over the flowing, decorative Urdu script for some minutes.

"An invitation," he said slowly, not looking at his wife, "to a hunting party in the mountains."

"Will you go?"

More than anything Keith wanted to stay with her, to sort out the difficulties and lies that lay between them. But hadn't Faraday demanded evidence? He thought he saw a way to get that evidence now. If Afzul meant to be away for some time, as he indicated in his letter, his house might be empty.

"I think I must accept his invitation," Keith said slowly. He wondered how much else to say. Should he confide in his wife his idea of searching Afzul's house while he was away on this hunting party? With a sinking heart he realized that he dared not trust her that much. Not while so many questions remained unanswered. And there wasn't time to answer them now. No. He would tell her that he was going hunting. After all, it was true enough. Only the quarry was not a mountain boar or the wild deer but something much more dangerous.

He dropped a kiss on her forehead. "I need to go," he told her. "It's part of my job. But I can't go if I am worried about you. Please, promise me to stay until I get back. Then we can talk."

"Then we can talk," Bridget echoed. The words sounded like her doom. But she could not refuse Keith, not when he looked at her with so much love in his eyes.

"Promise."

Bridget dropped her eyes. "I will stay until you return." And what then? She felt cold at the thought. She put her hands on his shoulders and drew closer to him, until he wrapped his arms around her and laid his cheek against hers for a long, tender farewell embrace.

"Be careful," she said when they separated again. "Do not trust Afzul."

Keith grinned. "I don't. I thought that was what we were fighting about."

"We are not fighting."

"Right." He gave her a quick kiss. "Now I'd better get the ladder out of the stables."

Afzul's letter said that he had already left for the suggested rendezvous. Keith changed clothes quickly, packed his hunting kit and left on horseback, making no particular attempt to conceal his actions from any possibly interested watchers. The messenger who had brought the letter, Afzul's personal servant, accompanied him as a guide.

On the way out of town, and for some distance into the mountains, Keith rode along the path indicated by the guide, occasionally commenting on the beauty of the autumn weather, the possibility of snow and his hopes for a successful hunt.

When the path narrowed to follow the line of a mountain stream between two cliffs, Keith's horse balked several times and shied as though something was making it nervous. Keith cursed the horse loudly and swayed from side to side in the saddle, yanking at the reins, kicking it in the side and generally making the situation even worse.

The guide spurred his own horse to come up beside Keith. "Perhaps the sahib should relax," he suggested with a deferential manner. "If the sahib permits, I will lead his horse through the—ouf!"

A wild sideways lunge of Keith's horse caught the man off balance as he was reaching for the bridle. Keith stood on his left stirrup and threw his own weight sideways at the same time, catching the guide with the point of his own shoulder in a driving thrust that unseated him. With a continuation of the same movement, Keith jumped from the saddle and was kneeling on the man's chest before he could catch his breath.

The guide brought up his heels and arched his back in a desperate attempt to throw Keith off. They wrestled in deadly silence until the guide got one hand free for a moment. As if by magic, a thin, deadly blade not more than three inches long appeared in that hand. Keith's fingers locked over his wrist as the blade descended on him and he threw his full weight on that arm, pushing the guide's arm out to one side over a boulder half-buried in the earth. There was a sickening crack as the man's elbow snapped under the sudden weight. Gray-faced, he let his hand flop open and let Keith retrieve the knife.

Keith unwound the man's turban and roughly hacked it into three pieces with the little knife. One piece served to bind the guide's feet together, while another tied his good hand to a tree.

"How many more of these little jewels do you possess, I wonder?"

Whistling softly through his teeth, Keith patted the man's body down and pulled off his soft leather boots. Three more weapons were thus disclosed: a dagger thrust down one boot top, a matching but smaller dagger in his cummerbund and a little silver-mounted pistol in the bosom of his loose-fitting undertunic.

Keith packed the weapons away in his saddlebags, reserving only the small dagger. It was worrying to find that the guide carried no more than the normal complement of arms for a town-dwelling Bashiri. Perhaps he had been wrong in surmising that Afzul's invitation to a hunting party was a plan to get him outside of the town and ambush him in the mountains. In that case, he had been monstrously unjust to the guide. But broken limbs would heal, and Keith didn't think he would ever have recovered from what he suspected Afzul had planned for him.

"Now," he said, sitting down opposite the man and balancing the smaller of the two daggers on his palm, "we can talk." No need to let this man know how much he was relying on blind intuition. If he acted as though he knew of a definite plan, he might get more out of him. "Where was the ambush to be?"

The man's lips were compressed over his pain and his dark eyes gave nothing away. "Near?" Keith continued aloud. "By the spring, perhaps? Or was it to be the very meeting place set by Afzul?"

A flicker in the man's eyes told him that he had guessed correctly. "Good. One more question only. Did Afzul go with the group?"

A stony stare was his only answer.

"No," Keith said aloud, "I suppose he would not. He is as cowardly as most Bashiris and would prefer to skulk in his house while others do his killing for him."

"Dog!" The guide spat in Keith's general direction. "Afzul Khan remained in the city to settle certain business matters, but he rides to join us. You are the coward, Angrezi. He ordered us most particularly not to kill you before he arrived."

"Ah." Keith gave a sigh of satisfaction. His guess had been correct, then. "I do hope—I do very much hope—that you are telling the truth."

He stooped over the guide and unfastened the cloth that bound his hand to a tree. He lifted the man's body over his shoulders by the good arm and started up the rocky slope, panting between phrases. "Because . . . I intend . . . to visit Afzul's house . . . today." He reached a plateau of rock out of sight of the road and

259

deposited the guide as gently as he could. The broken elbow must have caused the man agonies, but no sound escaped his lips.

"You are a brave man," said Keith. "It would give me no pleasure to kill you. But I shall leave you here, so bound that there is no possibility of escape. Now, if you have told me the truth about Afzul, then I may visit his house and leave again, and I will come to get you when my visit is concluded. But if he is there, he may possibly kill me, which would be most unfortunate for both of us."

As he talked, he was refastening the strip of turban, tying the man securely to a twisted cedar that grew around the ledge. "I understand the wolves get very hungry at this time of year," he added, watching the man's face carefully. There was no change of expression that he could see.

Keith sighed and used the remaining piece of the turban as a gag. "I hope to be back before nightfall. I do trust that your good wishes go with me."

He rode back to Guahipore by a circuitous route, leading the guide's horse, and left both horses tethered in the hills just out of sight of the north gate. For what he had to do next he could not afford to be encumbered with a horse.

Afzul's house was in the north quarter of the town, a maze of winding alleys and over-leaning housetops that made their own quarter look like a modern planned town. Keith was relieved to find the compound gate locked and the windows of the house shuttered. It seemed that so far, at least, Afzul was telling the truth.

A flicker of doubt crossed his mind. It seemed strange that Afzul should really have sent away his servants and shut up his house, if his real plan was to assassinate Keith in the mountains and return home.

Perhaps he wished to pass off Keith's death as an accident. Yes, of course. He would make all preparations as if he really expected to be gone for a month or more; his "unexpected" return would be caused by Keith's "accident."

Keith smiled to himself and swung himself up over the compound wall by the branch of a tree. He landed lightly on the packed ground of the outer court and glanced about him. Good—no movement, no alarm.

He worked quickly but quietly to loosen a shutter in the back of the house, trying to leave as little mark of disturbance as possible. When he was able to crawl in the window, he pulled the shutter closed behind him just in case Afzul had a watchman sleeping somewhere in the compound who might notice the open window.

Keith was familiar with the layout of the house from his previous official visits to Afzul. If Henderson's maps were here and not with Afzul himself, they would be in the richly decorated room on the second floor, opening off Afzul's sleeping chamber, where he entertained guests and kept up his correspondence. More than once Keith had seen him locking papers away in the elaborately inlaid writing stand with a hinged top that stood in the corner of that room.

After a few minutes' unsuccessful juggling with the lock of the writing stand Keith was forced, with regret, to break the catch with the point of his knife. He hated to break up such a beautiful piece of furniture, but he could not spend any longer fiddling with it. The absolute silence of the house was getting on his nerves. It did seem strange that Afzul had sent away not only his servants, but also his women and dependents, on such short notice. Could it be a trap? No matter—he'd come too far to turn back now.

Inside the desk he discovered not only the maps

drawn in Henderson's spidery pen with the dark brown ink, but also a thin bundle of letters, carefully folded so that only the seals and superscriptions showed. Keith stuffed all the papers inside his shirt. If the correspondence was of diplomatic interest, he could read it later. If not, perhaps its disappearance would lend credence to the idea that an ordinary thief had broken into the house—although Keith didn't have much hope in Afzul's believing that.

He closed the writing stand and gently pressed back into place the jagged strip of inlaid wood that he had broken off with the lock, trying to make it look as natural as possible.

His hand was on the silken curtain that separated the study from Afzul's private apartments when the sound of a door opening below made him stop and stand absolutely still.

Keith dropped the curtain and retreated back across the carpeted floor of the study with noiseless steps. How high from the ground were the windows here? Perhaps he could escape that way.

A moment later he heard voices that made him give up any notion of sneaking away through the window. One voice was Afzul's, as he had expected. The other was light and feminine.

They were speaking English.

Chapter Nineteen

AFTER KEITH'S DEPARTURE, BRIDGET FELT DISORIENTED and at loose ends. Their happy life in Guahipore was crumbling about her. She remembered Keith's silences —his anger and mistrust—and now, just when they most needed to be together, he'd accepted a hunting invitation from the very man he had most reason to fear!

Bridget chewed on her nails, imagining all the things that could happen to Keith alone in the mountains with Afzul. A quarrel, a fight, an accident? So late in the year, they could even be caught in a snowstorm. Afzul might not need to do anything at all. She paced the smooth earthen floor of the downstairs room until she could bear the inactivity no longer. Then, throwing a shawl over her head, she informed Mirza that she was going to see Aziza.

"But she has not sent the jampon!" protested Mirza.

"I'll walk," said Bridget. "I've not been acting the fine lady so long that I've lost the use of me legs."

And waving back Mirza's offer to accompany her, she set off alone through the bleak day.

For once, the visit with Aziza did nothing to calm her fears. Aziza was not in her usual merry, laughing mood that day. Her delicate features seemed pale and pinched; she huddled over a brazier of glowing coals and welcomed her friend with a wan smile.

Bridget dropped to her knees on the cushion beside her. "What is it ails you, Aziza?" She remembered an earlier comment of Aziza's and looked round to be sure all the slaves were out of earshot. "Will Habiba be trying to poison you again?"

Aziza shook her head. "No . . . I am worried. It was good of you to come so quickly. I scarcely thought you would have had my message yet."

"There was no message in it," Bridget said. "I came to you out of my own mind."

For a moment they looked at each other with identical worried frowns, then Bridget forced a smile. "It is a coincidence surely."

At the same time Aziza said, "My thoughts were calling to you before the messenger came."

"I must have missed Abdul with the jampon, and he on the road to fetch me."

"No doubt."

They lapsed into silence again, each preoccupied with her own worries. Finally Bridget took her friend's hand. "Aziza, what is wrong?"

Aziza, too, looked round to be sure no one else was in earshot. Then she whispered a tangled, confused story of bazaar gossip and harem plots into Bridget's ear.

"Wait you a minute." Bridget had some trouble

untangling the characters of this tale. "Leila's cousin, who is a grasscutter in the stable of Afzul-ul-Mulk, told the shawl seller in the bazaar . . ."

"No," Aziza said, "it's the shawl seller who is Leila's cousin, and her husband's third son is a grasscutter for Afzul's horses . . . oh, never mind!"

The gossip that had reached her, stripped of these details, was that Afzul-ul-Mulk was planning a coup to unseat the mehtar.

"Remember the riots on the day when the Angrezi soldiers came? He has been bringing more of his tribesmen into the town since then. They are to rise in the streets while Afzul sends a message to the Colonel Faraday, in the mehtar's name—may he live forever—asking him to come in and restore order in the town. Only before the Colonel Sahib comes with his soldiers, Afzul's men will break into the palace and kill us all. Then the Colonel Sahib will make Afzul the new mehtar."

Bridget's hands gripped the silk-bound border of the cushion. "How sure is all this? It may be only the idle talk of the loafers in the bazaar, and they with no work to keep them from mischievous thoughts," she said as steadily as she could. "How would they get into the palace itself?"

"Habiba," whispered Aziza. "She will let them in by a gate that she knows of. After, they will make it seem that they broke in from outside."

"Habiba! That's ridiculous," Bridget said with more confidence than she felt. "Surely she'd not be after killing her own husband? This is just bazaar gossip."

Aziza bowed her head. "No," she whispered, "that is the part I think is true. Habiba would do anything to put her son on the throne."

"Wait a minute," Bridget said. "My Urdu must be

worse than I thought. Were you not telling me that this plot was to put Afzul on the throne?"

"Yes. He is Habiba's son by her first husband. It was long ago—before I was born." Aziza seemed to find some relief in the telling of the tale. "The mehtar, may he live forever, had sons by his first wife who was dead. But he saw Habiba and desired her. Perhaps she was beautiful *then*," she added with a trace of spite, "for all she is such a dried-up old stick now. She was married already, but those Bashiri women don't keep purdah, so he was able to see her and even to talk with her. Her husband didn't give her a divorce, but a few weeks later he was mysteriously dead. So she married the mehtar, may he live forever, but she couldn't give him sons. Afzul is her only son. And now that she is getting old and the mehtar loves me better, she will do anything to keep her power."

Bridget sat back on her heels. "Of course." Why hadn't she put it together? Aziza had mentioned that Habiba was of Bashiri origin. Henderson had said that Afzul was half Bashiri. No wonder he was always about the palace and seemed to have so much influence! He would be like another son to the mehtar.

"Can't you warn your husband?" she asked.

Aziza only wept. "She will kill me—Habiba will—if I mention anything to him. I am afraid to say anything. That is why I sent for you. You Angrezi are not afraid of anything. I thought you would know what to do."

"We must tell Keith," said Bridget, and half rose before she remembered her own trouble. "Keith . . ." She did not even know when he would come back again, or whether he would come back at all.

"We will have to wait," she said, sinking down again. "Afzul has gone hunting."

"Hunting what?" asked Aziza.

And Bridget had no answer.

Soon afterward she left, having nothing but sympathy to offer Aziza or herself for that matter. Perhaps in the morning she could ride to the army camp and tell Colonel Faraday of the plot against the mehtar. But if he had not taken Keith's word, how likely was he to trust her own?

And if Keith did not come back?

Wrapped in her own thoughts, Bridget climbed into the jampon that stood ready for her outside the zenana gate without even noticing that the bearers were not the usual crew.

After a few minutes she noticed that they seemed to be trotting uphill, as if they were heading into the old quarter on the north side of town rather than through the flat southern quarter where her house was.

She put her head through the curtains to call instructions to the bearers, but they ignored her and picked up their pace, running uphill so fast that she was thrown from side to side inside the curtained jampon.

As soon as they paused she scrambled out backward without waiting for them to lower the jampon. Her feet touched the ground and an arm as hard as iron encircled her waist. She struck out blindly and her arms were caught and pulled behind her.

"It was thoughtful of you," said Afzul-ul-Mulk, "to go to the zenana. Much easier to take you from the palace gate than from your own house."

As he spoke, he pushed Bridget before him through the open gate of his compound. She stumbled forward, recovered her balance and dodged to one side. Afzul's hand cracked across her cheek with a stunning force that sent her to her hands and knees.

"If you scream," he warned her, "you will regret it."

He closed and latched the compound gate, telling the

bearers that they might go away now. Still kneeling, Bridget watched him. She was half-stunned from the blow, and she felt as if the whole side of her face was on fire. She put up one hand to nurse her cheek, surprised that it was not already swollen out of shape.

Afzul stood for a moment at the gate, regarding her with satisfaction.

"As I told you once," he said, "the only secret in the management of women, as of horses, is . . . knowing when to apply the whip."

He jerked her to her feet by one wrist. "Inside!"

Still half-dazed by the blow, Bridget stumbled into the house.

"Upstairs."

Instead of the usual ladder, there was a stone staircase leading to the upper rooms. Bridget mounted as slowly as she dared. She was sick with fear for Keith. Surely Afzul would not have dared to treat her this way if Keith were still alive.

At the top of the stairs there was a curtain of midnight-blue silk draped across the doorway in soft folds. Afzul reached around her to pull the curtain aside.

The room they entered was furnished only with rugs in deep, rich reds and blues, piled two and three deep on the floor and with large cushions covered in silk and velvet. Light entered through a small window with glass panes, a luxury Bridget had not seen elsewhere in Guahipore.

Bridget took two steps into the room and sank down onto an embroidered cushion very near to the door. It required no acting effort to let her head droop back against the wall as if she were totally conquered and submissive already to Afzul's will.

What frightened her was how close that was to the

truth. For months she had used every polite ruse to avoid being alone with him. Now she was not only alone with him but entirely at his mercy in this silk-lined room scented with musk and jasmine.

Afzul moved about the room, lighting lamps that added a warm glow to the cold light from the window, lighting piles of incense that sent even more cloying sweetness into the air with their lazily twisting columns of blue smoke. Then he came back and sat cross-legged before her.

With a great effort Bridget raised her head and looked Afzul in the face.

"Are you mad to bring me here?" she said. "My husband will surely have the great rage on him that he will kill you for this insult to his house."

Afzul chuckled. "Your husband? *I* am your new husband. The Englishman will be dead before night."

"Will be," Bridget repeated softly. She could not stop the blaze of hope that leapt to her eyes. So Keith was still alive! Then there might be some reason to fight after all.

Afzul chuckled again. "Do not look so happy. By now I am sure he is wishing for death. But my men have strict orders to keep him alive—just—until I come."

Bridget shut her eyes against the picture his words called up. Keith broken, tortured, mutilated—no! If she did not think it, then it was not so. Keith would not have casually ridden into Afzul's trap.

He had seemed very casual about the hunting invitation that morning.

Bridget shook her head so violently that her long brown hair fell loose about her face. "No!" she said in a fierce undertone. "No! No!" With each shake of her head the hair whipped across her face. When she would have brushed the fine, clinging strands away, Afzul's hand imprisoned her wrists. She shivered involuntarily at that warm, dry, confident touch.

One by one, he lifted the clinging strands from her face. His fingers brushed down her cheek with each touch. "Beautiful," he murmured. "You shall be the prize of my household."

His hand lingered over the swell of her breast. Bridget felt faint and weak. Her bones were turning to water and there was a rushing sound in her ears. There was a dizzy sense of unreality, as though she were floating, dreaming.

"First the whip," Afzul murmured, "and then the reward." He drew a carved box from a recess in the wall and opened it to reveal gold bracelets, heavy and cold as chains. He lifted Bridget's limp arms, each in turn, and fastened the heavy bracelets over her wrists.

She put up her hands to pin her hair back up, but again Afzul restrained her. "Let it float loose," he murmured. "You are lovely so. You will be lovelier tonight when you wear only your hair as a silken veil to your beauty." His low laugh sent shivers down her spine. "What a pity that I am a good Moslem! I will not take a woman whose husband is still living. But that will soon be remedied."

Keith. The thought of him was like a breath of clean, fresh mountain air sweeping away the perfumed closeness of Afzul's rooms. And with that thought, Bridget knew what was wrong with her. Just once before had she felt this dreamy lassitude in which she was unable to resist others' wishes . . . on her wedding day. Here, she had eaten and drunk nothing. But each breath of the air, heavy with perfumed smoke, made her feel weaker and dizzier.

"I feel . . . sick," Bridget murmured. "May I lie down?"

"Yes, of course. You may do whatever you please—if it pleases me. But it is good that you ask permission."

Bridget felt a cold shudder of horror at this glimpse of what her future might be: tamed and trained into obedience, like the falcon he carried on his wrist when he rode out.

He helped her up. The only couch was near the window. As they approached it, Bridget gauged the distance with a swimming head. She pretended to stumble and fell heavily against the window, one hand out and taking her full weight.

The glass shattered and a sharp pain stabbed her arm. She leaned into the opening and gasped in great breaths of the cold, reviving air. That and the pain cleared her head. While Afzul helped her get free of the broken pane, she managed to get hold of one of the shards of glass. It would cut her palm if she held it hard enough to strike with it, but it was a weapon of some sort.

"How badly are you cut? Let me see."

Bridget held out her cut arm, feeling somewhat sick with the pain and the sight of the blood covering it. But she was able to conceal her other hand and the glass shard in the folds of her skirt.

Afzul bound up her arm, swiftly and more competently than Bridget had expected. "You don't cry? That is good. I guessed right." His eyes glittered. He looked like some predator of the mountains, excited by the sight of blood. "When I have tamed you to my hand, you will be a fit mate for me." He caressed her face and neck. "Beautiful," he murmured, "fair-skinned, a pearl in my palace."

The blue smoke was drifting out through the broken window, and the cold and the winter light were coming in. Bridget felt quite herself again and terribly afraid for herself and for Keith. She knew the exact moment when Afzul's soothing caresses became something more. His eyes grew dark and wide and his mouth thinned. "But why wait for tonight? Your former husband is as good as dead now. The Prophet will forgive my impatience."

Bridget tore herself free of his hold and backed toward the stairs, holding the bit of glass before her. "You'll wait longer than that," she told him. Never taking her eyes off him, she hitched up her skirt and used a fold of cloth to hold the sharp-edged, deadly bit of glass.

Afzul laughed. "Not tamed yet! Don't run away so fast, little bird. I don't want you to hurt yourself."

His hand shot out and captured her wrist, twisting to force her to give up the glass. Bridget struggled, kicked in his grip and used words she had tried to forget forever when she became a lady. It was all useless. He was dragging her back across the room. But she still held the glass. In the hopelessness of defeat, she turned her hand inward upon herself. The unexpected movement met with no resistance at first, and the glass had stabbed through the tight cloth of her bodice when suddenly she was released and falling across the pillows.

"Keith!"

Bareheaded, dressed only in a loose shirt and trousers that left him freedom of movement, Keith backed off from his first impetuous rush that had knocked Afzul over and freed Bridget. Balancing lightly on the balls of his feet, the light of battle in his eyes, he waited for his enemy to stand.

"Go to the stairs," he instructed Bridget. "I don't want him using you for protection."

Afzul made a hissing noise between his teeth and

stood, weaving slowly back and forth as he approached Keith. "Dog and son of a dog. I do not hide behind women."

"No?" Keith circled his opponent warily, watching for an opportunity. "Then why do I find you hiding in your sleeping quarters with my woman while you send your servants to assassinate me?"

"A mistake," Afzul acknowledged. "I may have underrated you."

He was poised for the rush; something bright gleamed in his hand.

"Keith, take care!" Bridget cried. "He has a knife on him."

Keith grinned, reached toward his boot and held a small, sharp dagger. "So have I."

Then they closed on one another, and Bridget held her breath, watching. Afzul was taller than Keith by half a head, lean and wiry with mountain-bred strength, and in his hand he held the long, wickedly curved knife of the tribes. In his first rush, she thought Keith must be overpowered; but he slipped under Afzul's guard and came up, breathing hard, with a trail of blood along Afzul's side to mark where his knife had scratched in passing.

"You underrated me again," Keith gritted, circling just outside Afzul's range.

Another slashing pass and Keith twisted out of the way of death with less than an inch to spare. The descending knife caught and ripped his trouserleg from thigh to boot top.

As he turned back, so quickly that Bridget could not follow the motions, he seemed to be striking out with his right hand, but Afzul's raised arm met empty air, and a knife in Keith's left hand sank into his shoulder.

Afzul fell back to the curtained doorway, clutching

his shoulder with one hand. The hilt of the knife protruded between his fingers. He looked down in surprise.

"I know that knife."

"You might," Keith acknowledged. "I had it—and this other one—from the man you sent to guide me."

"He warned you?"

Keith laughed. "Let's say—he was not subtle."

"You killed him?"

"No."

"Good. I shall." Blood was staining Afzul's silk coat dark, but he held himself erect and kept his own curved blade up as a barrier between himself and Keith. "It seems I have indeed underrated you, Angrezi. Keep your woman. I have another game to play."

He slipped through the curtains and was gone.

Bridget had risen while they spoke. Now she started forward. "Oh, stop him!" she cried.

"Sweetheart, the odds are that he'll stop us." Keith wiped beads of sweat from his forehead and encircled Bridget with one arm. "The place seemed deserted as I came in. Do you know if he has people outside?"

Bridget shook her head. "I think . . . they are busy elsewhere." Was today the day of Afzul's plan? It seemed too likely. They would have to hurry. And there was so much yet unsaid between her and Keith and, once again, no time to say it. But one thing had to be said.

"Keith, you're never thinking I came here of me own will? 'Twas a trick of his brought me here, and I thinking the jampon was Aziza's to take me home."

"I know." Keith held her so close that she could feel his heart thudding. "I heard you talking with him. I was in the inner room when you two came in here."

Bridget felt herself shrinking away from him. When Keith appeared she had not seen from which direction he'd come. "You listened a long time then, and me in fear of me life and thinking you dead. Is it that way you are trusting me, that you must listen at doors to be sure of my honor?"

Keith bowed his head. There was really no explanation for that. He had listened. He had mistrusted her and wanted to hear her refusing Afzul in no uncertain terms before he revealed his presence. And she knew that.

"All right," he said after a while. "I was not sure." Something more needed to be added to that. "I am now."

Cold, useless words! He was fast enough at talking round other people, why couldn't he talk to his own wife? He put his other arm round her and held her close, hoping the embrace would say all he could not put into words.

She was the first to break away. She was smiling, but her chin trembled a little and there were tears in her eyes.

"We really do have to talk," she said. "Tonight." This time she would not let any excuse put her off. But for now there was more urgent business. "Keith, I think I know what Afzul is planning. And it's you and I must find some way to stop it."

Quickly she told him of the rumors Aziza had passed on to her. "I thought maybe . . . if we told Colonel Faraday . . ." She fell silent. The colonel probably wouldn't even care if the mehtar was killed. All he saw in him was a stubborn old man opposing British interests.

"Convenient for him," Keith agreed, "to have the mehtar put aside. But Afzul won't get his support."

275

"Why not?" Bridget asked bitterly. "It seems to me he trusts Afzul a great deal more than he does you."

Keith grinned and patted the crackling mass of papers in his shirtfront. "I have something here that may change his mind. And we won't have to risk going back to the house. There are two horses outside the north gate."

Chapter Twenty

THE SENTRY ON DUTY WAS INTENSELY CURIOUS ABOUT THE bedraggled pair that rode into camp demanding to see Colonel Faraday: the man with a knife gash ripped down the leg of his trousers and into his boots, the woman with her hair falling about her shoulders and a bright native scarf bound about one arm and a swelling bruise on her cheek. But regulations forbade his following them to Colonel Faraday's tent and listening to find out what was going on. He had to remain at his post, hoping that one of his fellows would see fit to eavesdrop and report the story to him.

Colonel Faraday's cheroot dropped out of his mouth and the legs of his chair hit the ground with a thud when Keith lifted the tent-flap and ushered in the first white woman he'd seen in Guahipore. A regular beauty, too, even if her face was bruised and her hair falling loose. Reminded him of a damn fine woman he'd had in

Madras in '24, the half-caste daughter of an Irish soldier and his washerwoman.

The bedraggled beauty lifted her torn skirt in two fingers and swept a curtsey that had Colonel Faraday out of his chair and bowing over her hand before he knew what he was doing.

"Honored, m'lady! Honored!" he exclaimed. For of course this must be young Powell's wife, the Lady Charlotte Fitzgerald that was. The colonel gave himself a mental shake and tried to stop his lubricious memories of Rosie—or was it Sadie?—O'Neill. Couldn't compare a street woman like that with a real lady.

"Honored!" he said again.

Bridget looked at the goggle-eyed colonel and felt very tired. Why was he staring at her like that when his business was with Keith? She retrieved her hand from his damp, flabby grip and bowed her head slightly, the way the real Lady Charlotte would have been doing it. The motion let a strand of loose hair fall into her face, sticking to her cheek. She put up a hand to brush it back, winced at the touch on her sore face and all at once realized what a picture she must make— disheveled, bruised, bandaged with Afzul-ul-Mulk's silk scarf and still wearing the heavy gold bracelets he had clasped about her wrists!

"It's sorry I am to be coming before you in this condition, Colonel," she apologized, "but my husband's business with you is urgent."

The colonel only beamed fatuously. "Not at all, Lady Charlotte! Not at all! Honored to have you gracin' my tent! Only sorry . . . no refreshment suitable for a lady . . . rough soldiers, y'know! Very rough life!" He swept a stack of papers off the spare chair, plumped up a cushion and yelled for the boy to bring tea and fruit.

Bridget rolled her eyes at Keith. "Try to get his

attention," she muttered under cover of the colonel's shouts to the messboy. "This could go on forever!"

The colonel returned to find his noble visitor seated at the side of the tent while the Powell boy was pulling sheaf after sheaf of bloodstained documents out of his baggy shirt.

"Don't mind the blood, sir," Keith said. "Just a scratch. These are what I wish you to look at." He unfolded the top paper and spread it out over the desk. The colonel glanced down.

"Yes? Some native scribbling? That brown ink's plaguey hard to read. What is it, anyway?"

Keith could not keep the triumph out of his voice. "You told me to bring you Henderson's maps. I found them in a locked desk in Afzul-ul-Mulk's house. Now will you believe he's not playing a straight game with us?"

"Maps? Nonsense!" Colonel Faraday made as though to brush the offending document off his desk but Keith's two hands firmly anchored it. "That ain't a proper map. Where's the little compass in the corner?"

Keith bit his lip to keep from smiling. "These are Henderson's field notes, sir. I think you'll find all the compass headings and distances are marked in the appropriate places. I grant that it doesn't make a very pretty picture, but I assure you that any competent surveyor could construct a regulation British army map from these notes."

"Oh . . . I see, yes. Well . . ."

Colonel Faraday was visibly nonplussed. He chewed on the ends of his mustache for a while and walked up and down the short clear space in the middle of the tent. Finally he wheeled sharply and addressed Keith again.

"Broke into his desk, did you? Hmph! Not quite the

thing, Powell." He marched up and down the clear space again, sucking in the ends of his mustache and blowing them out again as he muttered to himself.

"Never did consider these politicals were real officers," Bridget heard when he passed her.

"I suppose a chap loses the right instinct when he's around natives all the time," came out on the next turn around the tent.

"Sir!" Keith broke in at last, unable to stand it any longer. "Whether or not I acted correctly, sir, the evidence is before you now and you must act on it. Afzul has concealed valuable information from you, and at this very moment he is acting on a plot to assassinate the mehtar and use your services to establish himself as the next ruler of Guahipore."

"Must? *Must?* Don't use that tone with me, boy." Colonel Faraday flipped the map over and picked up the unopened bundle of correspondence which Keith had taken on impulse when he stole the maps. "And what's this, eh?" He slit the ribbon holding the papers together and the stack collapsed, papers skating all over the tent. Keith dived for some, Bridget rescued a stray sheet that came her way and even Colonel Faraday went down on his hands and knees to collect a double armful of thin white papers worn with many creases.

"Good Gad!" The colonel remained on his knees, staring at the papers he had rescued from the floor. "Powell! Come here!"

Keith stepped to Faraday's side and glanced over his shoulder.

"This what I think it is?" Colonel Faraday snapped out.

"Yes, sir. Cyrillic script."

"Oh. Thought it was Russian."

"Ah . . . yes, sir. The Russians use the Cyrillic script instead of our alphabet."

"Well, dammit, I knew that," Colonel Faraday said. He heaved himself to his feet and plopped the papers down on top of Henderson's maps. "Knew they have some kind of funny writing. Why couldn't you say it was Russian straight out? You read it?"

"No, sir."

"Well, dammit. What's the use of havin' you politicals pass exams in all sorts of native gibble-gabble if you can't read a simple letter when I need it? Oh, never mind." Colonel Faraday waved the top sheet around under Keith's nose. "This is evidence enough. The damned bastard's been corresponding with the Russians behind our backs. Playing a double game, by Gad! What's this you say about a plot to assassinate the mehtar? Can't have that sort of thing going on. Orderly!"

The colonel raised his voice and bawled out a stream of orders.

Within minutes the somnolent camp was transformed into a beehive of activity as the junior officers armed, mounted and assembled their men. Colonel Faraday stood before his tent and watched with satisfaction. While the men were forming into marching order, he dug an elbow into Keith's ribs.

"Know y'think I'm a useless old fart, m'boy," he said with a wink, "and y'could be right. But by Gad, there's one thing I've learned in the army and that's how to delegate authority!" With a sweep of his arm he indicated the military order arising out of chaos before them.

"Delegation—that's th' secret. Train y'r officers right, and b'Gad, you can damn near retire!" The colonel looked worried and chewed his mustache more

vigorously than ever. "'Course, that's only in peace-
time. Have to lead them into battle m'self. The men
expect it of me."

Keith remembered the quantities of men Colonel
Faraday had managed to lose during the Sikh wars and
pictured the havoc that could be created by someone
unfamiliar with Guahipore trying to lead men through
the winding streets and narrow passages of the old
town.

"With respect, sir," he said, "I beg to differ with you
there. You have already served your country in so
many vital engagements." Surviving most of them by a
combination of the devil's own luck and a healthy
willingness to retreat. "It would be nothing short of
tragic if your years of accumulated wisdom and experience were to be lost to the country in a minor skirmish
like this." Not to mention the men that could be lost at
the same time. "I think you owe it to your country to
delegate the leadership of this action to one of your
junior officers."

"Hmph." The colonel seemed to be thinking over his
words. "Something in that. Still . . . distinguished
action . . . like t'be associated with it, what?"

"You would of course lead the *official* entry of troops
into the city," Keith said quickly. "I was only proposing
that a minor scouting force should go ahead to, as it
were, reconnoiter. I could guide them." Once he had
made the mehtar's palace secure and dealt with Afzul,
Colonel Faraday was welcome to play whatever official
games he wanted in his report. Thinking of Afzul,
Keith smiled, and his fingers just touched the hilt of the
dagger stuck in his belt. He had his own plans for the
man who had insulted his wife—and they were not at all
official.

"Hmmph!" the colonel said again. "Very well. You

young fire-eaters! Dan Weaver can command the force. You go as guide or whatever you want. Understand, though—no official standing."

"I understand completely, sir." Keith bowed to the colonel.

"Keith—"

Bridget stopped her own outcry. Of course he would go. It was his job. She couldn't stop him.

Keith gave her one quick, hard embrace. "I'll be back," he told her. "You stay here. Understand?"

"I'll take care of your good lady, Powell," the colonel put in. "You . . . ah . . . report back to me when you've . . . ah . . . reconnoitered the situation."

Bridget forced herself to smile and to keep smiling as he rode away beside Dan Weaver on a borrowed mount. Then she went back inside the colonel's tent and sat stiffly upright on the spare campchair, answering his questions at random and letting the tea he ordered for her grow cold while she listened for the sound of firing from the city.

"Too far away," Colonel Faraday told her. "We can't hear what's going on from here."

On that word, a distant fusillade of musket shots beat a quick, ragged rhythm against the sky. Bridget half started from her seat, spilling the cold tea over her skirt.

"Means nothing!" the colonel assured her. "Think that rabble can stand up against a trained force of British soldiers? Finest fighting men in the world, b'Gad! Why, when I was first out here, in the Mahratta wars . . ."

He called for more tea and kept Bridget entertained with a steady flow of reminiscences through the long, still afternoon. He did not quite succeed in his kind intention of distracting her from what might be going on in Guahipore, but at least his monotonous conversation provided a soothing backdrop for her own thoughts.

"I suppose this is what all soldiers' wives have to go through," Bridget thought. "I've only been spared it this long because Keith is in the political service."

". . . seven companies of native infantry in the square," droned Colonel Faraday. "More tea?"

Bridget smiled and held out her cup. "And I don't like it! I wish Keith were not a soldier," she thought. "How interesting, Colonel Faraday," she said out loud. "And what happened then?"

It was almost dusk when they heard the sound of the returning regiment. Bridget dropped her cup and ran outside, straining her eyes to see Keith. There were so few—so very few of all who'd marched out a few short hours earlier!

"Weaver reporting, sir." A dust- and blood-stained figure swung off his horse and advanced toward the tent. "There was some street fighting but no organized resistance. I've left most of my men in the city to guard strategic points."

"Keith?" The question burst from Bridget's lips almost before Dan Weaver had finished speaking.

"Safe. He should be coming up with the rear of the column." Dan grinned. "You'll get a shock when you see him, but don't be worried. He came with us as far as the mehtar's palace. I think Afzul's Bashiri pals were expecting us to be on their side, for they made no resistance until it was too late. Once the palace was secure, Powell made off on his own. Private errand, he said. Came back with blood all over him. Somebody else's, he said. Not a scratch on him."

"See anything of Afzul?" Colonel Faraday asked.

Dan's eyes slid sideways. "Nothing official to report, Colonel. I think you'll not be troubled with him, though. You might ask Powell—"

"All right, all right," the colonel interrupted. "I'll have Powell give his report in private. Any losses on our side?"

"One." Dan cleared his throat. "Private soldier—name of Kelly. Some of the natives caught him in a part of the palace where he shouldn't have been. Looking for what he could pick up. But he made the mistake of going into the women's quarters. I'm afraid they killed him before I found out about it."

"Looting, eh? Bad business."

Dan nodded. "We brought his body back. I found this stuffed into his jacket pocket. Funny thing—none of the natives would claim it. Wouldn't even say who the owner was."

He fumbled inside his coat for a moment and drew out a blue stone set in gold. It sparkled in the last rays of the setting sun like a malevolent blue eye.

Bridget drew in her breath sharply as she recognized Afzul's sapphire.

"The man is dead, you say?"

Dan Weaver nodded. "Do not distress yourself, Lady Charlotte," he said. "We would have been obliged to shoot him anyway, for looting."

Bridget exhaled a shuddering breath of relief. She could never have wished such a death on John Kelly. But it was a relief to think that twisted hatred was gone from her life.

"No claimant, y'say? Queen's trove, then." Colonel Faraday took the sapphire from Dan. "I'll send this down with my report. Best not to let anybody know about it." He winked at Bridget. "Pity about regulations, eh? Stone like this should be about the neck of a

pretty woman, not locked in some government safe."
He made as if to hold it up to Bridget's throat, and she
shrank back from the cold touch of the pendant.

"What, no taste for jewelry, Lady Charlotte?" the
colonel teased her. "Now that's unusual . . ."

Bridget heard no more of his words, for her attention
was focused on a rider at the very end of the column of
men marching past. His shirt was one great crimson
splash of blood, his dark hair fell over his forehead, but
he sat as springily erect in the saddle as though he were
just setting off for a day's hunting. He dismounted
several paces from the tent and tossed his horse's reins
to a groom who stood ready.

Bridget felt as though her feet were glued to the
ground. She stood waiting, breathless, while Keith
covered the few steps between them.

Then he was before her, his face blotting out all the
rest of the world, and her hands fastened on his arms
and she knew he was warm and alive.

It was late that night before they were alone together. Colonel Faraday, in high good humor over "his"
victory, had insisted on Keith's and Bridget's attendance at a mess dinner where innumerable toasts were
drunk and a fair amount of the regiment's glassware
was smashed. He had summarily vetoed any notion of
their returning to Guahipore that night, although he
did permit Keith to send out a detachment to find and
free the guide he had left bound in the mountains.

"Not safe," he told Keith. "You may have disposed
of Afzul—very well—but there's bound to be some of
his friends will not be feeling so kind toward you right
now. And I need you alive. Weaver tells me you're the
one with the mehtar's ear. Got to hammer out treaties
and such. Once that's done, you can go and get yourself

286

killed any time you like. But Lady Charlotte stays with me . . . eh?"

He gave a ponderous wink and squeezed Bridget's hand. "What d'you say, m'dear? I'll wager you'll be glad enough of an evening of civilized company for a change, after all these months with nobody to talk to but the blacks."

Keith caught Bridget's eye and shrugged in rueful acquiescence. She smiled at the colonel as he called for yet another toast.

It was late that night before they could slip away without causing offense. All the officers had wanted to talk to Keith about local conditions and to Bridget—the first white woman they'd seen since leaving the plains—about anything at all. Finally, under the influence of Colonel Faraday's toasts, the atmosphere degenerated into one of cheerful ribaldry and the young officers forgot to censor the words of the ballads they were bawling out in an off-key chorus. Then Bridget's presence was more of an encumbrance than a delight, and she and Keith were able to go to their tent.

Bridget's head was aching with the hours in the crowded mess tent and the din of conversation. And Keith, who as a fellow officer had been expected to partake of all the toasts proposed by all members of the regiment, was none too steady on his feet as he made his way across the uneven ground to the tent the colonel had set aside for their use.

There was a brisk, wintry bite to the night air. They huddled off their clothes and slid gratefully into the chilly nest of blankets, cuddling close together to share heat.

"Tired?" Bridget asked.

Keith yawned. "Drunk. No, not so much as I thought! That cold walk must have sobered me. But I could sleep for a week." He opened his arms and pulled her close. "With your head on my shoulder."

For a moment Bridget let herself relax in his comforting embrace. Their body heat was beginning to warm the icy blankets; how easy it would be to slip into a comfortable dream in this cocoon of warmth! But she had taken the easy road too many times already, and each time it got her deeper in trouble. It was time to end that.

"Tomorrow you'll be busy?"

Keith nodded. "You heard the colonel nattering about treaties? I think there's a real chance. The mehtar was pretty cut up when he discovered Afzul's treachery. Kept saying he'd reared the boy as his own son. Anyway, he seems to've decided he'd rather trust us than anyone else. Thinks the British are his best friends. I think he'll agree to let us appoint a resident now."

Bridget clasped her hands. "Oh, Keith! You're to be a resident?"

Keith laughed and hugged her. "Not a chance, dear heart. A post like that will go to someone far, far senior to me. But I daren't let Colonel Faraday lead the negotiations! My knowing the local version of Urdu is an excuse to act as interpreter and keep the colonel under control. So yes, for the next few days I'll probably be busy with the mehtar."

"May he live forever," Bridget murmured sleepily.

Keith chuckled and kissed the tip of her nose. "May he live a darned long time, anyway—and his chances of that are better now than they have been for some time!"

His light kisses wandered from the tip of her nose to the corner of her mouth and then to the soft place just under her chin and the triangle where her pulse beat strongly at the base of her throat. Bridget sighed and stirred in his arms.

"Keith," she said.

His arms tightened about her. "Darling!"

"I . . . we have to talk."

"Go ahead," he cordially invited her. "I promise to leave your mouth free." His lips and teeth nibbled a tantalizing trail down to the peak of one breast where they fastened about the swelling nipple and sucked it into a hard point of ecstasy. The small tugging motions of his teeth sent radiating lines of pleasure through her body.

"Oh, I can't talk when you do that!" she moaned in defeat and submission.

"Hmm?" One hand traveled lower, seeking out the moist crevices between her thighs. Bridget clamped her knees shut and twisted away from him.

"What the—Darling, are you angry with me?"

Keith sat up, the blankets tumbling down about his waist. Bridget shivered at the touch of the freezing air, grabbed a blanket and wrapped it about her shoulders. Keith howled as her tug exposed the lower portion of his body to the air.

"No fair! Share and share!" He grabbed a corner of the blanket and huddled under it with her. A second blanket covered their legs. He put his arm behind her back and drew her close against his chest. "Look, if it's about Afzul—" he began.

"When you thought I was flirting with Afzul—" Bridget said simultaneously.

They stopped and stared at one another. Finally Bridget broke the silence with a sigh.

"The man in the garden," Bridget said at last. "It was Afzul's sapphire I was after giving him, true enough, and him throwing it about my neck the day we came back from the mountains, by token he meant to have it back someday and me with it. But it wasn't passing between us as a message. I gave it to that man because—"

Bridget stopped and took several deep breaths. She felt dizzy, almost exhilarated, now that she had gone too far to draw back.

"He was blackmailing me. He threatened to go to you and tell you that I wasn't Lady Charlotte Fitzgerald."

"And you thought I'd listen to a story like that?" Keith put his arm round her shoulders and hugged her close under the blanket.

"You should have," Bridget said quietly. "It was true."

"True or not," Keith said with a peculiar emphasis, "I wouldn't listen to some drunken soldier telling tales of my wife. You should know me better than that." Both his arms encircled her close, protecting her with the warmth of his body. His breath against her cheek stirred a trailing strand of brown hair that had fallen loose from her braids.

Bridget pushed herself a little bit away from him and stared in disbelief. "Keith, don't you understand what I'm after saying to you? I'm not Lady Charlotte! I'm an impostor!" She covered her face with her hands, afraid to see his expression. "God be my witness," she whispered, "I never meant it to go this far."

She waited for Keith to say something—anything. Braced for his anger, she was shocked to hear him laughing. "Ah—purely as a matter of academic interest," said Keith, his voice light and hatefully amused, "how far *did* you intend it to go?"

In a halting half-whisper, staring at the moonlit wall

of the tent, Bridget told him the whole story from the very beginning in Ireland, so far away. John Kelly's pursuit, her temporary escape into service at the Great House, the chance of coming with Charlotte to India. The shipwreck, and the doctor's mistake about her identity that she'd thought to use as a way to get on to India, safely away from John Kelly.

Bridget gave a shaky laugh at this part of her story. "You'll never believe how ignorant I was then! I thought India would be like a big city—like Dublin, only bigger—and that I could slip away and find work. I'd always been good at taking off Lady Charlotte in the servants' hall. I thought I could do it long enough to fool a few people who'd never met her." She hugged both arms round her knees and stared at the shadows. There was a sort of vicious satisfaction in recounting her folly, after so many doomed attempts to conceal it.

"I didn't know then," she said quietly, "how much more there was to being a lady besides fine talk and fine clothes. Things I'd never learned."

"I know," put in Keith. "You'd never ridden sidesaddle before, had you? For a long time I couldn't figure out why you had so much trouble riding in Calcutta when you did so well riding astride in the mountains with me."

"Sidesaddles!" Bridget had to laugh with him. "Well, there you are. How I thought I could carry it off, I'll never know. I'll tell you, it was a rare panic I was in all that week in Calcutta. Thought meself lost for sure, I did, when that old bishop came to call. It was the best piece of luck in me life when you broke the glasses on him."

And the very next day, that unexpected reprieve had rushed her into a situation she'd never expected to face, as she woke to find the plans for their marriage all arranged. "Keith, I was going to tell you. I swear to God I never meant to marry you!"

She could feel the muscles of his arm tensing behind her. Of course, this was the bit he never, never could forgive. "I tried to run away but Gul Ram stopped me, then I was going to tell you before the wedding, but I never got the chance, and Mrs. Lanyer had me that full of laudanum I didn't rightly know—"

She stopped the torrent of excuses. "No, that's not true," she said. "I knew what I was doing, right enough. But I . . ." She turned to him. His face, half-shadowed in the moonlight, was an abstract composition of planes and angles. She could not see his eyes. "I loved you so very much!" she burst out despairingly. "Oh, Keith, can you ever forgive me? I only wanted to be with you for a little while!"

Keith's face softened and he pulled her back close to him and kissed her on the eyelids and the cheek and the tip of her nose and her chin and every place he could reach. "Forgive you for what?" he said in a voice smothered by laughter. "For loving me? I should think so! You're a fine fool, Biddy Sullivan of Ballycrochan. And it's a relief to have a name to put to you at last. It's been a long time since I felt right about calling you by Charlotte's name."

Bridget jumped. She felt as shocked as if a pin had been stuck in her. "You knew?" she said loudly. No wonder he'd been laughing. Her face burned. What a fool he must have thought her. "You knew! How long? How did you find me out?"

Keith gave a lazy, contented sigh and settled back into the blankets, wrapping his arms about her so that she was forced to lie down with him.

"How did I find you out?" he repeated. "Hard to say. For a few days I just thought you were too damned nice to be Charlotte."

Bridget relaxed against his body. They made a little nest of warmth under the blankets, the two of them together. She was beginning to think that he didn't mean to throw her out after all.

His palm caressed the side of her hip in long, soothing circles that raised a shiver of desire deep within her.

"Then what?" she murmured sleepily.

"Oh, you looked enough like her, a girl changes, growing up. I did think she'd not shown promise of growing into such a ravishing beauty, but you never know. Then—"

"Wait a minute," Bridget interrupted. "Would you say that part again?"

"Didn't you hear me? I said I never thought Charlotte would grow up to be such a ravishing beauty."

Bridget sighed happily. "Thank you. Nobody ever called me that before . . . It'll be something nice to remember."

Keith squeezed her so tightly she squeaked for breath. "What do you mean? I'm going to give you lots of nice things to remember, years' and years' worth. I've got something nice for you right now, as a matter of fact." He held her close against his body and she felt his hardness rising against her thighs.

"Anyway," he said after he captured one of Bridget's hands and held it against him where it would do the most good, "I had a few suspicions in those early days. There were things you didn't remember, things you said that didn't ring true. But I wasn't entirely sure until that evening in Gul Ram's house."

"That evening?" Bridget repeated.

Keith laughed. "Don't tell me you've forgotten! Shall I remind you? It went like this . . ."

His hand roamed teasingly over the soft contours of her body, and he pressed one knee between her half-opened thighs.

"Let me guess," Bridget said. "Real ladies do it some other way?"

Keith laughed. "No. Not in my experience."

"I don't think I want to hear about your experience," Bridget said. Keith stroked her cheek and she turned her head to kiss the palm of his hand.

"No? Oh, all right. It was Miss Cherry." Keith grinned. "You *do* remember dear old Miss Cherry, don't you?"

Bridget gasped and sat up.

"Come back!" Keith implored. "It's cold down here."

"There never was a Miss Cherry," she accused him.

Keith lay back, pulling a blanket over his chest, and giggled.

"You made the whole thing up!"

The giggles turned into guffaws.

"You trapped me!"

Keith roared with laughter and reached for her.

"Oh, get away from me! Here I've been suffering agonies of guilt for months, and you knew all about it and were just watching to see what I'd do next!" Bridget remembered her desperate evasions and inventions on the subject of Miss Cherry. She had to laugh even as she nourished her rage. "A fine fool I must have made of meself! Was it fun, watching me lie and evade and pray for the grace to keep up the masquerade another day? Did you enjoy yourself, I hope? For it was no pleasure to me at all, let me tell you, and 'twould be a pity did neither one of us get some fun out of it! Oh, you—you—" She raged impotently at the air with her clenched fist.

Keith's strong arms imprisoned her from behind and pulled her back into the nest of blankets. She kicked and struggled in vain. "Get away from me! I don't like you anymore!"

Keith yelped as her heel caught him high on one thigh. "Another kick like that, and there'll not be much left of me to like! You'll have destroyed the best part entirely!" He rolled over on top of her, silencing her protests with a fold of the blanket and holding her down till her thrashing limbs grew still.

"And since you ask," he said into the sudden quiet, "no—it was not very much fun at all." He paused and watched the rage leave Bridget's eyes. "You see, I kept wishing you would trust me enough to tell me the truth."

"I nearly did," Bridget whispered. "So many times . . . but I was always afraid."

"Yes," Keith said. "So was I. Sometimes I stopped you, I think, when you were about to tell me."

"You? What were you afraid of?"

"That you'd have something to confess that neither of us could live with," Keith said quietly.

Bridget turned her face away from him to hide the tears that were falling into the coarse woolen blanket. "And I have," she whispered. "You can't—if word gets out that you've married a servant girl from Bally-crochan, it'll ruin your career."

"Not a bit of it!" said Keith emphatically. He straddled her body and turned her face back up to his by force. "You listen to me, Biddy Sullivan. When I said something we couldn't live with, I meant—oh, I don't know what I meant! Some horrible dark secret in your past. This is nothing! If you want to learn to ride sidesaddle, I'll teach you, though I'd just as soon you didn't risk your neck like that. If you want to have tea parties with the colonel's lady, I'll teach you that too. But you're not getting away from me on a flimsy excuse like this. I married *you*, not Lady Charlotte," he said, punctuating each statement with a light shake, "and I've got you and I'm keeping you! Is—that—understood?"

"Y-yes," Bridget got out between shakes. "B-but, K-keith, you c-can't—"

"Yes. I. Can." Keith pushed Bridget back down on the blankets and closed her mouth with a fierce, consuming kiss.

Chapter Twenty-one

THE SECURITY BROUGHT BY KEITH'S LOVE HAD VANISHED by morning.

All night Bridget had slept nestled in Keith's arms, warm and safe in his love. The relief of her confession and of finding that he didn't hate her for the deceit she'd practiced had been so great that she'd dropped off to sleep without a care in the world.

But in the restless hours before dawn, when Keith had rolled from side to side, muttering in his sleep and twitching the blanket away from her, Bridget woke to cold reality again. Unable to get back to sleep, she rose and dressed as quietly as she could.

It was cold in the tent. She peeped outside and saw that a fresh snowfall had come down on the peaks behind the city. If she had been watching the dawn from the upper windows of her own house in Guahipore, she would have exulted in the play of light and color that turned the white hills into a radiant display; she would have called to Mirza to put fresh coals in all the braziers, would have gone to the bazaar for quilted cotton coats and red-embroidered wool leggings. She had never been through a winter in Guahipore, but Mirza's tales of the indoor feasts and storytellings that occupied the long cold months had made it all vivid to her.

Now she supposed she never would see the winter in this strange foreign city that had become home to her. Now the white covering of the mountains extending nearly to the plain meant only that any day now the snows would sweep to the south, blocking passes and covering the hills. What would happen when the winter began in earnest? Colonel Faraday would want to get his men back to India before then, before snow filled the hills to the south and covered the trails. And she and Keith would go with him—to what?

Keith had said that his work in Guahipore would be over with the appointment of a resident. There was no telling where he'd be stationed next. Perhaps he could teach her to carry off the airs of a lady in society—but what if they ran into somebody who had known Charlotte Fitzgerald? The slight resemblance on which Bridget had traded so far could not fool anyone who knew Charlotte well.

"What's the matter, darling?"

Keith was stirring in the nest of blankets. In a moment he had pulled on his trousers and joined her at the tent-flap, looking comically like a small boy with his black hair sticking up in spikes above his forehead. He gave a jaw-cracking yawn and slipped both arms around Bridget, pulling her back against his naked chest. The heat from his body warmed her back.

"You'll catch your death, going around bare and shameless in this weather," Bridget said.

Keith leaned over her shoulder to leer at her. "One gets hardened to it. You should try it. I think I'll set up my own zenana and make you go around the house in those translucent gauzy pants the harem ladies wear. And I hear they've nothing whatever on top but a pair of gold spangles. D'you fancy yourself in gold spangles, m'dear?"

Bridget had to laugh at his lurid imaginings. "Run mad you are," she told him. "Where would Aziza be going about in no more than a bit of a veil and some gauze, the way she'd freeze to death huddled over a firepot? It's long trousers and a silk tunic the girls in the zenana wear, and the veil over their heads, the way they're covered more decent than an English lady with her petticoats that flip up in any strong wind."

"*Must* you destroy all my fantasies?" Keith complained.

Bridget looked down at her own clasped hands. "Yes . . . I think I must." She let the tent-flap fall and turned to face him. "Keith, I've been thinking."

"Always a mistake," Keith interrupted her. "Don't you want to learn to be a lady? Lesson one . . . always let your lord and master do the thinking. That's me," he added, thumping his chest, "in case you've forgotten." He sat down on the camp cot and pulled Bridget backward to rest on his lap. "Maybe I should remind you? Do we have time before breakfast?"

"We do not," Bridget said, "and we have to talk. Keith, you can't spend the rest of your life breaking the bishop's glasses."

"Wasn't actually planning to do it again," Keith said. "I'm not that clumsy, y'know. I could see you were scared to death of meeting the bishop, afraid he'd recognize you—wouldn't recognize you, rather—and that was the only thing I could think of on the spur of the moment."

"Yes," Bridget said. "It was slow of me to take it for an accident, so it was, but how was I to know you'd found me out so soon, and me trying every shift I knew to keep from showing my ignorance before you? A wonderful bit of quick thinking on your part and grateful I am for it, and I take back everything I said when I was out of temper with you last night." She frowned for a minute, remembering her anger when she'd discovered how Keith had let her make a fool of herself. "Well—maybe half of everything I said."

Keith laughed and nuzzled her neck. "That's my Bridget. Don't get too meek and mild, I wouldn't know you!"

"But, Keith," Bridget said, lifting one of his hands off her thigh and persuading the other away from the neckline of her dress, "if we go back to India, it might happen again, don't you realize that? Especially if we go to a crowded station with officers and civil servants and visitors coming through, bad cess to them! Will you spend the rest of your life breaking people's glasses or explaining why your wife wears a veil or . . ." She ran out of alternatives.

"Look on the bright side," Keith said, "we might never meet anybody who knew you—er, Charlotte. And if we do, don't you trust me to take care of it?" He began fiddling with the line of tiny jet buttons that ran down the front of her dress.

Bridget sighed. "Yes . . . no . . . oh, I don't know! Keith, it's *cold!*" She protested in vain as the front of her dress opened under his persistent hands to reveal her breasts swelling under a snowy, thin chemise of Indian muslin.

"I'll keep you warm," Keith promised, cupping her breasts in his hands. "Isn't that nicer than a dress?"

"Much," Bridget admitted. She leaned back against him and savored the strength of his masculine body, the quivering tension of a spring about to be released that ran through all his muscles.

"You do keep me warm," she said from that safety. "You take care of me. You'll teach me to be a lady. You'll make excuses for me. And you'll spend your whole life in fear that some visitor from Ireland will show up, point a finger at your wife and say—"

"This ain't our Charlotte!" Keith interrupted, his voice shaking with laughter. "Where is the strawberry mark on her left shoulder? What have you done with our innocent babe?"

"I don't understand," Bridget said. "What do you mean, strawberries?"

Keith released her. "Oh, it's just a joke. Sort of thing they say in the third act of a tragedy, you know—oh, I guess you wouldn't know. Never been to the theatre, have you?"

"No," Bridget said with a sort of flat despair. "I've never been to the theatre, I've never been to Paris, I can't speak French and the only time I was let touch a pianoforte was to dust the top of it! How will I play the lady for your friends in India? Keith, I can't let you spend your whole life wondering if some accident is going to expose me and horribly embarrass you!"

"Actually," Keith murmured into her neck, "I didn't plan to spend my *entire* life doing that. There might be time for a few other things . . . like making love to my wife."

At that moment an impatient "Harrumph!" from outside the tent startled them both. Bridget slipped away from Keith and turned her back to the tent-flap while she struggled to do up the front of her dress with cold fingers. Keith thrust his head into his borrowed shirt and went outside to greet Colonel Faraday.

There was no chance to talk at breakfast. Colonel Faraday dominated the mess table with his plans for a triumphal entrance into Guahipore with Keith and Dan Weaver at his side.

"I'm going with you," Bridget announced to Keith after breakfast, while he was struggling into Dan Weaver's second-best dress uniform.

"No place for a lady," Keith mimicked the colonel. "Harrumph, what?"

Bridget disregarded his attempt to make her smile. "I want to talk to Aziza."

Before the procession moved off from the camp she was close to regretting her impulsive decision. The dizziness that had been bothering her intermittently in the mornings was back, and there was a bitter taste in her mouth and her head was aching. Even the short ride into the city taxed her strength, and she was relieved when at last they reached the mehtar's palace and she could escape the formal reception to be ushered into the endless halls and interconnecting rooms of the zenana.

Aziza was reclining on a charpoy of red silk and gilt bamboo that swung from the ceiling on twisted ropes of gold chains, eating sticky sweets from a plate held by Laila. She jumped up, spilling the sweets, and ran to give Bridget a joyous hug.

"Oh, thank you, thank you, thank you!" she exclaimed. "I knew you and Powell Sahib would make everything all right."

All right for Aziza, perhaps, but all wrong for them. Bridget felt dizzy again. She sat down on the swinging charpoy without waiting for permission. Aziza perched cross-legged beside her, chattering and trying to pop sticky sweet fruit pastes into Bridget's mouth.

Bridget frowned at her first bite of the apricot paste. "Aziza, these taste bitter. Do you think . . .?" She left the question unvoiced. Surely Aziza would be on her guard, now more than ever, against Habiba's vengeance!

"Oh, no," Aziza assured her with a sunny smile. "Habiba will not poison anything again. She is dead. She took poison herself when she heard the fighting and knew that Afzul's plot had failed."

Dead! Bridget put down her half-eaten sweetmeat.

Aziza patted her hand. "Do not distress yourself. She is wise. If she had lived, the mehtar would have cut off her breasts and thrown her to the wild dogs. He does not pardon traitors." She twirled a new ring, an elaborate gold creation with little chains hanging from it, and a dreamy smile crossed her face. "Or perhaps he would have hung her from the city walls in a cage until the crows picked out her eyes."

The revolting image was too much for Bridget. Murmuring an apology, she jumped up from the charpoy and ran to a brass bowl in the corner where she lost the few bites of apricot paste she had consumed.

Aziza was all sympathy, insisting that Bridget lie down on the charpoy and drink hot mint tea while Laila fanned her forehead.

"I'm sorry," Bridget said weakly. "It's the strain . . ."

She could go no farther; her voice wobbled and cracked in the middle of the sentence.

Aziza gave her a sharp look and ordered Laila and the other slaves out of the room.

"Now," she ordered, seating herself beside the charpoy on a turquoise brocaded cushion, "tell me *everything.*"

Bridget confessed that the very success Keith had achieved was about to ruin their personal happiness. Once the mehtar agreed to allow a British resident in Guahipore, the British government would send in someone much more senior and important than Keith to be the resident. Keith would be stationed at some other place, and she would go with him.

"I do not like that," said Aziza. "You are my friend, even if you are a feringhi. Why does not Powell Sahib leave the British raj and take service with the mehtar, may he live forever?"

Bridget could not explain the impossibility of such an action. All she could do was reiterate that Keith would remain in the service of the British raj and would have to go wherever he was posted. "And if we go to some big station with a lot of Europeans, it is too dangerous. Somebody might find out that I am not Lady Charlotte, and then—well, it would be bad for Keith."

"I understand," said Aziza. "He would lose the favor of your queen."

It was as good a summary as any. Bridget nodded.

Aziza tapped one tiny, silk-clad foot on the carpeted floor. "Powell Sahib knows the truth now? You have told him?"

"Yes," Bridget surprised, "but how did you know? It was only last night."

Aziza kissed her forehead. "It shines from your face," she said. "Your spirit was cloudy before, because of the lie. Now your spirit is free and your eyes show the difference. That is good, that Powell Sahib understands. As for the rest, it is a small matter. Powell Sahib shall be the resident here, and you will stay in Guahipore as long as you like."

Bridget gave a weak, embarrassed laugh. "Dear Aziza! I wish that we could do that! But I've told you. It will have to be somebody much more important than Keith."

Aziza's eyes flashed in the way Bridget had come to recognize as a danger signal. *"No one* is more important than the man who saved the life of the mehtar, may he live forever! I will tell my husband that he must insist that Powell Sahib and no one else is to be the resident. Your government will agree I think, because you say that they want very much to have this treaty. And my husband will agree, because"—she giggled—"right now I am his favorite wife."

"Stay there," she ordered Bridget. "Laila will look after you. At a time like this, you need to rest more." Her eyes darted to Bridget's waistline. "Tight clothes," she muttered. "Truly, the feringhis are mad. Assuredly you will stay in Guahipore, even if I have to interrupt the mehtar's council. I cannot let you go back to India to be attended by some feringhi woman who does not know how to bring babies."

She laughed at Bridget's open-mouthed astonishment. "So? Why do you think you are sick? And your dresses too tight? We will have to sew charms for a boy inside all your petticoats now."

Firm, competent little hands pushed Bridget back down on the charpoy. "Rest now. I will arrange all." She slipped on a pair of high, carved wooden *pattens* and went down the hall of the zenana with short, clacking steps that echoed all the way through the interlocking rooms.

Bridget did not see Aziza again that afternoon. She

rested for several hours, dozing intermittently, and was wakened by a servant who came to guide her to the outer door of the women's quarters. There she rejoined Keith and Colonel Faraday.

Keith's face was alight with joy. She knew without asking what the upshot of their interview with the mehtar (may he live forever) had been.

"Darling, you'll never guess what has happened!" Keith exclaimed. He took her elbow and drew her to one side, several paces behind Colonel Faraday and Dan Weaver. "Let me tell you . . ."

Bridget smiled to herself and let him tell her.

"You don't seem very surprised," Keith said at the end of his recital.

"Yes . . . well . . . I have some news of my own," she told him. "Later."

They did not return to the camp with Colonel Faraday. Instead, they went back to their own house in Guahipore, preceded and followed by an escort of the mehtar's men, mounted men carrying small round shields and curved swords. They were mostly Guahis, with a sprinkling of fierce dark Bashiri faces. Keith told Bridget that the mehtar had said that the Bashiris who remained in his service were those of proven loyalty.

Bridget wondered briefly what had happened to the others and thought it better not to ask.

They reached their house just as the sun broke through the low-lying clouds of afternoon and painted the snow-covered mountains behind the city with gold and red. In the compound garden, drawn up like a guard of honor, were their three servants, Mirza, her mother and old Daud the gatekeeper, who had returned without explanation.

The house was swept and clean—by Guahi standards —and there was an appetizing stew of mutton and vegetables and herbs bubbling on the open fire in the cookhouse out back. Bridget sniffed appreciatively, turned over an anonymous dark lump of entrails in the corner of the cookhouse and decided that the exact makeup of the stew, like the fate of the disloyal Bashiris, was something it would be better not to ask about.

They retired early after dinner. The clay pots of coals which the Guahis used for supplementary heat were burning in two corners of the bedroom, taking the chill off the biting air that whistled in between the ill-fitting slats of the wooden shutters.

"Resident," said Keith for the eighth or ninth time, with undiminished satisfaction. "Resident of Guahipore! Your husband's a great man, Biddy, my dear."

He threw open the wooden shutters and, one arm about Bridget, drew her to the window to look out on the snow-crowned peaks of the hills above the flat roofs of the city. "There's work for us here," he said softly. "A lifetime of good work. And by the time I retire to Ireland, my love, I shall be a doddering old bore and you will be a white-haired *grande dame* whom nobody would think to question."

Bridget felt a stirring of unease at the mention of Ireland. For her, India had meant freedom and love. She had no desire to return to the hovel where she'd grown up. But Keith, second son to a great estate, might feel differently. "It doesn't seem right," she said. "I don't want you to spend your life in exile for my sake."

Keith laughed and hugged her closer. "What exile?" He pointed out the window. "There is my home. This is where we both belong, Biddy-Sullivan-of-Ballycrochan, and you know it!" He looked at her with a question in his light eyes. "Will you be lonely? I think there will be more of a foreign community here as time goes by, you know. We need to bring in a doctor—yes, and I want the mehtar to approve a system of secular schools and clinics—In ten years there'll be a little community. And by that time, you'll not be afraid to meet them. I'll see to that."

Bridget kissed him lightly on the lips. "There'll be an addition to the population sooner than that," she told him. "Aziza says seven months from now, and it's to be a boy."

Keith stared, laughed, grabbed Bridget by the waist and swung her into the air. Still laughing, he fell backward onto the bed, tearing the mosquito netting loose.

Some time later, they remembered to get under the blankets.

Epilogue

Guahipore, 1862

(Excerpt from a letter written by Lady Boyle to her friend, Kitty Conansburgh)

. . . During this hot weather Lord Boyle and I grew quite *ennuyee* at Simla and so conceived the daring project of a trip to Guahipore, where Keith Powell holds the residency amid his half-savage tribes of mountain men. While Captain Powell and my husband were out hunting in the mountains north of Guahipore, I stayed several days in the residency, where I was most hospitably entertained by Mrs. Powell—Lady Charlotte Fitzgerald that was.

You are too young to remember her, but I knew Lady Charlotte well when she was a young girl in Ireland, and I am quite favorably impressed by the way she has matured in later years. Though she and Captain Powell were mercifully spared the vicissitudes of the Mutiny, the native ruler being a steadfast friend of the

309

English, her life in this isolated spot cannot have been easy for someone used to the luxuries of Dublin and Paris.

Remembering how self-centered and bad-tempered she was as a girl, I had expected to hear a positive torrent of reproaches and complaints poured out upon my poor defenseless ears!

Instead, picture her seated among their four children, dispensing favors and punishments with an even hand; now hearing the young ones at their lessons, now romping like a child herself. Her husband's pet name for her is Biddy, "because," he says, "she is so biddable,"; *that* should give you some notion of how she is changed! And I declare, she seems even handsomer now than she did as a girl; such is the bracing effect of this mountain air!

The durzee has made up the Lyons silk you sent in a most becoming pattern . . .

Tapestry
HISTORICAL ROMANCES

Next Month From Tapestry Romances

PIRATE'S PROMISE
by Ann Cockcroft
GALLAGHER'S LADY
by Carol Jerina

POCKET BOOKS.

Home delivery from Pocket Books

Here's your opportunity to have fabulous bestsellers delivered right to you. Our free catalog is filled to the brim with the newest titles plus the finest in mysteries, science fiction, westerns, cookbooks, romances, biographies, health, psychology, humor—every subject under the sun. Order this today and a world of pleasure will arrive at your door.

POCKET BOOKS, Department ORD
1230 Avenue of the Americas, New York, N.Y. 10020

Please send me a free Pocket Books catalog for home delivery

NAME _____

ADDRESS _____

CITY _____ STATE/ZIP _____

If you have friends who would like to order books at home, we'll send them a catalog too—

NAME _____

ADDRESS _____

CITY _____ STATE/ZIP _____

NAME _____

ADDRESS _____

CITY _____ STATE/ZIP _____